As well as being a fiction writer, Laurence Fearnley is a curator and has written about many contemporary New Zealand craft artists. Fearnley holds an MA in Creative Writing from Victoria University and has previously published short stories in *Sport* and several anthologies.

Her second novel, *Room*, was shortlisted for the fiction award of the 2001 Montana Book Awards.

In 2004, Fearnley was part of the New Zealand Artists and Writers to Antarctica Programme. She currently lives in Dunedin with her husband and son.

ALSO BY LAURENCE FEARNLEY

The Sound of Her Body
Room
Delphine's Run
Butler's Ringlet

DEGREES OF SEPARATION

Laurence Fearnley

PENGUIN BOOKS

PENGUIN BOOKS
Published by the Penguin Group
Penguin Group (NZ), cnr Airborne and Rosedale Roads, Albany,
Auckland 1310, New Zealand (a division of Pearson New Zealand Ltd)
Penguin Group (USA) Inc., 375 Hudson Street,
New York, New York 10014, USA
Penguin Group (Canada), 90 Eglinton Avenue East, Suite 700, Toronto,
Ontario, M4P 2Y3, Canada (a division of Pearson Penguin Canada Inc.)
Penguin Books Ltd, 80 Strand, London, WC2R 0RL, England
Penguin Ireland, 25 St Stephen's Green,
Dublin 2, Ireland (a division of Penguin Books Ltd)
Penguin Group (Australia), 250 Camberwell Road, Camberwell,
Victoria 3124, Australia (a division of Pearson Australia Group Pty Ltd)
Penguin Books India Pvt Ltd, 11, Community Centre,
Panchsheel Park, New Delhi – 110 017, India
Penguin Books (South Africa) (Pty) Ltd, 24 Sturdee Avenue, Rosebank,
Johannesburg 2196, South Africa
Penguin Books Ltd, Registered Offices: 80 Strand, London,
WC2R 0RL, England

First published by Penguin Group (NZ), 2006
1 3 5 7 9 10 8 6 4 2

Copyright © Laurence Fearnley, 2005

The right of Laurence Fearnley to be identified as the author of this work
in terms of section 96 of the Copyright Act 1994 is hereby asserted.

Designed by Mary Egan
Typeset by Egan-Reid Ltd
Printed in Australia by McPherson's Printing Group

All rights reserved. Without limiting the rights under copyright reserved above,
no part of this publication may be reproduced, stored in or introduced into
a retrieval system, or transmitted, in any form or by any means (electronic,
mechanical, photocopying, recording or otherwise), without the prior written
permission of both the copyright owner and the above publisher of this book.

ISBN 0 14 302057 9
A catalogue record for this book is available
from the National Library of New Zealand.

www.penguin.co.nz

For Aaron, Becky and Neil

PROLOGUE

It is midsummer and snow falls, extracting colour from the landscape. The sky bleaches, becomes a shade of dull white; yet the ground is still, in many places, the colour of charcoal. In the hollows, where the snow has settled, the impression is of a brass rubbing: marks made by white chalk passing over a sheet of black paper. The scientist's tracks from the previous day have disappeared. He stands still, looking about him as if suddenly unsure of where he is. He has picked his way through this landscape so often, and yet now, without the thin, broken trail of trodden ground to guide him, he is momentarily disorientated. Ice forms on his face, creating a mask which, for the present, feels warm, shielding him from the cold. But, as he stands surveying his surroundings, his eyelashes begin to catch; weighted with ice they stick together, then tear apart as he squints against the light. His gaze finally falls on a pair of skuas that have dragged a penguin chick to the edge of the frozen lake, where they begin steadily, methodically, to rip it to shreds.

The skuas work together, one bird holding the fluffy brown chick's flipper as the other tugs at its breast. From time to time they pause and glance around, watchful, keeping track of the other skuas that hover nearby. Only when another bird comes too close do they cry out. For the most part they remain quiet, intent on feeding and on attracting as little attention to themselves as possible. In less than an hour the chick will be nothing more than a bloody red ribcage and a pair of pink legs still attached by the pelvic frame. In time its legs will fade to a pale yellow, the colour of parchment, but for now they rest on the ground like rose petal decorations on a wedding cake.

The scientist shuffles, adjusting his weight, and a rivulet of shingle falls away from his feet, sending a thin stream of stones across the ice-covered lake. He is aware of another man approaching: his colleague, a man in his thirties who walks slowly, his head bowed, eyes focused on the ground as he passes through the colony, pausing every now and then to write in his notebook. After several minutes he is within a few feet of the scientist and he stops and looks around, considerate, perhaps, of the older man's privacy, or maybe in deference to his seniority.

The older man watches as his colleague fumbles in his pocket, bringing out a plastic bag of brightly coloured jelly-beans. The newcomer offers the bag to him, saying, as he does so, 'Watch your teeth – they're frozen.' Although he declines the offer, the scientist's eyes remain fixed on the sweets; he is attracted by their garishness. The younger man speaks again. 'I'm off to my bed. It's late. I'm knackered.'

Nodding, the older man looks at his watch and turns to where the sun sits in the sky, a pale glow obscured by broken cloud, barely strong enough to silver the passage being made by the ice-breaker through the sea ice several kilometres from where they stand. It's almost two in the morning; the conservators have long since retired to their beds and will not leave their tents again until eight, just as he returns from his all-night bird watch. Mumbling 'Goodnight' to his colleague, he watches the young man's progress as he sidles around the lake, pausing to light a cigarette as he passes in front of Shackleton's hut, his dry cough cutting through the noise of the penguin colony, which is always, day and night, in the background.

He notices that the skuas have abandoned the carcass. Other birds have moved in but there is little left of the chick for them. Its blood is trampled into the snow, a spreading stain that briefly captures the attention of a group of six adult Adélie penguins. They hesitate and crane their necks at the scene in front of them before hurrying by, heads bowed. As they near the scientist they pause once more, then charge past, feet thudding as they skitter towards the edge of the colony and the trail that leads down the steep cliffs to the edge of the sea.

Above him now a skua circles the penguin colony, the white flash on its dark brown wings appearing almost as a tear, the same colour as the sky in which it flies. He watches as it passes overhead before striking out to sea.

As the skua disappears from view, his thoughts drift until he imagines himself airborne, flying over this land. In his mind he maps the place he has visited so often over the past forty years – the place he will soon leave for the very last time. He looks down on Ross Island and the surrounding sea, tracing a passage from the grey open water to the vast plain of white, ice-covered ocean. He reaches the tidy strip carved by the ice-breaker and follows it briefly, before overtaking the ship and continuing on his course towards the distant American base, McMurdo Station.

Below him now lie streets, power lines and buildings: a small settlement tucked between hills so black they could be slags of coal. Although the town is familiar to him, he is amazed, once more, by its ugliness. It is as if the people who built it followed a brief permitting them to select only the largest, most utilitarian buildings and, being unable to deviate from that plan, they decided – in an attempt to make the place distinctive – to select one building in every colour offered. Dull brown accommodation blocks sit within sight of ochre and green workshops; white communal areas face silver-grey hangars. Scattered around, filling in any remaining space, are hundreds of shipping containers of various hues, which lead in turn to the huge white fuel tanks that dominate the entrance to the town.

With the exception of one building – the chapel with its small bell-tower – there is nothing restful about the place, nothing homely or gentle on the eye. The scattered jumble of sheds assaults the senses. Strangest of all is the apparent lack of life in the town. Few people are walking the streets and those who do are walking briskly from one shed to another – a sudden flash of colour that is swallowed up by the building into which it disappears. By contrast, the town emits plenty of noise – the sound of music through loudspeakers, the drone of heavy machinery, the batter of helicopters preparing to take off, and the slow drawl of trucks making their way along the road, passing the oil tanks as they ferry passengers and goods to Scott Base or the airport beyond.

Still airborne, he follows a truck now, over the low pass towards the smaller settlement of Scott Base. Here the sheds are all green – the colour of frozen peas. Being smaller than the buildings of the neighbouring American base, they reflect a scale that is still human. The trucks are smaller than the giant machines that trundle, almost empty, back and forth from McMurdo. But even here, there is little to hold his attention. Below him, two figures walk out onto the sea, following a trail marked out with red flags. Occasional clusters of black flags flutter in the slight breeze, indicating areas that are dangerous. Beside one such flag, near a tide crack, lies a seal, asleep in the sun, oblivious to the boundaries set out by the human visitors.

The two figures, a man and a woman, pause and watch the seal for several minutes. He can hear their voices but from this height is unable to understand what they are saying. After a short while he sees the man hug the woman and then the woman steps back, as if amazed by the unexpectedness of the man's gesture.

Already, however, he is flying past the figures, leaving them behind as he turns in the direction of a small wedge of land, Bratina Island, which sits, darkly, on the ice shelf, thirty kilometres to the south-west.

At first, his flight continues across the white, flattened sea, featureless but for the swathes of blue-grey shadows that sweep the ground ahead of him. After a while the ground beneath him alters: the untracked expanse acquires markings, patches of water and stone appear, gaining in frequency and size until they become lakes, surrounded by dunes of grey shingle. The island is close now, directly below him. He can see people leaving the campsite, their progress to the northern end of the island momentarily interrupted by a skua that repeatedly attacks their stooped bodies as they scurry by.

It appears that the group is trying to reach a plastic pole

that has been placed in the ice a kilometre or so from where they stand. Although the distance between them and the pole is slight, they are having difficulty determining the best route. The hummocks that surround the island obscure their view and, as they walk, their passage is frequently blocked by large ponds. He watches as they walk back and forth along the edge of one such pond, looking for a place to cross. He sees the leader of the group jump and, like penguins hesitating at the shoreline, the remaining figures continue to walk to and fro for several seconds. Then without warning they leap, one after the other, and hurry to catch their guide. Suddenly he can hear laughter and, drawing closer, he hears a softly spoken voice ask, 'So, have you found inspiration yet?' More laughter follows and he finds himself joining in: the sound is infectious; it makes him feel young.

Still smiling, he turns back to Ross Island. His gaze takes in the vapour cloud that rises from Mt Erebus as he glides over tide cracks and pressure ridges, which diminish as he draws closer to the large snow-groomed strip that serves as the runway. Out of the corner of his eye he is aware of the lumbering hulk of an aeroplane preparing to land. A Starlifter. It approaches slowly, its descent so gradual that it is almost impossible to tell the exact moment of its touchdown. He watches as it crawls to a standstill, turns and then taxis back to the collection of sheds. A fresh busload of passengers is gathered there, waiting to embark. He hears a man in uniform shout, 'Okay, folks, we're good to go!'

Not yet ready to join them, he turns his back on the group and returns to the place he has not yet quit, Cape Royds. He hovers for a moment, observing his own figure standing just as he left it on the edge of the penguin colony, head tilted, gazing out towards the thin grey strip of horizon, waiting and watching for the skua to return from the sea.

SALLY

Located in the roof of the aeroplane, high above her, was a door marked Emergency Exit. Sally couldn't take her eyes off it. Leaning back, with her head resting against the red webbing of the seat, she imagined the circumstances in which the door — which had to be at least six metres above the floor — would come into use. She glanced down the length of the plane looking for more exits, but could see none. She registered the four rows of people who filled the Starlifter:

men and women dressed in either red, black, or blue and yellow. Her eyes went back to the exit. Remained there.

Sally became aware that the woman next to her had begun to fidget. She was trying to remove her jacket but because there was so little space between their two bodies she could barely move her arms, and now one of them seemed to be stuck mid-length down her sleeve. It began to flap uselessly as she attempted to break free. She reminded Sally of a bird with a broken wing trying to get airborne. The woman gave up, rested for a second, and then began again, this time pushing her arm back into the sleeve before trying to slip the coat off backwards, over her shoulders. She looked like a diver squirming out of a wetsuit. The brown paper lunch bag that had been balanced on her knee fell to the floor, landing on the boots of the woman opposite. Encumbered by so much clothing, even bending down to retrieve the bag was difficult. Polypropylene vest, shirt, polarfleece salopettes, windproof salopettes, fleece jacket, large padded jacket . . .

'Shit!' Sally could see her neighbour speak – she lip-read the word even though she was unable to hear it spoken. Her own ears, like those of most of the other passengers, were fitted with bright yellow foam earplugs.

'Shit!'

Sally heard the voice this time, and smiled in the woman's direction. She didn't know her name but had sat opposite her at breakfast that morning at Scott Base. She had said hello but nothing more because the woman had been talking to her neighbour. The conversation, Sally remembered, had been about cats. About how the woman was looking forward to seeing her pets again. She was telling her friend about a game she sometimes played. She would shine a red laser pointer onto the cat's paw or tail and watch it spin round and round as it tried to catch the light.

The woman had smiled as she spoke, adding that she

found cats less complicated than people. No matter who you were, she had said, you could count on a cat for company. Her friend had nodded but replied that she preferred people. Sally had said nothing. She had listened but had felt dislocated, as if finding herself in some foreign backpackers', among people whose language she could not understand. She had only been away from the base for ten days but now everything about the place seemed odd, every light too bright, every voice too loud and every person or piece of furniture one too many. She'd wanted to contain herself. Walking down the corridor she had noticed that her arms were folded firmly across her chest, as if she was holding herself in, protecting herself from anyone who might have passed her. It was a feeling that had remained with her throughout the day.

At eleven, when she had returned to the cafeteria for a cup of coffee, she had chosen a seat away from the other people and was sitting by herself, gazing through the window, when she heard a woman's voice say, 'We can't have you sitting by yourself!' Sally had smiled, introduced herself, and wished the stranger would go away. Instead they talked. It was the woman's first full day in the Antarctic; she had arrived the afternoon before, later than scheduled because the plane had been delayed. Sally had nodded and felt somehow old. As if she had aged because she had already spent two weeks on the ice and was due to leave later that same day. The woman had asked her what she thought of the place and Sally had replied, 'Fantastic.' She had hoped her reply would discourage further conversation but the woman had agreed. 'It is fantastic, isn't it?'

Sally had glanced back to the window but the woman continued. 'It's more than that. When you first step off the plane and see all that featureless, limitless white space around you and it's impossible to determine any sense of scale, it's overwhelming.'

Again Sally had glanced towards the window and this time she felt sorry. Sorry that she was so intent on protecting her memories and keeping everything to herself that she couldn't even permit herself to talk to this woman. She held on to the silence between them, then, fearing the woman might ask her a question, enquired, 'Why are you here?' The question sounded ambiguous in her ears. She felt embarrassed by the bluntness of it. But the woman sensed only one meaning.

'I'm studying marine sediments on the McMurdo Ice Shelf.'

'Oh.'

There was another silence. A pause that was familiar. It had occurred before when Sally had spoken to scientists passing through Scott Base. It was a silence that came from not knowing what to say next. Despite her interest in everything that was going on and her desire to learn, it was as if she didn't possess the necessary vocabulary to keep the conversation going. In any case, she'd discovered that most research projects couldn't be turned into easy conversation. There were two options: the subject could be dropped or, alternatively, it could be developed, not so much into a conversation but into an explanation, a lecture on a subject she would only ever half grasp. Not for the first time it struck Sally that since arriving in the Antarctic she had often felt stupid.

As if sensing Sally's hesitation, the woman had continued. 'In fact, with luck I'll be flying out to Bratina Island this afternoon. It's about fifteen minutes from here – by helicopter.'

Sally interrupted. 'I've just come from there.'

The woman smiled at her. 'Really? What did you think? Incredible, isn't it?'

'Yes. Fantastic.'

The plane was gloomy. For the first time in days Sally was struck by a lack of light. A few bulbs were positioned overhead but towards the back of the plane, beyond the passengers, where the cargo was stored, it reminded her of a cave. The overall feeling was one of being deep inside a ship. With so many bodies pressed into such a tight space she imagined a convict ship. It was hot, too. Sweat trickled down her back, an avenue of water between her shoulders.

Her neighbour was shuffling again. She was standing up, her boots carefully positioned between the feet of the two women opposite, when the upturned toes of her blue mukluks caught in a trouser leg, causing her to lose her balance. She stumbled and fell onto Sally. 'Sorry!' she shouted. She pushed herself up and fell again, this time onto the knee of the woman opposite. Then, regaining her balance, she stepped over the legs of two more people, Distinguished Visitors, until she was standing at the front of the plane, facing a US Air Force crew member who had been watching her. Sally watched as they talked. The man leaned down, his mouth almost pressed to the woman's ear as he spoke. She saw her neighbour smile and the crew member gave her a rough, playful jab – a 'Get out of here!' shove that caused him to laugh. Then the woman removed her jacket, placed it on the end of the seat, and went into the women's toilet.

Sally turned away and glanced across the row of bodies. The man she had spoken to while waiting at the edge of the runway was standing on his seat, reading. Only by standing on his seat with his back against the metal supports could he hope to find enough room to stretch his long legs. Here and there, other passengers took up similar positions. It was nothing out of the ordinary – she had seen the same thing on the flight down to the ice. He was wearing a red jacket with his name printed onto a Velcro strip attached to his chest: William. Like delegates at a conference, everyone at Scott Base had a name tag. And like some defiant teenager, Sally had removed hers during her first day, only to discover later, when she went to collect her coat from the row of pegs in the hallway, that she couldn't find it. Where there had been only one or two coats, there were now over thirty, all blue – identical in almost every respect. As she'd stood looking at the jackets she had experienced a momentary panic, as if she was a child who had mislaid something an adult had instructed her to guard.

Earlier, while waiting for the plane to arrive, when Sally had spoken to William, she had noticed him stoop as she talked. Because he was wearing a red jacket, she had assumed he was American. But when she'd asked which part of the States he was from, he had said Vancouver. Then, in her haste to make amends, she had added that she had relatives in Vancouver. Without looking at her, he had nodded, and said that he was from Nelson, originally. The other member of his research team was a New Zealander. His event, he said, had been funded by the University of Auckland, so, officially at least, he was still a New Zealander.

'So, why the red jacket?' Sally had laughed. She had been told that anyone wearing red was attached to McMurdo. He'd touched his coat then as if he'd forgotten what clothing he'd put on that morning but said nothing.

It was then that she had realised he wasn't bending over to listen to her but to look at a piece of bright blue ice by his foot. She had watched as he prodded it with his toe, then told him something she had learned herself only a few days earlier: that very old, dense ice didn't absorb colour from the blue end of the spectrum. The colour blue was reflected back. William gave no indication of having heard and some time passed before he looked up and said that he thought the ice was blue because the dye was seeping out of his mukluks. He had stamped the toe of his left boot into the ground as if to prove it. Immediately, another small patch of blue appeared.

Sally had chatted for several more minutes. Then she

realised she wasn't having a conversation so much as asking a string of questions while being asked none in return. William had spent the past three months at Cape Royds studying the skua population. It was his ninth season on the ice. His last. He had shrugged, added, 'Back home to winter in Vancouver the day after tomorrow,' then turned away and pointed towards a grey smoggy line tracing across the sky. 'Looks like the plane's here.'

More people had begun to gather around. The red, black and blue jackets were joined by a small number of khaki camouflage suits, those of the US armed forces. All faces were turned to watch the approaching Starlifter, eyes shaded by an uneven salute of raised hands. It was as if the group had transformed into a silent, misshapen colony – the kind you see in films where people abandoned on a space station are watching the approach of an American-led rescue team.

As the Starlifter passed in front of them, its wheels only metres from the ground, Sally had noticed a black wedge of land: Bratina Island. She had often been troubled by her perception of space in the Antarctic. It seemed to her that the place was somehow open-ended, without limit, and that there was simply no scale by which to judge distance. Even now, despite all that she knew, the island appeared to be so close that it might have been on one sideline of a sports playing field while she was standing on the other. In reality, however, she knew the island was close to thirty kilometres away.

She had turned back to William, but he had already wandered away and was standing by himself. She lost sight of him and didn't notice him again until they boarded the plane. He was one of the last men to file into the cabin; his standing body now signposted the demarcation between male and female passengers.

Sally watched as he glanced up from the book he was holding and looked across to a younger man who was trying

19

to take photographs through one of the few windows in the plane. Unable to position himself, the photographer twisted in his seat, his hand raised so that his camera faced the window. Without knowing what the camera was pointing at, he pressed the shutter. He repeated the process several times, then turned back in his seat, shaking out his arm as if loosening up before a big race.

A few other men stood on their seats, random outcrops scattered along the length of the plane. Others – the majority – sat slumped, looking straight ahead, their legs slotted into a space between the knees of the person opposite like fingers and hands clasped together in prayer.

There was a jolt as Sally's neighbour returned to her seat. For the first time since being in the plane Sally noticed the woman's name tag: Marilyn. She recognised the name; indeed, she had heard her voice on the radio almost every day during her visit, but hadn't known the woman by sight until now. So that was Marilyn, the Scott Base communications operator. Sally felt startled by her discovery. The girl looked nothing like the image she had created in her head. Rather than the plain, or at least ordinary girl she had pictured, Marilyn was striking. Her eyes were almost the colour of turquoise and her hair, which was long and straight, was auburn and glossy – not at all the mousy brown Sally had imagined. But most remarkable of all was the girl's skin. It was not just pale but almost translucent, delicate, like that of a newborn baby. For the first time in her life, Sally felt she had come face to face with someone who possessed a 'fragile beauty'.

Marilyn's hand edged under Sally's leg as she searched for her seatbelt. There was a tug as the buckle wrenched free and swung across the back of her hand, hitting her knuckles.

'Sorry,' she mumbled.

Again, Sally was struck by the fact that 'sorry' was such

an easy word to see. If she was suddenly to fall deaf, her earplugs lodged in her head, she imagined that for the first few days of her new life, 'sorry' would be one of the few words she could be certain to understand. Most other words would be lost on her. She smiled in Marilyn's direction. So that's Marilyn, she thought once more, before sagging into her seat and pulling the hood of her coat over her eyes. Instantly she was alone; she had created space.

MARILYN

Marilyn pulled her brown paper lunch bag onto her knee. Reaching in, she pulled out two sandwiches, one marked Tuna, the other, a sandwich with a filling of orange-coloured cheese, marked Veg. Just the smell of the tuna was enough to make her feel queasy. She placed both sandwiches to one side and plunged her hand back into the bag, feeling several small plastic packages with her fingers – chocolate or muesli bars, she guessed. The women from McMurdo, who sat opposite her, had already started to eat.

Marilyn gave a slight smile. At least she'd succeeded in getting on to the plane behind them, she thought. It had taken all her nerve to hang back and not step ahead in the queue. There were four of them, all big women, and all as determined as she had been to stay out of the plane for as long as possible. One of them had even smiled and nudged her forward, saying, 'Off you go,' as if doing her a favour. Perhaps she expected Marilyn to believe that it was better to be jammed between two people in that stuffy space than to get on last and have the empty seat to one side. Marilyn had managed to stick it out, though, and if it hadn't been for the Distinguished Visitors, she would have been the last person to board and she would have had the space to spread out in.

She frowned in the direction of one of the DVs, a businessman from Wellington. He had kept all the passengers on the airport bus waiting for twenty-five minutes while he had taken video footage of Mt Erebus. She had heard that he was one of the richest people in the country. He was certainly one of the most ill-tempered and rude. Even though she'd spoken to him often during the past few days, and had organised numerous conference calls back to New Zealand on his behalf, he had made no attempt to remember her name or thank her.

At least, thought Marilyn, the Americans hadn't been sucked in by him. They had had no idea who he was. When he'd finally boarded the bus they'd clapped – slowly. All the seats had been taken so he'd had to crouch on top of the pile of bags in the aisle. He was just making himself comfortable when William, the skua scientist from Cape Royds, had asked him to move because he was sitting on some valuable computer equipment. In the end, the DV had had to relocate to the floor. Probably the first time he'd ever been on a bus and there he was squatting on the floor like a woman going to the toilet.

All the other New Zealanders had been watching, their eyes fixed on him while trying not to smile. The way he was crouching must have made Ursula think of toilets too, because, without warning, she had suddenly brought up the subject of female urinary devices. What she had missed most while out in the field, she'd said, was being able to simply pull down her pants and sit on a proper toilet. She'd never quite got the hang of peeing through the urinary funnel into a plastic bottle. All the women joined in then. Everyone had a story about how hard it was to relax and pee while standing up. Even the artist, Sally, the woman with the interesting face and cool streaked grey hair, had contributed to the conversation, saying that she had quite liked using her personal pee bottle because she had discovered that holding on to it as it filled was the quickest way to warm her fingers in the morning.

'Except wanking. That's quicker.' Marilyn recalled that there had been a moment's silence when Phil had come out with that. A few of the men even looked down, as if something on the floor had suddenly attracted their attention. The rich guy, she remembered, had simply covered his mouth with his hand and looked annoyed.

Marilyn glanced at the businessman. He had his laptop out and was staring at the screen. It was probably a DVD. A DV with a DVD, she thought. She smiled wearily as she watched the Distinguished Visitor, her gaze lingering on him as it dawned on her that she didn't know what the final 'D' of DVD stood for. The meaning of the term DVD, like a lot of things, was something she had never bothered to think about. The word lodged in her mind and she found herself repeating DVD, DVD, DVD as if uttering a mantra. DVD: Distinguished Visitor's Doodah. She glanced at the man, half expecting a reply or, at least, some indication of his having guessed what she was thinking.

The DV was still wearing his jacket, a brand-new black coat with fur trim – the type usually reserved for people based at the South Pole. All the DVs had brand-new gear. They weren't expected to make do with twenty-year-old mismatched blue-and-yellow suits. Anyway, it was silly to insist that everyone wear all their extreme-weather gear on the plane. They'd be lucky to survive a plane crash and, as far as she knew, corpses didn't feel the cold.

She glanced around, took in the US soldiers and frowned. They didn't have to wear layers and layers of clothing but were simply kitted out in standard khaki camouflage. The rumour going around was that most of the soldiers had come straight from Iraq, where it had been over forty degrees Celsius most days. She'd overheard two soldiers talking when she'd first arrived at the start of the season and it was pretty clear from their conversation that they didn't want to be anywhere near the ice. She recalled hearing one of the men say, 'Man, I just don't want to be here right now,' and his friend had nodded and looked depressed. As far as they were concerned, going to McMurdo was a punishment. They wanted to be at home with their families. She understood that now and, moreover, she almost agreed with them. Being on the ice was like being sent to prison, or some distant penal colony.

She glanced in the direction of one soldier who hadn't lifted his head from his hands since boarding. He should be pleased to be going home, she thought, and yet he was sitting there as if he couldn't face the thought. She sighed. Perhaps, like her, he was feeling uneasy about going home for some reason. Or perhaps he was being sent back to Iraq, or some other place where his khaki uniform would be put to proper use. Around McMurdo the only soldiers she'd seen had stood out from their surroundings like cowpats on a frozen field.

The real South Pole guys were different from other people. Marilyn smiled. She'd been in the shop at Scott Base when two Americans wearing black anoraks had wandered in. Everyone had noticed them. The atmosphere in the whole shop had altered, grown quieter. She'd said hello and then, because she'd had nothing else to do, she had helped them locate the map of the Ross Ice Shelf they were looking for. She found out that the shorter one was an astronomer and the other guy a mechanic. She'd wanted to ask the astronomer how it was possible to see the stars when they were surrounded by twenty-four-hour sunlight, but she hadn't had the nerve. She suspected it was a stupid question so had kept it to herself and talked to the mechanic instead. He had kept asking her questions – what was she doing at Scott Base? How long had she been there? Did she get over to McMurdo very often? He even said he might see her around. He was going to be in McTown for ten days before going south again.

The way he said 'going south' had made her think of her boyfriend, Chris. He often talked about going south – to visit his family in Mosgiel. But she was trying not to spend too much time thinking about him, or their approaching wedding. When she'd first arrived, the reality of their separation had made her feel alone. It was the first time she had been parted from him and it had been almost unbearable. More recently, however, the thought of going back to him had made her anxious and depressed.

It had been Chris's idea that she apply for the job. He'd pointed out the advertisement one Saturday morning as they'd sat eating breakfast. But she had been in a hurry to get back to her own flat and her two cats, and hadn't taken much interest. It had been another two days before she had read the advertisement carefully and realised she was qualified for the job.

Even then, she'd been reluctant to apply. There were so

many practicalities to consider. She'd have to find someone to look after her flat and cats if she was going to be away for several months. Then there was Christmas, and the fact that she'd miss being at home with her family. There was also the issue of the climate. She would have to trade a warm summer for a frozen one. And finally there was Chris. She didn't know how she would cope without him for an entire summer.

Although she felt embarrassed to admit it, she needed him. He was so different from her. Whereas she often felt awkward and shy, he was always friendly and outgoing, confident. It was old-fashioned, she knew, but she felt protected and safe whenever she was with him. By contrast, she usually felt lost and vulnerable when they were apart. It was as if she didn't know how to look after herself. When she was alone, she sometimes had the impression that she was occupying a different world from the one she inhabited when she was with him. Her world was slightly obscure, ill-defined, as if nothing in it was real or straightforward. Moreover, her world was in a constant state of suspense and she always felt she could not control her future. It often felt as if she was simply waiting for something bad to happen.

In the end she had decided against applying for the job, and it had taken all of Chris's optimism and persuasion to get her to change her mind. She completed her application only because he had made her believe, finally, that it would be too good an opportunity to miss. She had listened to him and felt guilty. She wanted him to feel proud of her but she'd been relieved – happy, even – when she was turned down.

Chris, however, was disappointed. He spent an entire weekend at home, refusing to go out or talk to anyone. When, finally, he did talk, he put it to her that she'd sabotaged the interview on purpose. He insisted on going over the questions she'd been asked, getting her to repeat her answers over and over again until she could hardly remember what she'd said. All she did know was that she would have said almost anything just to get him to stop but whenever she'd tried to change the subject – by suggesting they take his dogs down to the beach for a run – he'd shaken his head and asked her, once more, to describe what she'd said *exactly*. She'd tried to make him understand that it didn't matter; at least this way they'd be able to spend the summer together, even 'go south' to his parents' for Christmas, if that was what he wanted. But Chris just wouldn't leave it alone. He was so disappointed. She could feel his disappointment and in the end she began to wonder if she had indeed ruined the interview on purpose.

Chris would have loved to go to the Antarctic – that was the problem. With his skills and employment background he would never be accepted. Marilyn had not been able to find out why he was so attracted to the place. When she'd asked him to explain, he'd looked at her and said simply, 'Because it's special.' She'd wanted to ask what was so special about a lot of ice and a couple of ugly green sheds in the middle of nowhere, but she'd seen that he was almost close to tears and had left him alone.

'He'll come right, don't worry,' her mother had comforted her. In a way he did come right, apologising for his over-reaction before going on to tell her that he'd once heard Sir Edmund Hillary give a talk and it had been so inspiring he'd wanted to go to the Antarctic ever since. He'd laughed then, saying he'd only been seven at the time, but the image of Hillary driving a tractor to the South Pole had been locked in his mind ever since.

Months later, when the applicant who had taken the position of communications operator broke his leg just days after arriving at Scott Base, Marilyn was recalled for a second interview. Chris was beside himself with excitement. 'Be positive,' he'd advised. 'Make them believe that you not only *want* the job but you're the best person in the world for it.'

At first, Marilyn had been so nervous that when she was asked why she wanted to work at Scott Base, she'd replied, 'Because my boyfriend says I should.' She'd seen a collective look of concern cloud the faces in front of her, and it was only through some miracle that she'd managed to retrieve the situation, stressing she was good at her job and that she took her responsibilities very, *very* seriously. And, although it wasn't true, she remembered to mention that she had 'people skills' and that she could always be relied upon to stay calm in a stressful situation.

Like some fairytale monster, the interview panel had nodded its multiple heads and then one of the members had spoken independently, asking how she felt about being the only civilian communications operator on base. She hadn't understood the question and it had had to be explained to her that all the other communications operators had been recruited from the armed forces; in fact, if successful, she would be one of only a handful of civilians ever appointed to the position.

She could remember the 'Oh' of her response and her puzzlement at why the position had been advertised in the papers in the first place. But she remarked only that she imagined army people to be as 'civil' as anyone else. A few heads had smiled at one another and one had laughed out loud, agreeing that, yes, in general, the members of the armed forces were good blokes. Even the women!

Marilyn had taken that as a cue to laugh, joining in with some of the heads, ignoring the one or two who were frowning. More relaxed now than before, and remembering what Chris had told her, she had gone on to refer to Sir Edmund Hillary's Antarctic expedition, joking that she'd grown up on a farm near Rangiora and knew how to drive both a tractor and a bulldozer and that, like him, she would be able to run supplies across the continent if necessary. Then she had fallen silent. There was nothing else to say. The interview panel didn't appear to notice she had finished, however. Despite its smiling faces, she got the impression that some of the heads were waiting for her to say something more. Watching them looking at her had made her self-conscious and she had coughed and said, 'That's all. The end.'

It was only later, through her roommate, Andrea, that she discovered that one of the panel members had taken her suggestion about driving across Antarctica seriously. She didn't know how Andrea had come by that piece of information and she had been too taken aback to ask. However, the fact was, she got the job, and for the first time in weeks Chris had hugged her and told her she was bloody fantastic and that he was proud of her.

'You wait,' he'd said. 'It will be an amazing experience.' He'd lifted her off the ground and swung her around, adding, 'You'll be the best comms op they've ever had. You'll run rings around those army guys, just you wait.'

Marilyn had smiled at his confidence in her. She found it touching, too, that he referred to her as comms op. There was something about the title that identified her with Scott Base, as if she had already been there and was familiar with the place. Marilyn had laughed in response to Chris's joy but had felt a knot tighten in her stomach. Going to the Antarctic was out of her league. She knew, with absolute certainty, that she didn't want to go.

Chris was still wound up when the day of her departure came around. He insisted on taking her to the airport, even though it meant leaving home at four in the morning. Marilyn could remember the drive in from Woodend, how the sky was almost black, with only a faint glow of orange from the city lights to brighten it. She hadn't given it much thought at the time but had realised later that that would be her last proper night for several months.

She recalled, too, that the sprinklers had suddenly started up and begun to water the lawns outside the Antarctic departure terminal. The spray had caught in a weak beam of light that glowed dully from the building's entrance and she had spent several minutes watching the repetitive motion of the sprinklers as they waved back and forth across the grass. She had felt strangely calm, almost hypnotised by the sight, despite the fact that Chris hadn't been able to stop talking. She was only vaguely aware of his voice, his constant stream of instructions and suggestions, and she took one deep breath after another as if capturing the smell of damp grass for the last time. Finally, as she turned away to join the others in the departure hall, she captured another sound, that of a rooster crowing in the approaching dawn.

When she'd first arrived at Scott Base she'd wanted to appear friendly and sociable and had told Andrea all about Chris; the fact that he was always busy, could never sit still – not even for an instant. She'd mentioned their plans to get married in the autumn, the way Chris had taken it upon himself to organise a reception for their families and friends, even though the money he earned as a prison officer back in Christchurch was not really enough to cover the cost of such a huge event. Still, she'd managed to laugh, he's one of those people who never lets reality get in the way of a good time. That was one of the things she liked about him – his optimism and the fact that he was never down.

When questioned by Andrea she'd talked about her hobbies, how she loved going down to the beach where, she said, she could happily walk and beachcomb for hours and hours. She loved the smell of the sea, the way the water glistened in the sun and the sound made by the waves breaking. Sometimes, she added, she'd just sit and watch Chris surf or boogie-board. As long as she could watch the sea she was happy.

She'd thought at the time she was just telling her new roommate a bit about herself, but in no time at all complete strangers seemed to have heard about Chris and her home environment, and the more she tried to keep that part of her life private, the more she was forced to share it. She'd also had to put up with heaps of teasing: stuff like 'So, who wears the handcuffs in your family?' Most of the time she knew people were just having a laugh, that nothing was meant by the comments, but she had found them embarrassing and intrusive all the same.

Marilyn recalled that the South Pole mechanic had ended up buying a kid's T-shirt. It was blue, with a penguin on it – the type you could buy from any tourist shop in Christchurch. She hadn't asked who he was buying it for. He had tried on a couple of hats, too, and she'd helped him choose. It was blue-grey and she had told him it matched his eyes. He'd said something like, 'Since when did you notice the colour of my eyes?' She was about to answer when her supervisor, Christine, had walked in and asked her to take over the radio shift from Alan, who was sick. Christine had kept on talking, and by the time she finished the two Americans were heading out the door, leaving to catch the shuttle bus back to McMurdo. Marilyn had only just had time to call out, 'It was nice meeting you,' before they were gone.

It might have been nice, getting to know the Americans. Moreover, Chris would have been impressed if she'd managed to make friends with someone from the South Pole. Not that there was anything wrong with the New Zealanders at Scott Base. Most of them were nice, once you got to know them. Over the past few days, before she'd left, quite a few staff members had spoken to her, telling her how sorry they were for the way things had turned out. It was almost as if they felt slightly responsible for what had happened. It had made her feel better, knowing that not everyone thought she had lost it. It was almost as if they could imagine what she was going through. Not that they had to deal with the consequences, she sighed.

It seemed funny now, remembering back to those first days at Scott Base. In the beginning she'd felt intimidated by the other staff members. The people who had been so friendly towards her during the past week had back then struck her as distant and scary. They had appeared to know everything about the place – how it worked and where they fitted in. She, by contrast, knew nothing. She'd had to learn everything – even simple stuff, like rinsing the dishes and using the steriliser, had seemed complicated back then. She was so sure that she'd break something or mess things up. She was completely lost.

It was lucky that Andrea and Christine had been around when she arrived. They'd made those first few days bearable. Even so, she shuddered at the memory of the first time she had walked into the dining room. She recalled the way she had stood facing the water cooler, slowly pouring herself a glass while all the time her heart was beating at a million miles an hour as she tried to figure out where she would sit. Coming into the room she had noticed that everyone was sitting in groups, deep in conversation, laughing and joking as if they had known one another for years. She'd looked for an empty seat, somewhere where she could sit by herself, but there had been none available and she'd had to squeeze in between two men who were talking to each other. They'd paused just long enough to say hello and then continued with their conversation. Marilyn kept her eyes on her plate the whole time she was at the table, but even so she'd got the impression that she was intruding.

After her meal, she recalled, she'd wanted a cup of coffee

but hadn't known how to operate the espresso maker. She had stood by the machine reading the instructions, and she could feel the eyes of everyone in the room upon her. She hadn't known what to do. She knew that if she walked away without anything she'd appear even more stupid than she already felt, so in the end she'd made herself a cup of tea. And then she hadn't known where to put her tea bag. The rubbish bags, as far as she could tell, were colour coded and she'd been worried about putting it into the wrong one. She'd waited for someone else to make a cup of tea so she could follow their lead.

She'd finished her drink and was watching the last of the diners wash their plates when Andrea had walked over to her. She had felt such a sense of relief that she'd almost cried. Up until then she'd been so worried about what to do with her dishes that she had been too scared to go to the sink. She had watched the others rinse their plates and then stack them on a metal dish rack. Whenever the rack had become full someone would slide it into a large metal machine, press a few buttons, wait a few minutes and then pull the tray of plates out and restack them in piles by the counter. She had been watching surreptitiously for over fifteen minutes, trying to figure out how the buttons worked, but so far she hadn't managed to get a clear view. All she knew was that if she timed things right she could do her plates just after the tray had been emptied and that way she could avoid using the machine. She was almost ready to go to the sink when Andrea turned up. Instead of simply chatting, like any normal person would, Marilyn recalled the way she had instantly blurted out her fears about the dishes and how, in response, Andrea had laughed and told her it was no big deal. 'They're just dishes,' she'd said. 'Don't worry about it.'

That evening Andrea had taken her down to the bar and introduced her to everyone. Even then, she recalled, there were a couple of people who didn't return her greeting. They more or less ignored her and carried on with their conversation as though she didn't exist. She remembered how she had made a note of their faces so she could avoid them in the future.

She hadn't felt much like talking but had been content to listen to what the others had to say about life at Scott Base. Then Andrea and Christine brought up the topic of relationships. They agreed that it was difficult to maintain a relationship with anyone back in New Zealand. And, Christine had continued, it was pretty inevitable that sooner or later you'd wind up having it off with someone on base. It was depressing, she'd added, knowing that eventually you'd end up having sex with someone in the linen cupboard or some other less-than-romantic place. You didn't even have to like the person, she'd continued. That's what made it so sad. In fact, it made her depressed just thinking about it. It was pathetic, really, the way people just slept with each other for no good reason. It was almost like it was expected of you.

Andrea had nodded in agreement but had excused the behaviour, saying that people were only human after all, and it was easy to get lonely. She also added, quite casually, that as far as she was concerned what went on down south stayed down south. Christine had smiled, as if reminded of something, and then told them a story about some film people she had once worked with in Queenstown. Apparently they'd spent the entire summer repeating, 'What goes on on location, stays on location.' 'That used to pass for intellectual conversation,' she laughed.

Marilyn had laughed with the others but in truth she hadn't been sure she'd understood what they were on about. It was Tobin, she remembered, who had whispered, in a voice that only she had heard, that Andrea knew about all these things – she had researched the topic. He'd smiled and then explained in a louder voice that he had known Andrea for a long time. He knew her well, he'd said. They'd even spent the past two seasons together.

'Not *together* together,' Andrea had suddenly corrected him. Marilyn had been surprised by the tone in Andrea's voice. It had an edge to it, a sharpness. Several of the other people seemed to notice it, too, because the group fell silent for a moment and there had been a feeling of tension in the air.

Tobin had looked at his glass before responding, quietly, 'Right. Not *together* together – whatever that means – just together.' He'd looked at Andrea and for a second they'd held each other's glance and neither of them had smiled.

Eventually, Tobin had continued to speak, saying that lots of people around the base shared Andrea's viewpoint on relationships and that, curiously enough, most of those people were women. Women, he'd added, didn't seem to care too much if they cheated on their boyfriends back in New Zealand. They had some kind of emotional blockage that made it possible for them to divide their lives into two separate components, with a Scott Base segment and a New Zealand segment.

An argument had followed, Marilyn remembered. It had seemed that Andrea and Christine couldn't let Tobin's statement go unchallenged and had become quite worked up when he countered that he wasn't being sexist, he was simply stating a truth. The women at the base, he insisted, played around a hell of a lot more than the men. It was a fact.

'So, who exactly are they playing around with?'

Tobin had simply shrugged in response to Andrea's question. 'Not me. That's for sure.' He'd smiled in Marilyn's direction and, although everyone except Andrea had laughed, Marilyn had felt out of her depth. She guessed there was a private joke going on. In the end she'd smiled in order to appear polite but had been relieved when the conversation turned to the topic of cocktails.

A few hours later, someone she hadn't been introduced to appeared to revisit the subject of relationships, saying that what was accepted as normal behaviour in the Antarctic was a bit different from the rest of the world. The Antarctic and New Zealand, she'd said, might as well be two completely separate and unrelated planets. There were quite a few people around the place, she added, who even found it difficult to function back in the real world. They were the ones who tended to come back, year after year. She'd nodded in the direction of an older man who sat alone, reading. 'That William's one of them,' she'd said. 'He's based at Royds but had to come back to get some equipment fixed. He's returning to Royds tomorrow. I've never spoken to him but Tobin told me the other day that he's been coming down to the ice for over forty years – since the late 1950s. He used to stay in Shackleton's hut and probably knows more about the place than anyone but he never talks about it. The rumour is that he rarely talks at all. He's only comfortable with birds – can't deal with people any more.'

Marilyn had nodded and smiled as if she was already attuned to the pitfalls of a place like the Antarctic. She found herself glancing in William's direction and wondering if it was true that he couldn't talk to people. Perhaps, she thought, he just didn't have anything to say. If all he did was look at birds, there couldn't be too much for him to talk about. Maybe he just knew that his work would strike most people as boring. She could understand that. She'd often had the impression that she was the most boring person on the planet – maybe he felt like her. She'd watched him for a few seconds, then shrugged. What did she know? She'd only just arrived.

The evening had wound up shortly after that. It was mostly Christine and Andrea who had done all the talking and suddenly even they appeared to run out of things to say. At one point, shortly before they'd all stood up to leave, she heard Christine mention Tobin's name and say something about how he'd recently broken up with his partner back home. She'd been surprised by Andrea's response, the way she'd snapped, 'I'm not interested,' before glancing away as if wanting to bring the conversation to an end. Andrea had sat silently following that brief conversation and it seemed to Marilyn that she was brooding over something.

Back in their room, Marilyn recalled, Andrea had become even more thoughtful, suggesting that there might be times over the coming summer when each of them would need to have a little space to themselves. Although they shared a room, there might be the odd occasion when they'd want a bit of privacy. Either to be alone or with someone else. It had been a very matter-of-fact statement, and because of that, Marilyn had felt comfortable enough to reply that although she was certain that she, personally, would not be bringing anyone back to the room, she would always be happy to give Andrea as much space as she needed.

Marilyn looked at her neighbour. Even though the woman had pulled the hood of her jacket down over her eyes she could see that she had fallen asleep. Her mouth was all slack and her head kept falling forward onto her chest. Marilyn wasn't sure why the woman had come to the Antarctic. She'd been told she was part of the visiting artist programme, but that was as much as she knew.

In truth, she wasn't sure what to make of the artists they sent down. When she first arrived she'd met a man from Auckland whose art project appeared to consist of building snowmen. Although his snowmen were supposed to be based on early Antarctic explorers – men such as Captain Scott – none of them had facial features or, for that matter, any features at all. Constructed from lumps of snow, ice and scraps discarded in the waste, they were titled 'No-men'.

One evening she'd noticed that the artist was giving a talk about his work, and, hoping to learn something, she'd tagged along. Right from the start, however, she had felt self-conscious, unable to make sense of what he was saying. Despite listening carefully, she got lost in his talk of polar explorers, myth-making and paradigm shifts. Whether paradigm shifts were good or bad – and what they had to do with snowmen – she wasn't sure, and she listened hard, reliving the apprehension she had felt at school whenever her science teacher had paused mid-lesson to ask her to expound on some scientific theory in front of the class.

Storing each of the artist's words in her brain but still feeling lost, she had glanced around the rest of the audience and noticed that one or two of the scientists were simply gazing into space or doodling on their notepads. Gathering confidence, she wondered whether the artist was making sense to anyone. Perhaps, she had concluded, he was a phoney – not a real artist at all. But phoneys didn't get articles written about them in books and, as he had pointed out, his work had been described in over sixty publications throughout the world.

As the lecture drew to an end, the artist had taken a deep breath and fallen silent for several seconds. It was an embarrassing moment. Marilyn hadn't been able to tell if he'd lost his train of thought or if he'd finished. Once more she had looked around, but as no one else appeared to have noticed any change she had sat still, waiting for the artist to do something. Scratching his head and tucking his greasy hair behind his ears, he had eventually resumed his lecture. He described a cemetery gate he had seen years before, in the small southern town of Palmerston, and began to explain some theory he'd developed about memory. It seemed to Marilyn that he regarded his theory as pretty clever. The bottom line appeared to be that he had seen a sign reading 'Lest we Forget' on the cemetery gate, and had got it into his head that he could give it more meaning by rewriting it as 'Let's Forget'. And that was it. Before stepping down, however, he read some quotes from two men: Walter Benjamin and somebody Wittgenstein, and then ran his hands once more through his hair, frowning as a noticeable hunk came away in his fingers.

When it came time for questions no one said anything. Eventually, one of the scientists asked if he'd been to art school, or had any formal training. Marilyn got the impression that the artist was annoyed by the question because all he said in response was, 'Yes.' Another awkward silence had followed as the members of the audience shifted in their seats or stretched and yawned. Finally, after more than a minute had passed, the artist spoke again, explaining that *like them* he was university educated and that, like *one or two* of them, he was an associate professor. Most people had nodded, with one or two appearing slightly impatient, as if daring anyone else to ask any more questions. Waiting for Phil to give the vote of thanks, Marilyn had felt uneasy, dreading what he might say. It had come as a relief, therefore, when he had said, 'Well, so much for that. The bar's open. See you there.'

A few people clapped. Then everyone had gone, leaving her alone to help the artist put away the chairs and tidy away the projector. Even though she'd tried to think of something to say, some interesting point to raise, her thoughts had frozen up and in the end she'd left, saying she might see him in the bar.

She'd thought about the artist occasionally – after he'd returned to New Zealand – on her evening walk around the base. She still didn't understand what he was getting at. To her, his snowmen looked like snowmen. Even close up they didn't appear to be anything special – just the type of snowmen on any Christmas card or Advent calendar. Everywhere she turned there seemed to be groups of them and when the light around the base was especially flat it was hard to distinguish them from their surroundings. Finally, everyone had got sick of bumping into them and, recalling the words 'Let's forget!', had voted to bulldoze them.

They'd had a party the night they destroyed the No-men. It was one of only a few parties she'd ever been to. She'd never felt confident in a room full of strangers. She didn't have much to say — not compared with the others, anyway — and she had stood off to one side for as long as possible, just watching and taking the occasional swig of beer. It was such a weird place, she'd thought. The environment was so ugly, so cold and featureless — with nothing really going for it. She missed the beach, the warmth of the nor'westers and the smell of the pine trees at the end of her street. She was just thinking of leaving the party to phone home when Tobin had walked up and handed her a drink.

'It's an ice-breaker,' he said, 'I mixed it myself. Try it.' For a minute she'd stood awkwardly, a bottle of beer in one hand, the blue 'ice-breaker' in the other. She'd felt self-conscious, knowing that everyone would see that she had two drinks. The ice-breaker had been good, though. It was very sweet and it suddenly made her realise how thirsty she had been since arriving at the base. Throughout the past ten days she had had to carry a bottle of water around with her all the time. It was as if she could never get enough to drink. Especially when she was working. For the first time in her life she had gone hoarse — from talking on the radio.

She discovered that alcohol was much cheaper at Scott Base than at home. This had made it possible for her to buy a few drinks, and after a while she'd been able to relax and join in one or two conversations. She remembered how she'd gone outside with Tobin for a walk. It had been sunny and almost warm as they looked at the various sites where the No-men had been. Tobin had made her smile by telling her stories about the artist. He had been assigned to take care of him and it had been his job to make sure that no harm came to him, the base or the environment.

They strolled down onto the sea ice, following a road that was marked by red flags. They walked for ten minutes and then stopped to watch some Weddell seals beside a large tide crack. Their fat, dark bodies reminded Marilyn of slugs. She didn't know why but she had suddenly found herself confessing to Tobin that she didn't like being in the Antarctic. She told him she hated not being able to do simple things like walk along a beach. It gave her so much pleasure, she'd said, to paddle in the edge of the waves and feel warm water wash around her feet. She couldn't get over the fact that everything around Scott Base was either white and frozen or black and stony. She'd expected it to be like that, but even so, she hadn't been prepared for just how depressing it was, how little colour there was. Everything was black and white – and green, she'd added, looking back at the huts. She felt out of place. In fact the truth was, she didn't know – couldn't really understand – why anyone was even in the Antarctic. There was something unnatural about people living in a place that was permanently frozen. The Antarctic, she'd concluded, wasn't meant for humans.

Tobin had listened without interrupting and when she finished he did something completely unexpected. He didn't say anything but just hugged her. He put one arm around her shoulders and held her against his body for a second. She'd been so surprised she hadn't known what to do. It confused her and if it hadn't been for the fact that Tobin had smiled and said that they ought to head back before they got cold, she could imagine she might have just stayed put, rooted to the spot.

She'd still felt unsettled when she got back inside. She'd wandered around for a bit, looking at the posters that dotted the walls of the corridors. Everything seemed strange and quiet all of a sudden, as if she was the only patient in a deserted hospital ward. There had been no one around and in the end she'd decided to phone Chris, just so she could hear someone's voice. She'd needed to hear a familiar sound. It was only when she heard his croaky voice whispering into the phone that she'd looked at her watch and realised that despite the sunlight outside it was three in the morning – just as it was in New Zealand.

Her attention was suddenly caught by the woman next to her. Her head had fallen forward so sharply that she had bitten her lip. A trace of blood appeared and she was wiping at it with the back of her hand.

'Are you all right?' Marilyn shouted the words and then remembered she had a packet of paper handkerchiefs somewhere in her pocket. Passing one of the hankies to the woman, she repeated, 'Are you all right?' The woman nodded as she took the tissue. Marilyn smiled and said, 'My name's Marilyn, by the way.'

The woman nodded and replied, 'Sally.' She dabbed at her lip, then smiled and added, 'Hello.'

SALLY

They'd only been in the air for half an hour but the travel-sick pills had made Sally groggy. Her body seemed to be trapped midway between bored wakefulness and uncontrollable sleepiness. Her thoughts were dulled and disordered, swinging from an awareness of her current surroundings to a vague memory of the past two weeks. She'd ended up taking two pills, the first one half an hour before the time of their scheduled departure, and then another three hours later when they'd finally heard the words 'Good to go' and boarded the plane.

She supposed she'd drifted off to sleep, though she felt as if she'd been awake the whole time. She had felt the constant shuffling of the woman next to her and had been aware, too, of a sticker attached to the wall of the plane opposite her seat. She'd read it several times: 'Find your G-spot! Georgia, USA'. Each time she glanced away, tried to focus on some other part of the plane, her gaze would be drawn back to the words, until, in the end, she convinced herself she'd been looking at the sticker the whole time. Then her head had jerked violently forwards and suddenly she'd woken up.

Her mouth felt dry. She had a water bottle somewhere. She'd put it on the seat between herself and Marilyn when she'd first sat down so it must still be there. It was probably just hidden in the layers of her coat. Her fingers crawled over the space next to her thigh but she felt nothing. She was just lifting a corner of her jacket when she felt a tap on her arm. It was Marilyn.

'Is this what you want?'

Sally nodded and took the bottle.

'Drink as much as you want. I think you can get more at the front of the plane.'

Cupping her hand around Marilyn's ear, Sally yelled, 'Thanks.' She took a swig from the bottle and smiled. Even the water was warm. It tasted like the stuff she kept in the boot of her car for emergencies. She took another gulp, then stopped. She'd better hold back or she'd have to go to the toilet. Squeezing past the other passengers would require more skill and effort than she was capable of mustering at the moment. Better to try and stay put for as long as possible.

Even the heat of the plane seemed to be acting like a weight on her body. That sense of weight was familiar – she had felt it before, in her tent at Bratina Island. There was a difference, though. The light. Whereas the interior of the aeroplane, with its scattering of dull orange bulbs, brought to mind some dark alley, her tent had always reminded her of summer. The constant golden yellow light that had encapsulated her as she lay awake in her sleeping bag, watching as the thin nylon of the domed tent walls billowed in the wind, had brought to mind fields of wheat swaying in a warm summer breeze. She recalled the noise, too – a sound like sheets flapping on a clothesline, and the squeak of the windsock as it spun above the wanigan.

While camped on Bratina Island, she would wake many times during the night. Each time she would be unable to gain any visual clue as to the time. Once, she imagined that she had been asleep for hours, only to discover that it had been less than twenty minutes. Another time she had woken and, not realising that the faded red cloth of her sleeping bag cover had worked its way up over her face, had momentarily panicked, thinking something terrible had happened to her vision, that the bright glow against her face was the result of blood filling her eyes. She had been aware of her heart beating as she fought her way free, and the relief once she surfaced and discovered that nothing about her surroundings had changed. Everything was exactly as she had left it.

She had pulled her neck gaiter over her eyes then, and looked at the dark band it created immediately in front of her, contrasting with the narrow shafts of light that seeped in at its upper and lower edges. She had kept her eyes open for a while, enjoying the experience of darkness and the soft shush made by her eyelashes against the warm fleece fabric. She'd stayed motionless for perhaps ten minutes before sitting up and pulling the gaiter back down around her neck and looking once more at her watch. It was a quarter past four.

She'd felt restless, as if she should simply get up and go for a walk around the camp. If she walked for only a few minutes, past the other tents, she would arrive at a place on the hillside where she could watch the skua and its chicks. It would give her something to do. She sat up and glanced around. Her clothes lay in a neat pile next to her sleeping bag. She took her fleece jacket from the top of the pile, then lay back down. She felt tired and the thought of getting dressed, of having to climb into her clothing and boots before leaving the tent, seemed too difficult. It was easier simply to lie down and stare at the tent walls.

She was aware of a new sound, a sound like rain but sharper somehow. She listened and then, unable to pinpoint the noise, leaned forward and unzipped the tent door. In front of her, the sky appeared to have been draped in tinsel. She guessed it was snowing but instead of large soft flakes she saw tiny ice crystals, diamond dust, shattering the sky as they caught and twinkled in the light.

Sally blew on her hands, suddenly aware of the difference in temperature between her sun-warmed tent and the cold air outside. She glanced at her watch once more and sighed. Her three companions wouldn't be up for at least another three hours, possibly four. Moreover, her own impatience to get going was constantly challenged by an equally strong desire to stay warm. She'd wait. In three hours she would get up and take the others a hot drink. That's what she'd do. She wriggled down into her sleeping bag, pulling the draw-cord tight above her head. When she tilted her face she was aware of a small circle of light. Apart from that, she was conscious only of the nylon of the sleeping bag against her mouth and a slight dampness from her breath.

Some time later she awoke with a start, still enclosed inside her sleeping bag. Beneath her longjohns and vest she felt damp, sweaty. She was conscious, too, of her body's smell. It was an acrid smell, unfamiliar, a mixture of perfume, sweat and damp polypropylene. She took a deep breath, as if, like some animal, she could identify her body by its smell, and then unfastened her sleeping bag and sat up. The tent still glowed orange – the same light as when she had first gone to sleep. Nothing at all had changed in the ten hours she'd been in bed.

As soon as she left the tent her fingers began to feel cold. Her shoulders, too, felt tense from the cold and she was reminded of the year she'd once spent in Scotland. The winter there, she remembered, had been the bleakest she had ever experienced. The damp, chilling cold had produced a permanent sensation of tightness in her chest as she walked through the streets of Glasgow's West End. She recalled the weekends spent sitting and reading inside the hot-house in the botanic gardens, the only place where she felt comfortable, cradled within an atmosphere of warmth as light flickered through a canopy of ferns and palms, separating her from a city that appeared to be in a continual state of melancholic, subdued half-light.

The air inside the wanigan was no warmer than that outside. Whatever heat it had had the previous night had seeped away, leaving the space chilled. Sally was aware of the sound of her footsteps as she covered the few feet from the door to the workbench. It brought to mind every garden shed or tramping hut she had ever stepped into – there was a noise that belonged exclusively to those huts and always unfolded in a particular pattern. First, the sound of boots being kicked against a doorframe to remove loose stones, then the noise made by the very first step into the hut, which marked the move from solid ground to a floor that seemed almost to sag under a person's weight. The hollowness to the steps was matched by the feeling of being suddenly within an unoccupied space, the emptiness magnified by coldness. It was as if she was experiencing the sound of coldness and it wasn't until she had lit both the gas burner and the primus, and heard the increasing roar of the latter, that she was able to relax.

She glanced about the hut, walked over to the window and stood reading the names scrawled on the wall. 'Two wonderful weeks with good companionship and exciting science spent with Custard Smith, Choucroute Villeneuve and Don Quichote. Thanks. University of Konstanz, Germany.' 'K300 RNZE: Stevo, Thomo, Po, Jimo and Jacko ... Go catch me a penguin mate ...' Her eye returned to the name Jim and she was immediately transported back to Dunedin and her own children. They would be sitting up in bed, next to Manu, as he explained, once more, where she had gone – and when she would be back. Her thoughts settled on the image of her family but were interrupted by the sound of the billy lid, which had begun to clatter. Reaching absentmindedly for the boiling water she felt a sting as the wire handle branded a line across the palm of her hand. She looked at the red mark and, beside it, a long white line – a burn from the previous day.

She carried three cups of tea outside. It was not yet eight and for a moment she felt self-conscious, uncertain whether she should be going to the others so early in the morning. Standing outside Craig's tent she paused while she thought of what to say.

'Cup of tea?' She spoke quietly and felt foolish as she stood in the cold, anticipating an answer. She waited and heard nothing. She moved on to Karen's tent and repeated the question. A voice answered from the tent. 'Thanks.'

'I'll just put it outside your door.'

Again, the word 'thanks' reached her as she wandered back towards the wanigan, Craig's tea still in her hand. Suddenly, she felt silly. Even though she didn't know Craig, there was no reason to suppose that he wouldn't be pleased to have a drink. Perhaps he had simply not heard her. She returned to his tent, said, 'I've made a cup of tea for you. Do you want it?'

There was a noise like a shuffle and his voice mumbled back, 'What?'

She had woken him. Her heart sank. 'Hot tea?' She glanced at the plastic mug and noticed that the drink was no longer steaming. 'I'll put it outside your tent. It's there if you want it,' she added, turning as Craig's voice mumbled, 'Thanks.'

She smiled. All she had done was make a few cups of tea and she had wound up feeling as awkward as a child going door to door selling sweets for a school fundraising project. She could feel her heart beating as she made her way to Brent's tent, the last mug of lukewarm tea in her hand. Again the call, 'Cup of tea?' And this time an enthusiastic response: 'Great. Thanks.'

'I didn't know how you like it – so it's white, no sugar.'

'Thanks.'

She hesitated, expecting Brent's face to appear at the opening to his tent, but apart from his voice there was no indication that the tent was occupied.

'It's a nice day. Sort of sunny but cold.'

'Cool.'

She waited a moment longer, glancing into the distance as if the sight of the mountains and glaciers might prompt further conversation, then said, 'I'm going back to bed – it's warm in my tent.'

There was no reply.

Sally was lost in thought, her mind wandering over that first morning on Bratina Island when she felt a body jostle against her legs. Looking up, she saw William. He passed in front of her, stumbling over the legs of the other passengers, as he made his way towards the front of the plane. Deciding to make the most of the path he had made, Sally quickly unbuckled her seatbelt and followed, falling immediately onto Marilyn, who was staring straight ahead as if in a hypnotic daze.

William stood facing the stairs that led to the open door of the flight deck. Sally could see past him, through the opening, the large windows of the cockpit, which gave the impression of a large conservatory in an otherwise dark villa. 'Hello again.'

William nodded but said nothing.

'Are you waiting to use the toilet?'

She watched as William shrugged.

'Noisy, isn't it?' She yelled the words, but again William gave the impression of not having heard. She realised she would have to stand on her toes and speak directly into his ear if she wanted to make herself understood, so instead she simply gestured towards the toilet door. He shook his head, indicated that she should go on, and turned back to the flight deck. It created a strange impression: a grown man facing a distant window like a child trying to see past the heads of adults in a crowd.

He was still standing, staring towards the open blue sky, when she returned.

'I bet they have a great view up there,' Sally shouted, and saw William smile. Perhaps he had heard, though it was more likely he was just being polite.

'I bet there's a great view from the flight deck.' She spoke more slowly and this time William frowned before replying, 'Yes.' He said something else but she couldn't hear.

'It's hot, isn't it?' she shouted.

He looked at her, his expression blank.

'I said it's hot! Stifling. A sauna!' She watched his face for signs of a response but he gave none.

Raising her hand in a slight wave, she began the journey back to her seat. Ladders, she thought. That's what the passengers reminded her of. A game she had been forced to play at primary school, where two teams had sat facing each other, their legs stretched out in front with the soles of their shoes touching as one member of each team ran – stepped – over the legs of their teammates.

As she sat down she saw Marilyn look in her direction. 'What did William say to you?' Sally moved closer in order to catch the question. 'The old guy,' she heard. 'What did he say?'

'William? Oh. Nothing much. Why, do you know him?'

A slight frown crossed Marilyn's face. 'I know most people.' She paused, appeared to study Sally's face, then added, 'By radio, I mean.' Sally nodded but felt uneasy.

'I was once told that he couldn't deal with people any more,' Marilyn continued after a long pause. 'In fact, I heard from some carpenters who went over to Cape Royds at Christmas that he had practically stopped talking, hadn't spoken to his research assistant for weeks. But there's always stuff being said about people that's not true. I visited him out there and he was nice. In fact, he came to my rescue once.' Marilyn looked at Sally and, seeing no response in her eyes, repeated more loudly, 'I said he's normal!' Sally nodded, waiting for Marilyn to continue. 'He's a world expert on skuas.' Marilyn raised her eyebrows. 'Strange, eh?' She leaned forward, as if about to shout something important. 'I mean, fancy spending your whole life studying skuas!'

Although she didn't know William, Sally felt herself wanting to jump to his defence. 'I quite like skuas.'

'What? Wait.' Sally watched as Marilyn removed a yellow foam tube from her ear.

'Skuas – they're probably very interesting birds.'

Marilyn looked at her, an expression of disbelief crossing her face. 'Skuas? You've got to be kidding.'

WILLIAM

There was a noise William had never managed to describe to his own satisfaction: the sound made by several thousand penguins at the Cape Royds colony. He had given a lot of thought to describing the noise; its description had occupied his mind as he walked through the colony. Recently he had even begun to wonder whether the sound – or, rather, its description – had become an obsession. Even now, as he stood in the front of the aeroplane, contained by a noise and half-light that made him feel as if he was actually inside – or even part of – the aeroplane's engine, his thoughts somehow managed to drift back to the penguin colony.

The noise, he recalled, was constant. Moreover, there was a density to it: a bass note over which a swell travelled like ocean waves. The surface sound was cheerless, as if a duck was trying to imitate a kookaburra. But individual birds, when singled out from the rest of the colony, made a different noise, one he imagined would be similar to that made by a seagull if it could bark like a dog. William frowned. It was the best he could do. He had never really been one for sound, anyway. He had never been able to understand music and, as a result, had always preferred silence to the sound of any instrument. It had always struck him as a strange twist of fate that Alice, his wife, should have made a career out of music.

'Opposites attract,' she had told him once, shortly after their first meeting over forty-five years ago. She had even set out to prove her theory with a quiz modified from some popular psychology questionnaire printed in a magazine. 'I'll say a word and you say the first thing that comes into your head, okay? North.'

'South,' he'd replied.

'Positive …'

'Negative.'

'Man …'

He had smiled, he vaguely recalled, as he submitted himself to her barrage. 'Woman.'

'You see,' she'd concluded, 'that proves it.'

He'd shaken his head. Her test had proved nothing and she knew it.

'Rubbish,' she'd countered. 'Opposites attract. You try it.'

'Love.' He could remember saying the word. It was the first time he had used it in her presence and here he was throwing it at her like a challenge. There'd been a long pause while he'd waited for her reply. She'd frowned. She knew what she had to say, but appeared to William to be reluctant to utter the word 'hate'. He felt he was taking advantage of her, being unfair, bending the rules in order to provoke her. He continued to watch her face, anticipating her reply, teasing the answer from her mouth with every second that passed. He pictured her frown, the way she screwed up her face and then the way her mouth had finally relaxed into a smile as she answered, 'Marriage!' She was triumphant. Although she had failed to prove her point, and lost the game, she had succeeded, nevertheless, in manoeuvring him towards a more satisfying conclusion, one of her own design.

'Marriage,' she had repeated.

And although he had nodded – 'Yes. Love and marriage' – he had felt a slight chill, as if her words really did signal a clash of opposites.

He was to recall his sense of unease less than three months later. They were on honeymoon when Alice had revealed that she had fallen in love with him after only a few minutes of making his acquaintance. It was a confession that had seemed both to delight and embarrass her. 'I don't believe in love at first sight,' she'd explained. 'In fact, I wasn't even aware of what was happening at first. It was as though the decision to fall in love with you wasn't mine to make, but then, once the *falling* had taken place, I became part of the process. My input was to *be* in love with you. That's how it happened.' She'd smiled, gently stroking her fingers along the curve of his brow bone, then asked, 'What about you? How did you fall in love?'

It was a question she should never have asked, and if she'd known him better, she wouldn't have. He felt uncomfortable hearing talk about love. Even when he proposed to her he avoided the word, and now her question struck him as somehow presumptuous. But, having just made love to her, he felt torn by a sense of duty, as if she was entitled, in a way, to hear the words. Her head was resting on his chest and she was gazing towards his face, waiting for his reply. She was smiling in anticipation, oblivious to his discomfort.

The idea of falling in love, of being in love, didn't make sense to him. Moreover, the very notion of 'love' was something he wasn't sure of. He knew that other people – his wife, for example – not only believed in love but seemed to gain strength from it, but to him the term 'love' was no more tangible, or relevant, than 'God'. Both words struck him as unsatisfactory; they elevated humans above animals and he was not prepared to do that. That, he had decided, was human arrogance at its worst.

He'd stroked her hair and replied, 'You once said that opposites attract.' She'd smiled and looked away. He recalled her silence and the pang that went through his chest as he saw himself failing her exam. He remembered the sense of shame coupled with irritation as he resolved never to be caught in a similar situation again.

'Excuse me, sir!'

William started, shaken from his memory. A man in army uniform was standing next to him, holding out his jacket.

'Would you mind very much holding onto this for me? Just for a minute, while I use the bathroom?' William nodded, took the coat from the man, who added, 'Something I ate last night ...'

William nodded again, and watched as the soldier stepped past him and into the toilet. He knew, as he watched, that the other passengers were also watching. They'd all know that the man was having trouble with his bowels. Using the crew toilet, when a bucket had been set up at the back of the plane for the male passengers, was as good as advertising the fact to the world. It embarrassed William to be privy to the soldier's problems. He felt, too, as if the passengers were now observing him, focusing on his body, as some kind of stand-in for the American.

William examined the man's jacket, turning it in his hands until the soldier's name became visible. Lester. His name was Lester. He couldn't have been much more than twenty years old. It was difficult to be sure, of course. Army personnel always looked young on account of their crew-cuts and uniforms, but William guessed that Lester was a similar age – perhaps a little younger – to himself when he had made his first trip to Cape Royds in the summer of 1959.

His shoulders shuddered involuntarily as if he was experiencing, once more, the cold of that first season. It was the sensation of cold that had remained with him all these years. During the last season there had been times when he had almost laughed out loud as he pictured himself as a young man, wearing the Aran jersey Alice had knitted for him. Apart from the fact that the colour of the jersey had been completely impractical – its cream wool a blank page onto which every stain and trace of dust had documented the day's events – its sleeves had been several centimetres too short. In the cold at Cape Royds this became a constant niggle and he was forever trying to invent new ways to cover the gap above his gloved hands.

It was only during the last season, however, that he had had any real reason to recall that jersey. Before, if queried, he would have had to admit that he hadn't seen it in years. He certainly hadn't spotted it since moving to Canada. It was nowhere among the cartons and books that littered the basement study of their new waterfront townhouse.

Alice never ventured into his study, referring to it as 'the teenager's room' on account of its cluttered disorder. But the room worked for him. With a bit of time and effort he could locate most things.

When they'd first married he'd been slightly irritated by the fact that he could never keep her out of his study. She was always inventing some reason to visit. He'd feel her presence before he saw her, a shadow or slight movement behind him as she stood holding a drink in her hand, an offering meant to validate her interruption. 'I've just made myself a cup of coffee, do you want one?' she'd ask as she stepped closer to where he was hunched over some paper or other. 'What are you reading?' she'd ask, then stand just behind him, looking over his shoulder as he tried to concentrate on the page before him.

'Nothing much. Just a paper on skuas,' he'd say, waiting for her reply.

'Oh.'

It was only after several years of this that her response was followed by a sigh. At first it had been an 'Oh!' of enthusiasm. His words had appeared to her as an invitation to sit down, to spend a few minutes talking about the colonies around Cape Royds and elsewhere in the world. She had been intrigued, back then, by the fact that the South Polar skua migrated such huge distances. That the birds from Ross Island would fly to the North Pacific. Once, he remembered, she had noticed an article written by an African bird-watching group which had identified a South Polar skua off the coast of Senegal. She'd wanted to know what it was doing there, and when he had explained that it was almost definitely on its way north, to Scandinavia or Greenland most probably, she had murmured, 'Jeepers.'

'Wouldn't it make a great holiday,' she'd continued, 'to follow the migration of the skuas? Don't you think that would be an incredible trip? Something we could do together one year?' He'd nodded but felt no particular desire to make the journey. The idea of turning the migration of skuas into some kind of personal pilgrimage – or, worse, honeymoon – struck him as sentimental.

However, it was a subject to which Alice often returned during the first few years of their marriage. In fact for a while, he recalled, it had been one of her main topics of conversation. He hadn't recognised her motivation in so often bringing the discussion around to skua migration. He hadn't caught on to the fact that she was intent on remaining ever present in his thoughts, that she had somehow imagined that a skua-watching holiday would be enough to keep them together. It was as if she believed that if she could display an interest in the things he found interesting, he might, in turn, find her interesting. He hadn't been able to read her thoughts, and by the time he had worked it out it was too late. The inconceivable had happened. The marriage had changed, and she had moved on and created a new life for herself – one that appeared complete without him.

It wasn't until some weeks after the birth of their first child that he'd first heard her sigh. 'I guess you're too busy reading about skuas to give me a hand with Ralph?' she'd asked one Sunday morning. Her tone, he remembered, was light, full of humour, as if she actually expected him to turn around in his chair, arms outstretched, and take the baby from her.

The next time she'd asked for help there was a note of resignation in her voice, a sense of foreknowledge – a sigh she could not conceal.

The problem was, he was busy. He felt under constant pressure, barely able to keep up with the demands of his university position, his teaching commitments and the bureaucracy and logistics of his ongoing research projects. Still, that first sigh had made a mark on his body. He had looked up from his desk and smiled at her as she stood in the doorway, Ralph cradled in her arms, and lied. 'I'll be there in a minute. I've just got to finish this paper.' He remembered that she held his gaze for a moment and that in that moment he had felt uncomfortable, guilty. She had then turned away, gone back to the kitchen, where, he guessed, a bottle of milk would be warming or a pile of nappies sat waiting to be folded.

After the birth of their second son, Hector, William resolved to stay away from the house whenever he had work to do. As long as he stayed in his office, he reasoned, he could work efficiently, without interruption, and would therefore be able to finish early and return home to his family. He could work in peace, cocooned from the frustration and guilt he experienced whenever he walked through the front door of his home to be met by his wife's question: 'Did you have a good day?'

'Sir?'

William's mind jolted back to the present as he registered that Lester was standing in front of him, hands extended.

'Sir? Can I have my coat, please?'

William nodded as he passed the jacket back to the boy. The soldier took it and stood awkwardly, as if trying to think of something to say, some follow-up remark that would enable him to go back to his seat without appearing rude. William watched as Lester glanced towards the flight deck. He expected him to make some observation along the lines of what the Sally woman had said earlier but instead Lester asked, 'What is it you do down here? I mean, down on the ice?'

William hesitated before answering. 'I've been studying South Polar skuas.'

'Excuse me?'

Lester leaned closer and William was suddenly aware of a smell. It was a scent he had almost forgotten – of trees and wood. Aftershave, he guessed. He felt vaguely moved by the smell. He couldn't quite understand why the soldier's aftershave should have any effect on him but an image of home unexpectedly sprang to mind: a photograph of his wife and grown children standing in front of the weekend cabin they had built two summers ago while he was away on a research trip.

'I'm sorry, could you repeat what you said just now? I couldn't hear.'

William started, his thoughts still with the photographic image as he replied, 'I've been studying siblicide ... among South Polar skua.' He took in the blank expression that crossed the soldier's face and repeated more loudly, 'Siblicide.'

'Suicide? Those skuas commit suicide?'

'No, *siblicide*!'

'Oh.'

In his imagination William heard his wife's sigh.

SALLY

Sally looked up as a good-looking soldier passed in front of her. She glanced at Marilyn, saw that she had also turned to follow the soldier's progress, and their gaze met. They smiled in mutual recognition, then she heard Marilyn ask, 'What were you doing in the Antarctic?'

Sally indicated that she had her mouth full, that she would have to finish what she was eating before replying to the question. As she chewed, however, she was aware of a strange sensation – that the orange cheese in her mouth was simply bending from the pressure of her teeth rather than breaking up. It seemed to take forever before she could reply.

'I'm a composer.'

A fleck of cheese sprayed out of her mouth as she spoke, but Marilyn appeared not to notice.

'Oh. I thought you were an artist.'

'What about you? Sally asked. 'You're a communications operator, aren't you? I've heard you on the radio, I think.'

Marilyn frowned, as if troubled by Sally's comment, but said nothing to elaborate. Her silence, however, suggested that she didn't want to talk about herself. For several minutes both women appeared intent on the food they were eating. It was Marilyn who eventually resumed the conversation. 'Did you get any good ideas while you were away?'

Sally nodded.

'Good.' Marilyn paused, looked once more into her food bag, before adding, 'That's good. I'm glad.'

Ten days ago, on Bratina Island, the glaciologist Craig had asked a similar question. 'You're looking for inspiration, then?' he had said as they walked up the hillside towards the summit of the island. 'That shouldn't be too hard to find in a place like this, should it?'

Sally recalled that she had agreed simply because it had seemed the easiest thing to do. She hadn't wanted to admit that as far as her work was concerned she had no idea where or how to begin. In fact, she wanted to say, she wished she was a scientist. She thought that, compared with her, scientists had it easy. At least they knew what they were doing; they had a framework – a project – on which to focus, a particular location on which to concentrate, and material they could process using established scientific methods. A composer, on the other hand, could only hope to take a stab at some undefined 'thing'. What's more, she wanted to argue – though she didn't know who with – scientists had the luxury of making regular trips to the Antarctic. They could return year after year to work on their projects, whereas she was expected to come up with a finished piece after only fourteen days in the field. Thirteen days, if you took into account the fact that the flight down had been postponed a day due to bad weather. Bloody scientists, she wanted to say. You don't know how lucky you are!

As she followed Craig, the words 'You don't know how lucky you are' echoed through her head. Her feet, previously so clumsy in her too-large boots, suddenly seemed lighter, as if marching in time to the tune she now hummed.

Gradually, her feeling of anxiety over her work was replaced by a stronger one: of joy at being in the Antarctic. Never before had she felt so happy to be somewhere. Not just happy, she realised, but content. At that moment she felt completely cut off from her life in New Zealand, and yet, instead of feeling adrift, as she had expected, she felt secure, completely at ease – as if for the first time she was free to be herself.

'You don't know how lucky you are!' She sang the words out loud, perhaps louder than she imagined because suddenly Craig had stopped walking and she had stumbled into him. She stood facing him, the sound of her breath striking her as absurdly loud in comparison to his.

'What's that song? It's not something you composed, is it?'

Sally tried to read Craig's expression for signs of mockery. 'No, it's Fred Dagg – a character created by a New Zealand comedian over twenty years ago.' Craig nodded but looked past her, his gaze focused on something behind her back.

'I don't really remember Fred Dagg.'

Sally started at the sound of Brent's voice. She hadn't heard his approach and was unaware that he had caught up and was standing just below her, with Karen on his left. Although they must have been hurrying to catch up, neither of them was puffing. They weren't even red in the face.

'The original shows,' Brent continued, 'were way before my time.'

'Well, I don't have a clue who you're talking about.'

Craig wasn't from New Zealand so he couldn't be expected to know who Fred Dagg was, but hearing him say so made Sally feel old. Old enough to remember every Fred Dagg sketch she had ever seen, old enough to have bought a Fred Dagg album when it first came out and, moreover, to have memorised, more or less accurately, the words to most of his songs. Although reluctant to hear the answer, she felt compelled to ask, 'How old are you, Brent?' She noticed that Brent didn't hesitate before answering, 'Twenty-five.' He was so young he thought nothing of the question. She turned to Karen. 'What about you?'

Karen took longer than Brent to reply. There was something awkward in her response, thought Sally, some hint in her manner that suggested she felt self-conscious. 'Twenty-eight,' she eventually replied.

Sally felt disconcerted. She felt older now than on the day she had first realised that she was entitled to celebrate Mother's Day *as a mother*.

As if reading her thoughts, Craig turned back to her, saying, 'I guess that makes you the oldest, then.' Sally shrugged, her smile barely creasing her face.

Several minutes passed, the chorus of the Fred Dagg tune still rotating in her head, before she could bring herself to ask, 'Well, how old are you, then, Craig?'

Craig paused and it occurred to Sally that he was teasing her, holding back the information that now seemed so meaningful. Eventually, smiling, he replied, 'Thirty-eight.'

He watched her as he spoke, and as the silence between them grew, his smile broadened. Sally tried to return his smile, then turned to face the track, her feet trudging heavily up the scree slope. The cheeky bastard, she thought. She had been so certain he was at least three years older than her.

Twenty minutes later they had reached the summit of the island and were standing in a loose group looking down on the ice shelf below. It was an incredible sight. In the near distance were hummocks of dark gravel interspersed with ponds that reflected the blue of the sky. Further away, the landscape appeared flatter and white, a plain of ice that led Sally's eye towards Ross Island and Mt Erebus in one direction, and the Royal Society Range in the other. The view far exceeded anything Sally had imagined. It was not so much the vastness of her surroundings but the unexpected variety of landscapes – the sense that in whatever direction she looked she would see something that could only be described as spectacular.

Her eyes rested on the mountains, which rose, blue, from the clouds around their base. She had a sensation that distance had been foreshortened, as if she was looking at the range through the zoom lens of a camera. She had seen pictures of the Rockies, the massive flat-topped mountains near Banff, yet these mountains, although similar in some respects, struck her as more solid: enormous, ranging into the distance as if without end. The glaciers that caught and held the shifting shadows made by the clouds appeared to her as lakes that had been tilted so that their entire contents could be viewed.

She turned, and turned again, trying to take in the enormousness of the view, until finally her eyes settled on a patch of ground in front of her, the black stony gravel at her feet. It seemed more manageable to focus on what was close by. She'd been mistaken in thinking that the immensity of the space around her had made no impact. She kept her eyes focused on the ground, afraid that if she looked up, the others would see that she had tears in her eyes.

'What do you think, Karen, about those polygons?'

Sally raised her head at the sound of the unfamiliar word. She glanced across to Craig but he was standing with his hands raised to his forehead, sheltering his eyes from the glare of the sun.

'They're big, aren't they?' replied Karen.

'Yeah, that's what I thought.' Craig laughed as he spoke, then, turning to Sally, repeated, 'They're big.'

All around Sally the hillside was patterned with furrowed markings, which brought to mind the shell of a massive tortoise. Although she wasn't certain, she thought it was these patterns that Craig and Karen had described as polygons.

'Listen, Sally,' Craig said, 'can you do me a favour and walk down a bit and stand in the centre of one of them? I need you for scale.'

When she reached the place he had indicated she stopped. How was she meant to stand? She was aware of being watched – the way she felt whenever a car stopped for her at a pedestrian crossing. She'd never been asked to represent scale before. Should she stand with her hands by her sides or simply relax comfortably? She wasn't even sure whether she should face the camera. She glanced back to the three people she had left, who now stood watching her, and felt embarrassed, as if she was the butt of a joke. It would be better, she decided, if she turned her back on them. That way she could give the impression of not being involved, of being nothing more than a marker.

She wondered how she would introduce a sense of scale to her own work, and then shivered. It was freezing. Her clothes, sweaty from the walk up the hill, now felt like cold hands against her back. Her face, too, felt stiff; her bottom jaw, when she moved it, seemed to creak. Craig must have got his photographs by now, she thought. She'd give him ten more seconds, then go back. It wasn't until she turned around that she realised the others had disappeared. Apart from the knowledge that they couldn't be far away, there was nothing to suggest the presence of any other human – anywhere. For as far as the eye could see – in any direction – she was it.

'When I was a kid,' said Craig, picking at his meal that night, 'we had this music teacher called Miss MacDonald and she was pants.'

Sally looked up from her dinner. 'What do you mean, "pants"?'

Craig took a sip of wine before replying, 'Rubbish, you know. Crap.'

Sally and Brent shook their heads.

'And if something's "a load of pants",' Craig continued, 'it's particularly bad – like this dinner, for example.'

Sally looked at the food in front of her, a yellow-brown stew that had been heated from a packet labelled Chicken Nasi Goreng. She took a bite and the glob squelched between her teeth. Yeah, it was definitely pants, she concluded, smiling.

'The reason I hated music so much,' Craig went on, 'was because we had to start each lesson with a thing called "movement". Movement simply consisted of Miss MacDonald banging a drum while the class pretended to grow from acorns. We started off scrunched up in a kind of foetal position, and then had to uncurl our bodies and thrust our way through the earth before slowly standing and stretching like big trees –'

'And at that point Miss MacDonald would beat the drum faster ...' Sally interrupted.

'How did you know?'

'Because I remember my own primary-school teacher doing the same.'

From the other side of the table Brent joined in. 'We had to wiggle our fingers to make leaves on the trees.'

'So did we!' Craig laughed. 'Even as a six-year-old I knew it was totally stupid.'

'I just remember feeling embarrassed,' said Brent. 'The girls quite liked it but the boys hated it. Every time we had to crouch down we'd pull faces at one another and half of us would end up being sent to the corner to stand with our faces to the wall.'

'So,' said Craig, facing Sally, 'is that the type of thing you put your students through?'

Sally laughed. She pictured the faces of her Stage III composition class and wished she was brave enough to start her lectures with the acorn exercise. 'Not yet,' she laughed, 'but I might suggest it at the next staff meeting.'

'Anyway,' said Craig, as he prodded a perfectly formed baby carrot on his plate, 'what's your music like? Are you any good?'

Sally shook her head. 'No, I'm pants.'

There was a moment's silence as Craig turned the small, unnaturally orange carrot on his fork. 'No, but seriously, you must be all right, otherwise you wouldn't be here. They're not going to send someone who's rubbish all the way to the Antarctic, are they?'

Sally shrugged but said nothing. Of all the things she would like to talk about, her own work was not one of them. Although she didn't mind chatting about her teaching position, she was reluctant to discuss her own work as a composer. In many ways she felt ambivalent about what she did. Although she took her work seriously, she was unable to believe that the result justified the hours she put in. There was, she worried, something slightly ridiculous – something akin to Craig's memory of a child pretending to grow from an acorn to a tree – about being a composer. Occasionally she had been struck by the absurdity of what she did; that she would spend days hunched over a tape recorder, gathering sounds from the environment which she would then manipulate by computer to create a composition. The New Zealand Symphony Orchestra had twice commissioned work from her, and her compositions had been performed at electro-acoustic festivals throughout the world, but she continued to feel insecure about her work, and vaguely suspicious of her chosen field.

Her former husband had always urged her to find a real job. Regardless of the fact that he had known – and, she had thought, respected – her decision to establish herself as a composer, he had encouraged her to get work. Even now – seven years after their divorce, six years since her lecturing appointment – she could recall the exasperation in his voice during one particularly gruesome argument when he had accused her of being a 'fucking useless music-writing bitch'. It was one of the few times they had quarrelled and his outburst had left them both stunned and humiliated. In the hours and days that followed, she was to give a lot of thought to his words, and although she could never quite bring herself to forgive him, she could not shake from her mind the suspicion that he had been right.

After their marriage had collapsed, she found herself consumed by guilt. She knew that if she'd simply given in, found a job, helped to pay the mortgage and contributed financially to the partnership they might have remained married. Her unease intensified when, the very week she was forced finally to accept that she and her daughter could no longer survive on her earnings as a full-time composer, she was invited to apply for a lecturing position at the university. She recalled her excitement, her sheer joy, on being offered the job, and the fact that she had accepted on the spot, without even waiting to hear the conditions of employment or salary.

On that day, she remembered, she had felt enormous relief. Her work was finally being validated by others. No longer the useless music-writing bitch, she was now someone who could earn a living doing the one thing she wanted to do.

Her pleasure in that knowledge was marred by only two things: the first was that she had 'sold out' by becoming attached to the academic world, that she was no longer 'pure'; and, more important, her fear that, paid or unpaid, she wasn't terribly good at what she did. In her mind she was still a 'B' music student struggling to fluke an 'A'.

She was still deep in thought when Brent's voice intruded. 'I saw your application for the Artist in Antarctica Programme.' Craig and Karen turned to face him as he continued. 'Yeah, I read that stuff about you being a sonic artist.'

Sally groaned. She wanted to protest, to say, 'It's not what you think,' but before she could open her mouth Craig had joined in. 'You're a *sonic artist*? What does that mean?' And then, almost as an afterthought, he added, 'I would never have the guts to call myself something like "sonic artist".' He paused, looked at Sally closely. 'I mean, even if I was a composer I couldn't imagine myself using a term like that. I wouldn't be able to keep a straight face.' He hesitated, smiled good-naturedly in Sally's direction, and shrugged. 'I'm not putting it – or you – down or anything,' he said. 'It's just that … well, I don't know. What do I know about these things?' He smiled once more. 'I'm merely an ice artist.'

A brittle smile crossed Sally's face. She was aware that the eyes of three people were now focused on her. She cringed. Something about their expressions made her feel as if she had been singled out as the night's entertainment. Why on earth had she allowed herself to be persuaded into using a term like 'sonic artist' anyway? She had never used the term herself but her referee, the head of the Music Department, had insisted she use it in her application because it was more eye-catching than 'composer'. 'Composer', he had said, was fusty. It conjured up images of middle-aged men wearing black roll-neck skivvies. That remark, uttered by a middle-aged man wearing a black turtle-neck jersey, had struck Sally as bizarre. Still, he had insisted.

She caught Craig's eye and felt her cheeks redden. It was easy for him to smile. Like Karen, he had come down to study the McMurdo Ice Shelf. Sally wasn't quite sure what he was doing exactly, but she had gathered from a remark made by Brent that he was examining the gravel that covered the area around Bratina Island. Clearly, there must be more to it than that, but whatever his project was, it was probably worthwhile. Brent's presence in the Antarctic was also legitimate. He was a professional mountaineering guide who had been assigned to look after the group's safety out in the field. In short, all three of them had proper jobs, while she was visiting the Antarctic as a 'sonic artist'. It wouldn't surprise her if everyone assumed her trip was just a perk, a free holiday to the ice.

She had just opened her mouth, ready to speak out in her own defence, when Karen said, 'I've been to one of Sally's concerts.'

Sally started; she could barely believe her ears. No one went to her concerts. Or rather, people did attend her concerts, but only students and friends. Not, as far as she knew, perfect strangers, and certainly not people she could ever imagine meeting again at some later, completely unrelated, gathering. She wouldn't have thought it possible but the evening was going from bad to worse.

It had surprised Sally to hear Karen speak; she had barely said a word all evening. Unlike the others, she seemed to be more at ease listening to the conversations of others. All day she had been friendly but shy, unwilling to be drawn into small talk or discussion on any topic that touched upon the personal. But now here she was describing a concert she had been to.

The evening, Sally recalled, had been intended as a showcase for student work, but due to a last-minute programme change, two of her pieces had been included. Given the lack of rehearsal time, the musicians, both final-year students, had coped well. She had felt proud of them. It had been possible to feel proud of their performance while at the same time feeling nothing at all about the music they played. It was as if the work, two pieces she had spent months labouring over, no longer had anything to do with her. By the time of the concert, the works were already a thing of the past, barely able to elicit any emotional response from her.

Now, however, she found herself listening to Karen's recollection of the performance with an intense interest she had not experienced during the performance itself. Although she remained silent as Karen spoke, she was conscious of following every word, absorbing the information in the same way that she might respond to a horoscope read aloud from a magazine. She experienced the sensation of not quite believing what she heard, while at the same time anticipating some insight into the very nature of her being. Unsure of whether to feel embarrassed or flattered, she found herself lowering her gaze, her head resting in the palms of her hands as she focussed on the half-empty plate before her.

As Sally listened it became clear to her that her insecurity was such that although there was something deeply personal about her music, something she was reluctant to share with the public, she needed it to be played before an audience in order for her to gain any impression of its worth. But hearing the concert described so favourably by Karen made her feel as if she had been caught out in the act of lovemaking by a complete stranger. Although mortified to be spied on, she could imagine the contradictory satisfaction that might result from the stranger's soft murmur; an approving remark, congratulating her on the fact that she had nice tits and a cute arse.

'The second work,' Karen continued, 'was called "What's the point of being forty if I can't do what I want".' Sally heard her own foot begin to tap gently against the leg of her chair, a sign of her growing discomfort. Karen had got the title wrong and although it was a minor detail, Sally felt an overwhelming desire to correct her. It didn't seem right to simply let the mistake pass.

She mumbled, 'It's not important, but the piece was called "You need to accept that I'm forty now and stop treating me like a child".' Her voice wavered as it dawned on her that the title was far too long, bordering on the pretentious. Nevertheless, she continued. 'It was a work I wrote in response to something my teenage daughter said. She's seventeen now,' she added. 'I meant it as a kind of joke, I suppose.' She hesitated, then added, 'Needless to say, my daughter didn't find it particularly funny.'

She paused, took a breath and looked around the table. Brent was the first to speak. 'I know this is completely unrelated to what Karen has just been saying, but do you really have a teenage daughter? I don't want to sound like a wanker but you don't look that old.' Sally felt the tension leave her body. Laughing with relief, she replied, 'Oh, is that right?'

'That's kind of cool,' interrupted Craig. 'Not that you've got a seventeen-year-old daughter, obviously, but that you can write music. I wouldn't have a clue where to begin with something like that. Can you see what I mean? I can't imagine being able to sit down with a blank sheet of paper, or a blank screen, or whatever, and simply start from scratch to produce something. It amazes me that anyone could do that.'

Sally felt taken aback. She hadn't anticipated a positive

reaction. She'd hoped, at best, for a kind of neutral silence, but had been ready for something negative – condescension or straight-out hostility. She smiled. In fact, she could feel her entire face relax into a grin. Once again she caught Craig's eye, saw him smile briefly in her direction before turning to face the window.

'Mind you,' he said, 'what do I know about music?' He paused, turned again to face Sally, and held her gaze. The corners of his mouth curled into a smile. 'I wouldn't know a good tune if it kicked me in the arse.'

It had been difficult falling asleep that night, Sally remembered. When she awoke the following morning she felt weightless, almost light-headed, and she had found it exhausting to get up and take drinks to the others. She was surprised to experience a feeling close to anticipation, however, as she stood outside Craig's tent, a cup of coffee in her hand. 'I've made you coffee,' she said, and waited for Craig to pull back the flap of his door. If anything the temperature was colder than the previous day and she felt her face begin to stiffen from the chill. She hesitated, anticipating a response from Craig, but when, moments later, there was still no sound coming from inside his tent, she said, 'I've leave it by your door.' As she began to trace her footsteps back to the wanigan she heard a mumbled 'Thanks'. She stopped, turned to face the tent but, seeing no one, continued to walk away. For some reason, one that she could neither define nor understand, she felt disappointed.

Later that morning she had followed the others as they went about their work. The walk across the landscape surrounding the island was unlike anything she had encountered before. Low hummocks thinly covered in gravel stretched out before them, extending into the distance like a desert of blackened dunes. Between the mounds, filling each hollow, were ponds.

While some of the ponds were only a few metres across and easy to navigate, others stretched for hundreds of metres, their shorelines disappearing from view as they hugged the base of each low hill.

From what Sally could understand, they were to locate poles that had been placed on the ice shelf several months earlier. Karen and Brent walked ahead, tracking the location of each point by global positioning system. Occasionally they would pause to study the readout on their individual GPS. After a brief discussion Karen would gesture ahead, remarking in a voice barely audible to the others, 'It should be 1.2 kilometres that way.'

Had they been able to fly, thought Sally, the task would have been easy. As it was, they could never be sure of which route to take to each marker. The height of the hummocks prevented them from seeing more than a short distance, and even when they stood on the summit of a hill they could never be sure of the perimeter of the pond nearest to them. Time and again they set off in one direction, only to discover that one pond had merged into another and so on, until the presence of what was now a lake forced them to walk back the way they had come. At these times they would often pause, and Sally would gaze around uselessly as Karen focused on the GPS and mumbled, 'The marker's 1.4 kilometres back that way.' A silence would follow as each of them took in the gesture of Karen's arm, a signpost as firm and direct as any roadside marker, and then, once more, they would resume their trek, slowly pacing out a course that appeared to Sally as haphazard as that made by an insect climbing a sand dune.

As she walked, trailing the others, Sally became more and more aware of the damage caused by her footprints. It was strange, she thought, that she could have spent so many years wanting to come to the Antarctic, so many years feeling drawn to the place, filled with a longing that she never imagined would be satisfied, and yet here she was, in the location of her dreams – and she was literally destroying it. Even though she placed each step carefully, planting her boots into the hollows made by the others, there was no getting around the fact that she was scarring the dunes, leaving tracks that might never disappear. Far more permanent than any headstone, her footprints, that scraggly line trailing clumsily behind her, might be the one, everlasting testament to her time on earth. She recalled a pair of feather-soled moccasins she had once seen in a museum display in Dunedin. Made by a Native American, the shoes had been labelled 'Revenge slippers'. Fashioned from feathers, they rendered their wearer invisible, permitting him to kill his victim while remaining undetected. More relevant, however, from her point of view, was the fact that the slippers left no tracks.

A new thought suddenly crossed her mind. In a matter of days she would leave the Antarctic and never return. The image of her departure struck her as final, like death. She glanced around and, for an instant, was struck by a sensation of having already left Bratina Island. It was as if she was looking back at herself from a distance, reliving the memory of this particular morning while still being present in it. She felt unsettled, suddenly lonely – as if she had lost something precious, and yet, as far as she was aware, she felt no attachment to the place. It was not as if some spiritual thread linked her to the Antarctic. Indeed, she had always been scornful of anything to do with spiritualism. As far as she was concerned, there was nothing 'out there', and being in the Antarctic wasn't about to change her mind on that score.

At that moment, Craig's voice broke through her thoughts. 'What are you thinking about?' he asked.

She hurried forward, catching up before replying, 'I was just thinking about our tracks.'

Craig nodded, 'Yeah, they're a bit untidy, aren't they?' They rested for a minute, allowing the others to walk ahead.

'What about you, what were you thinking?' Sally asked. It was the type of question she would normally never ask but, for some strange reason, being in such a spectacular place brought out the banal in her. Simple – even silly – conversations humanised the place, rendered it less overpowering. But, more important, she wanted to talk to Craig in order to extinguish the slight sadness that had settled inside her. She waited for him to answer, hoping that whatever he said would cheer her up.

'I was just wondering if I locked the door to the hut when we left this morning.'

It took Sally a second to appreciate the absurdity of the remark, then, smiling, she replied, 'You'd better go back and check.'

Craig glanced towards the island, which appeared wedge-like in the distance. 'Perhaps the footprints will disappear once the wind picks up,' he said.

They stood still, quietly taking in the view. Brent and Karen had already disappeared from sight, the sound made by their feet on the stones no longer audible. Sally was glad they had gone. She wanted to rest for a minute and enjoy her surroundings. She also felt a desire to prolong her conversation with Craig. She liked being with him. There was nothing irritating about his teasing and, although it seemed almost too clichéd to admit, she found him interesting. Despite the fact that she didn't know what to talk about – that she couldn't chat about his work and didn't want to say anything about her own – she liked his company. And, although she might have been imagining it, she had sensed a slight tension whenever she had spoken to him – an attraction, perhaps. She smiled, feeling foolish for allowing herself to believe such a thing.

If nothing else, she liked the sound of his voice. It was quiet and created a sense of intimacy; it was the type of voice she found attractive. She had been attracted to a voice only once before in her life and that voice, she recalled, had belonged to a woman. The woman's name had been Alice and she had been the mother of her flatmates, two brothers with whom she had shared a house in Glasgow more than eighteen years ago. She had long since lost contact with Ralph and Hector. Alice was Canadian, but the boys had been born in New Zealand, with links to Scotland through their father's father, a remarkable man by all accounts, who had died at the age of ninety-two in the home of his birth on Islay.

Ralph and Hector had often spoken about their grandfather, the influence he had had on their lives, and yet they had remained almost silent when it came to the subject of their own father. In the year Sally had spent with them, she learned only that their father was an academic, that his name was Bill and that he had neglected them throughout most of their childhood years, preferring instead to concentrate on his research. From the dismissive tone of the boys' voices, Sally assumed 'birds' referred to both the type and number of women their father had favoured throughout his lifetime.

Their mother, Alice, however, was clearly much loved and respected. Her voice, Sally recalled, was sexy. There was no other word to describe it. Despite the fact that she was Canadian, her voice appeared to be almost without trace of an accent – low and slightly knowing, as if she was one step ahead of everyone else, party to some kind of private joke. Sally had fallen in love with Alice's voice, and whenever possible she would allow dinner to drift into supper just so she could hear her friends' mother speak. In Sally's ears, Alice could have made a bus timetable sound like an exotic journey.

Alice had visited the boys on two occasions, and during the second visit Sally had discovered that she wrote music. Only after days of conversation did she find out that Alice's work had been critically well received in her home town of Vancouver, and that she was visiting Glasgow at the invitation of the university where Hector studied. Thinking back to those evening conversations, Sally recalled that Alice had named her sons after two of her favourite composers. 'If it had been left to Bill,' she once said, 'both boys would have been called John.' She smiled as she spoke and it had struck Sally that despite the boys' reluctance to talk about their father, there remained a great deal of affection in Alice's voice whenever she mentioned him. 'Bill was never very interested in names,' she continued, 'although if we'd had a girl I think he would have wanted to call her Adele, or Adélie, perhaps, after one of his beloved birds.'

It had taken several more days before Sally had confessed to Alice that she, too, was interested in writing music. 'I'm not very good,' Sally had explained. 'It's something I'm interested in but I don't know where to start, really.' She had been working part-time at an antique auction house, earning barely enough to meet her share of the rent. Most mornings she would rise in the pre-dawn gloom and travel the length of town, from the West End to Bath Street, where she would put on her dust-jacket and join her workmates in the staffroom of Swann's. She would sit quietly, watching, as each morning Mrs Mullen cooked a full breakfast of bacon, sausages, eggs and tomato for the men employed by the firm. She would listen to Mrs Mullen, the steady stream of words that flowed from her mouth, statements obscured in a Scots accent so thick that it was only the usual 'Are you nay eating today, hen?' that she could be sure to understand.

It had been a Sunday morning, a windy, cold day in November, when she had finally confessed to Alice her intention to be a composer. They had gone for a walk and had wandered into the Botanic Gardens, seeking shelter from the sleet inside the hot-house. It had been so cold, Sally recalled, that she had had trouble breathing. Her chest felt so tight, so cramped from the chill that she had barely been able to speak. Now, however, she sat next to Alice, watching a young girl run circuits inside the glasshouse, her excited screams of 'Banana, banana!' filling the air. She had fallen into a dream when she heard Alice say, 'Listen, if you want to be a composer, just get on with it. Don't make excuses.' Sally had been startled by the urgency in Alice's voice. It was the first time her voice had sounded anything other than calm, relaxed. 'There's never going to be a right time to begin. It's like having children – there's no such thing as a right time and if you think about it too hard you'll just find yourself paralysed by indecision.' She had smiled, before adding, finally, 'Although I loved and respected my husband very much, still do, I realised quite early on that he would never be a "family man". Accepting that was very painful to me at first because I had always hoped to be included in every aspect of his life. I was young, times were different and I had looked to him to make me complete. But, you know, he was immersed in his research, travelling a lot … He was under constant pressure, I think, wanting to establish himself. Anyway, my life felt kind of empty. I had two kids; we were living in New Zealand – away from my family in Canada – and I was unsettled. So I turned to music. It started as a kind of therapy but then the bug bit me and I was off. Bill encouraged me right from the start. He felt guilty, I suspect, about the state of our marriage, so it was a relief, I guess, that I had found something with which to replace him. That's how he would have seen it, I'm sure. He probably didn't anticipate I would do so well, though. Poor chump!'

As suddenly as she had spoken, Alice fell silent. She had been embarrassed by her outburst, Sally later realised. It was the only time either Sally or Alice referred to Sally's desire to be a composer. The conversation had quickly shifted to other topics. They had talked briefly about Ralph's apprenticeship in a well-known restaurant and Hector's intention to travel, following the completion of his studies. At one point Sally had asked Alice about her husband's relationship with the boys. The question, she remembered, was met with an awkward silence. Alice had appeared uneasy, unsure of what to say. Eventually she'd shrugged and replied, simply, 'I honestly believe Bill did the best he could, but the truth is, he lost them years ago. I'm not sure he realises that, and I hope he never does.' She sighed, then smiled faintly. 'I think the boys used to think of Bill as some strange migrating bird, something that would spend a few months a year by the nest, you know, and then fly away, leaving the chicks to fend for themselves.'

She laughed and shook her head, but seemed to become lost in some memory of a distant past. They had sat in silence enjoying the warmth and the musty, earthy smell that filtered through the air, reminding them both of places far away from where they now sat.

'It's good here, isn't it?' Sally started at the sound of Craig's voice. 'It's not quite what I imagined, though.'

Sally nodded. Like most people, she supposed, she had pictured the Antarctic as being white. To find herself in a landscape dominated by grey shingle hummocks was unexpected. It didn't make the place any 'less', but it certainly distanced it from her visual dictionary of standard Antarctic images. How different things would have been, she mused, if as a child she had flicked through the pages of her Ladybird book and seen illustrations of Scott's party struggling over grey, stony ground on their way to the Pole. To have seen the Antarctic represented as something akin to the mounds of coal piled up at the Christchurch gasworks would, undoubtedly, have changed her perspective on events. Instead of heroic explorers, she would have imagined a group of chimney-sweeps trying to reach the Pole, their blackened faces caused not by exposure to blubber smoke but to common coal, the type burned in the kitchen back home.

She smiled, barely aware of Craig's voice as he continued. 'I always wanted to come to the Antarctic. Ever since I was a boy growing up in Hong Kong I had this thing about going to the South Pole.' As he spoke, he kicked absentmindedly at a clump of ice that had rolled down the slope and was resting by his feet. 'I didn't even see snow until I was fourteen.' He laughed before describing to Sally his first experience of snow: the yellowish, gritty slush that settled in the gutters along London's Oxford Street on New Year's Day. He had been travelling with his family to Scotland to visit his grandparents but had been forced to spend a night in London because of a missed flight. After Hong Kong, London had appeared grey and dismal, he told Sally. He had taken an instant dislike to England and his opinion had only softened because of the snow. If he hadn't seen snow, held it in his hands, he would have vowed then and there never to step foot in Britain again.

As Sally listened, memories of her own brief visits to London came back to her. She remembered her homesickness upon seeing a man wearing a Manawatu Netball Club sweatshirt step out of a bus she was boarding. She recalled the way she had watched him as he walked down the street and how she had wanted to stop the bus and run after him, just so she could talk to him, hear an accent that reminded her of home. She had welcomed the freedom of travelling by herself, of living with strangers – and then she had seen that sweatshirt and the desolation of her homesickness had cut right through her, forcing her to confront reality.

'I wish I could just nip home and tell my wife how good it is here.' Craig smiled as he spoke, and for an instant Sally thought he was making a joke. 'It's not that I want to go home,' he said, 'but I'd like to go back for a few minutes just so I could tell Liz that it's brilliant back here. That it's better than I imagined.'

Sally didn't know what to say. It was as if Craig's words had made her understand just how much she enjoyed being away from her own partner and children. She felt renewed. Everything around her was extraordinary and new and that, in itself, made her feel more alive, more alert than she had for years. She could see only beauty in her surroundings. She glanced at Craig and saw that he was waiting for her to respond. 'I didn't know you were married,' she mumbled. She looked away, embarrassed by the clumsiness of her remark.

'Did you not?' shrugged Craig.

Sally shook her head. She frowned, annoyed with herself for being surprised that Craig had a wife.

'Don't you ever have that feeling?' asked Craig.

Sally wasn't sure what feeling he was referring to, so remained silent, hoping that he would elucidate.

'I'm crap at putting things into words,' he eventually said, 'but it's like some things are just too good for only one person. You need to share them, or gift them, to someone else, just so you get maximum pleasure from the experience. He paused, looked around. 'I'm always imagining bringing Liz here …' His voice drifted to a standstill.

He looked at Sally, puzzled by her lack of response. 'Don't you have any desire to share this?' He hesitated before slowly repeating, 'Don't you ever feel like that?'

Sally shook her head. 'No, I'm always glad to be alone. I like the idea of holding on to certain experiences, protecting them – keeping them secret, maybe?'

Craig gave the block of ice a kick and watched it roll into the pond with a splash. He shrugged and laughed. 'Christ, you're a miserable git, aren't you?'

They began to walk once more, and although Sally knew that Craig had spoken without malice, she felt perturbed.

Perhaps she did appear miserable to others. Her husband had always accused her of having a 'grumpy gene'. She wondered how she could redeem herself in Craig's eyes and then pushed the idea away. He was just having her on. She shouldn't take herself so seriously all the time.

Several minutes passed before Craig spoke again. 'So, how's the old sound map going? Have you found inspiration yet?'

'I don't remember telling you about a sound map,' she said. 'How do you know about that?'

Craig laughed. 'I asked Brent about your project and he showed me your application.' He paused, registered the expression on Sally's face and added, 'You don't mind, do you?'

Sally frowned, but felt a certain amount of relief. At least now she wouldn't have to describe her project to the others. If, one by one, they simply discovered her intention to create a sound 'map' of the McMurdo Ice Shelf, she would be spared the embarrassment of having to explain it. She could keep the project to herself.

'I ought to sue you,' she said. 'That information was strictly confidential.' She saw Craig nod and glance away guiltily. His expression reminded her of Manu's dog whenever it had been caught stealing food off the kitchen bench. Perhaps she had been a bit hard.

Then Craig turned back to her. 'Karen's read it, too.' He laughed out loud at her reaction. 'Well, if you're going to be following us around, it's only fair that we should have some idea of what you're doing.' He stooped to pick up a shell from near his foot. He held it for a moment, turning it in his fingers, then passed it to Sally.

As she took it she glanced at his face but his gaze was already somewhere else, focused on the distance.

'Do you know the name of that glacier?' he suddenly asked. 'The sexy-looking one over there.'

Despite the fact that Sally was certain she didn't know, she looked to where he was pointing. 'Which sexy glacier?'

'The big curvy one over there.'

She shook her head.

Sally could feel her hands beginning to grow cold. The tips of her fingers were stinging, reminding her of biking to school in the 1970s. She recalled those winter mornings, the way her knees turned red from the cold, despite her attempts to hold her kilt flat against her thighs with one hand. Those long bike rides had been miserable. Unlike her friends, she hadn't been allowed to wear dark pantihose with short white socks. She'd been forced to wear regulation oatmeal-coloured knee socks. Her socks alone, she recalled, had succeeded in identifying her as a 'brain box'. The word 'nerd' hadn't existed back then.

'I haven't seen you get out your tape recorder.'

Sally faced Craig, her eyes squinting against the bright light. 'I've taken it out a few times, actually.' She paused, her mind on the sounds she had collected the previous day. Recording sound, for her, had always been an extraordinary experience – one she never grew tired of. To sit quietly, listening to the environment, its sounds filtered through headphones, was completely absorbing. In some ways it brought to mind the experience of being underwater: the way that, immersed in water, all sound became exaggerated and other-worldly. Even the most inconsequential, commonplace noise was amplified. Like a dripping tap heard from where one lay in bed during the early hours of the morning, it held the power to obsess. She felt compelled to locate the source of the sound, and yet, more often than not, its exact location remained elusive, obscured by other fragments, a constant detritus of noise which she visualised as swarming particles of light seen behind closed eyes. At times she had become so engrossed in what she was recording that she lost all sense of time or place, creating for herself a new world, one that was sensed aurally, indefinable by size or shape: a landscape that existed within its own time-scale – one that was only recognisable in retrospect, as it passed by, not one she could ever anticipate or predict.

The Antarctic had been different from any other environment she had recorded. The moment she distanced herself from the camp she was aware of an absence of background noise. Even the wind, which had always been a problem in New Zealand, was often strangely absent, the air around her cold and still, the air currents undetected by the microphone.

She turned to Craig. 'Whenever I use the recorder here I'm faced with the problem of there being so little to record. There's almost no sound.' She paused, wiped her nose, which had begun to drip. 'It's silent.' They stood watching each other while straining to hear some distant noise. Sally raised her hand once more to her nose and the rustle of her jacket seemed explosive in the motionless air. She saw Craig frown and realised that he was intent on listening.

After a short while he seemed to relax, his shoulders dropped. 'You're right. Nothing. It's almost spooky, isn't it?'

Sally could see her face reflected in Craig's sunglasses and she felt slightly uncomfortable, as if she was being observed. 'I've never been in such a quiet place before,' said Craig. Sally nodded. The whole environment could be defined in terms of what was missing: life, heat, smell, sound ... There was no night to mark the end of day – in fact, thought Sally, it was almost impossible to gain any sense of time. Everything about the place seemed both empty and continuous, circular. For one of the few times in her life she had a real sense of being on a planet that was round rather than flat.

She was about to speak, attempt to break into the silence in order to make something human of her surroundings, when Craig suddenly said, 'I read an article in the *Guardian* the other day which said it was almost impossible to find anywhere silent in Britain. Apparently there's so much noise from industrial development and motorways and stuff that a lot of the birds can no longer hear or distinguish the calls of potential mates.'

Sally looked once more at her reflection and noticed the shape of her body captured in Craig's lenses. She even looked small, she thought. 'Yeah, well, England's fucked, isn't it?' she replied. 'Just like the rest of the world.'

They walked on, eventually joining the others at the edge of a wide channel that had cut through the ice. They listened as Brent assessed the width of the gap, encouraging them to leap from one side of the pond to the other, but, despite his encouragement, no one was willing to go first. The distance appeared too great and the landing place, a thin film of shingle over ice, too high and steep.

At last, clearly impatient, Brent leapt. He faced them now, rolling a cigarette as he urged them to follow his lead. Imagining that they must look as ridiculous as penguins flapping back and forth along the shore before diving into the sea, Sally jumped. Almost immediately she felt her right shin slam against something hard and sharp, as her left foot landed in the water. A terrible pain shot through her leg and, slumping with her head in her hands, it was all she could do to gesture that she was all right. A groan escaped from her lips as a wave of nausea hit her, draining her body of strength. When eventually she looked up, she saw Brent's concerned face staring down at her and she recalled the foolishness she had felt as a child whenever she had fallen and hurt herself in public and was trying not to show it. Now, like then, she just wanted to cry.

Karen and Craig were nowhere in sight – searching, she guessed, for an easier place to cross. Her left leg was wet from the knee down, and a small tear in her trousers identified the spot where her right leg had hit the hard ice bank.

'I was always crap at sport,' she said as she reached into her pack for the spare pair of socks she had brought in case of emergencies. Brent nodded but said nothing. She watched as he replaced the cap on the film canister he had been using to catch the ash from his cigarette, then turned her attention to her left boot and began slowly to unlace it.

'Are you married?' The abruptness of Brent's question made her look up. Why, she wondered, were Craig and Brent both so intent on talking about marriage and wives? She felt as if she had somehow found herself stranded on a desert island with only castaways – people who had forgotten society's conventions regarding privacy and etiquette – for company. It surprised her that, without any preamble, someone could ask such a personal question. Yet she found herself answering as if it was nothing out of the ordinary.

'I was, but I gave my husband the boot a while ago. I live with my boyfriend, now ... and my teenage daughter from my marriage, and Manu's and my two young sons – and Manu's dog.' She hesitated, aware that she made her divorce seem inconsequential when in reality it had been anything but. Nothing had prepared her for the rift: the slow realisation that her husband resented her continuing presence in the house and that, although he had always known of her decision to become a composer, he felt bitter because at no stage had he been consulted. Whereas she had been able, once, to brush aside his comments about her lack of employment – had regarded them as little more than teasing – she had realised, with time, that he meant everything he said. He had revealed his true feelings when he stated, flatly, that he had indulged her 'musical hobby', and he had been serious, too, when he complained that his wages were being wasted on crèche bills, recording equipment and travel. She remembered, with perfect clarity, the tone of his voice whenever he asked, 'How much did that cost?' and how those few words became the most frequent and most feared in their increasingly stilted conversations.

In her mind, she had played endless variations of how she might repay him for all the money he had invested in the relationship, while never once acknowledging her contribution as wife or mother. Theirs, she realised, was not a comfortable middle-class marriage. It was a marriage in which the husband felt used and aggrieved towards a wife who refused to pull her weight.

For months after, she had clung to her belief in the marriage, hoping to be saved by their past – a history of goodwill that would resurface and see him embrace her with the words, 'I'm proud of you. Things aren't easy but we'll make it – together.' But the words never came. Instead, month after month, bills and bank statements would be laid on the table, set between the knives and forks at their evening meals. And as they ate in silence, their eyes would scan the withdrawals as if reading a set menu of unpalatable food, each course less appetising that the one before it. But even then, even when faced with the most obvious of solutions, she hadn't known what to do. She had felt too misunderstood and hurt to react, and so had stayed in the marriage, grateful for the grudging financial security he provided and sick with herself for being so weak and needy.

'What about you?' she asked Brent. 'Are you married?'

She watched as Brent shook his head, and then reached for a stone that had caught his eye. 'I was planning to get married,' he said, allowing the stone to drop, 'but my girlfriend was killed last spring in an accident.' He leaned forward, selecting another stone, which he threw into the pond. 'She was caught in an avalanche.' He hesitated. 'She was skiing with a couple of friends. She'd wanted me to go with her but

I'd been guiding all week and just felt like spending a few days at home, chilling.' He nodded as if confirming what he had just said, then mumbled, 'I should have gone. If nothing else, it would have made it easier to explain to her parents where and how she died. It might have helped them.'

Sally looked at him. His reply had been so unexpected she didn't know how to respond. She imagined the faces of the girl's parents at the news of their daughter's death, and her eyes began to well up with tears; she could feel their damp warmth against her cheeks. 'I'm sorry,' she said.

Brent cleared his throat. 'It's okay,' he said. 'It's just one of those things.'

The insides of Sally's ears felt damp, clammy, as if they were sweating. She removed her earplugs and was startled by the loudness of the Starlifter's engines. She found the noise of the aeroplane's engines overpowering, as if she was standing at the foot of a waterfall, engulfed by the roar of water.

She glanced at Marilyn, who was sitting perfectly still, staring straight ahead, her hands resting across her stomach. There was something about Marilyn's expression that unnerved Sally. Her eyes were wide open and yet they gave the impression of being sightless, as if she had died and no one had bothered to close them. Sally hesitated. She didn't want to disturb her neighbour, but she really needed another paper hanky. As if he was taunting her, she noticed that William, who was still standing at the front of the plane, had suddenly reached into his pocket and pulled out a large white handkerchief. Sally watched as he raised the handkerchief to his face, blew and replaced it in his pocket. She smiled at him but he didn't see, or, if he did, he chose to ignore her, keeping his eyes lowered, focused on the floor.

There was nothing for it. 'Marilyn?' She spoke softly, as if trying to wake her neighbour gently from a dream, and then, realising the futility of trying to be subtle, she shouted, 'Marilyn!'

Marilyn started. Her head turned from side to side, her expression confused as if she was coming out of a deep sleep. It was an expression Sally had seen before – on Manu's face when he was woken by the alarm clock. He set the alarm every night but, inevitably, Sally would find herself waking several minutes before the old-fashioned bell went off. She never turned the alarm off, however, but waited and watched, anticipating the moment when Manu's eyes would jolt open and his body jerk as if electrocuted.

'Marilyn? Could I get another hanky off you, please?' She watched the woman reach first into one pocket and then the other. She saw her frown, then search once more before raising an empty hand. 'I can't find them,' she apologised. Marilyn sat very still for a moment, once more looking straight in front of her as if in deep concentration, then added, 'Hang on a minute; they might be in my lunch bag.' Her forehead creased with the effort of trying to reach the paper bag, which had slipped to the floor. Then just as she was lifting it to her knee, she suddenly lurched forward and vomited. Sally watched in horror as Marilyn sat upright, her eyes startled, wide open and her mouth hidden by a spew-covered hand, before her body convulsed and once more she was leaning forward, this time retching into her lunch bag. She kept her head lowered, her mouth gulping and her body trembling like a bird that had flown into a window.

Despite the suddenness and violence of Marilyn's sickness, Sally found herself entranced by the fact that the whole episode had occurred without sound. It reminded her of the times she had flown to Europe and watched an entire film without bothering to wear the earphones for the soundtrack. There was something vaguely surreal about what she had just seen. And then the smell hit her. A pungent, acrid smell that brought to mind parmesan cheese tinged with the sweetness of nutmeg.

When Marilyn looked up, her face was whiter than any face Sally had ever seen. By contrast her eyes looked almost black, like two pebbles pushed into a snowman's head. She looked afraid. Sally watched as Marilyn scrambled to her feet, her hand wiping at her mouth as she tried to break free from a length of webbing, part of her seatbelt, which had caught around her wrist. She noticed that like her, all the other women were watching and yet no one appeared able to move, to go to Marilyn's aid. Everyone simply drew their legs back and pressed against their seats, withdrawing from Marilyn as she made her way to the toilet at the front of the plane, the soiled paper bag still clutched in her wet and sticky hand.

MARILYN

Marilyn sat down on the toilet and breathed deeply. Everything will be all right in a minute, she told herself. It was nerves. Just nerves. It wasn't the first time she'd been sick with nerves. Throughout the past few weeks she'd felt constantly sick. In fact, she reasoned, she ought to be used to it by now.

She'd experienced a kind of stage fright the first night she'd had to read the news over the radio. The bulletin was scheduled for nine-thirty and, she remembered, she'd felt nauseous throughout the afternoon leading up to the event. Not only had she been required to read the news but she also had to write it, and she'd never done anything like that before.

She'd thought she might have found a quiet moment to work on the bulletin that afternoon but all day she had been busy taking calls from New Zealand and various field parties. Everyone, it seemed, had wanted a message relayed to someone on the base, and her voice had grown hoarse from all the times she had had to talk over the paging system. What's more, it appeared that no one ever listened to her, so she was constantly having to backtrack, repeat telephone extension numbers and reconnect calls that had been cut off through no fault of her own. Time and time again she had felt like a chef trying to prepare a meal for ten people while simultaneously supervising a group of children who were talking and running about in the kitchen.

At nine-thirty, she knew, everyone would tune in to the news report. For scientists at Cape Royds, Cape Evans or in the Dry Valleys her bulletin would be the only link to New Zealand and the rest of the world. It was a terrible responsibility, and as the day wore on she had become increasingly angry with Chris for getting her into this in the first place. More than anyone, he knew how much she hated public speaking. He had witnessed her panic when once she had had to speak at a friend's wedding. He knew she couldn't cope in front of an audience and yet he had just forced her into a job that involved speaking in public on a daily basis. It was incredibly unfair. More than fifty people would be listening to her bulletin, ready to laugh at every small mistake she made.

At least Christine had given her a few ideas. Sports stories were meant to be popular, and so were stories of a humorous nature. Apart from that, it was always a good idea to try to include local New Zealand stories, especially from the provinces. 'It doesn't really matter what you say,' Christine had tried to comfort her. 'Just think of it as a cross between the *Herald* and the *Woman's Weekly* and you'll be fine.'

Even though she had delivered her first bulletin over three months ago, Marilyn could still recall every item, word for word. She'd just begun the major news story of the day, about Iraq's apparently non-existent weapons of mass destruction, when the phone rang. She tried to ignore it but it kept ringing and in the end she'd had to break off the broadcast. She could recall that she'd said, 'Hang on a sec, I'll just get this call,' and then the call took far longer than she had anticipated so that by the time she got back to the news she'd completely lost her train of thought. Instead of resuming the main story she started on another item, one about parking wardens in Dunedin wanting to improve their public image. Reading that story she realised how trivial and unfunny it was, and because of that she started to get flustered. She glanced down at the list of items before her and it had dawned on her that none of her stories was actually newsworthy. So she abandoned her script and tried to recall something she'd read on the Net that day. She remembered something about some stranded whales but couldn't remember where they had beached or how many of them there had been. She thought maybe about sixty, somewhere around Abel Tasman National Park – but then it could have been further north, somewhere around Gisborne. Just as she was trying to get the story straight in her head, the phone rang once more and this time the call was urgent. Someone needed to get in touch with one of the scientists out at Cape Hallett and she had had to abandon the bulletin again while she patched the caller through.

Some minutes later, as she returned to her report, she suddenly visualised the faces of fifty people sitting waiting for her, listening to her – and she froze. Her words caught in her throat, and although she could see the script in front of her, she couldn't make the words enter her brain and escape from her mouth. For as long as she lived she would remember the story. She had chosen it because it had taken place at the beach at Woodend – her beach. It was a story about two teenagers who had made a raft and been swept out to sea. She'd recognised the name of one of the boys because she had met him only a few weeks before at one of Chris's scout group barbecues.

Such was her longing for home that reading the story she had felt engulfed by the images it created. She could picture the large driftwood logs that dotted the sand dunes. Some of the logs, she knew, were blackened on one side from fires that had burned in their shelter. She could imagine the tracks the logs would make in the sand as they were dragged down to the edge of the sea, and she could feel the waves slapping against her body as the makeshift raft struck the surf on its journey seawards. Clearer than any of these images, however, was the one of the moonlight forming a path across the water. In her mind it glowed as strongly as any beacon, guiding the two boys out to sea, to a place where everything would be slow-moving and peaceful. The sound of the waves lapping against the raft played softly in her mind, in stark contrast to the thumping of her heart, pounding in her ears. She managed to whisper, 'Just one minute please,' and then she turned away, ran from the room and down the long corridor to the toilets, where she retched. And then, wiping her mouth, she had walked back to the radio room and read the weather report.

Her ears, she remembered, had throbbed with the sound of imagined laughter. In all directions she could hear people laughing, choking back sobs as they regaled one another with stories of the incompetent new newsreader.

It had been hours before her shift had ended, during which she'd had to sit at the desk and continue with her work as if nothing out of the ordinary had taken place. As the night progressed, calls in and out of the base dwindled and for long periods she had little to do except torment herself by continually replaying the bulletin in her mind. And as she reconstructed her words, she was overcome by a feeling of humiliation. The certainty that she had made a complete fool of herself was coupled with a feeling of resentment towards both Chris and the Antarctic. In her confusion that night she had understood only one thing: what it was to be engaged to a prison officer. The fact that he was someone who made a living from punishing people took a hold of her, inviting her to see, for the first time, the kind of person he really was. Although her thoughts were twisted, she saw clearly that night that it was his fault she was trapped at Scott Base. He had done this to her and, she realised in despair, he would do nothing to help her break free. He had abandoned her.

At dinner the following night she had been aware of everyone in the room looking at her as she entered. She'd felt their eyes piercing her body and heard the quiet sniggers that travelled, wave-like, from person to person, table to table, across the room. She'd found a seat by herself and had eaten quickly, her aim to get food into her stomach as quickly as possible so that she could return to her room. Once, glancing up, she had seen Andrea gesture, indicating a seat that had been vacated by the base carpenter. Andrea had been smiling, laughing almost, and Marilyn had looked away, embarrassed by the expression of pity she had imagined on her roommate's face. She didn't feel like talking to Andrea; she was too upset.

She'd barely seen Andrea that day. She'd arrived back from her shift just as Andrea was waking up. They'd talked briefly and then Andrea had gone, leaving her alone in the tiny room they shared. As Marilyn sat on the edge of her bed she became increasingly irritated by the amount of Andrea's clothing scattered across the floor. She had the impression that most of it had simply been torn off and discarded by a whirlwind. There was one exception: a black bra that was draped carefully from the window latch. There was something deliberate about the way its straps had been twisted around the window fastening. It was as if it had been placed in the window as a signal to someone passing by. Where in fairytales people might place a candle in a window as a beacon for strangers, the bra, thought Marilyn, had been arranged so that anyone glancing towards the window would know exactly what was going on inside.

She sighed. The room smelt musty, like a bathroom full of damp towels. As she lay back on her bed her eye caught sight of something small and shiny. She reached across her duvet and retrieved a ripped shred of gold foil. She held it in her hand, turning it every now and again, watching the torn fragment spell 'urex' as it rotated in her fingers. It made sense, she supposed, that they had chosen her bottom bunk for their … The words stuck in her throat. Her roommate, she thought bitterly, had spent the night having sex with someone on *her* bed, *her* sheets.

No wonder Andrea hadn't mentioned the news bulletin. She'd been too busy screwing to listen to the radio. Marilyn laughed, a hollow gurgle that caught in her throat. She should be pleased that at least Andrea hadn't heard her make a fool of herself. Marilyn stood up. Despite the fact that she had worked through the night and just wanted to sleep, she felt dirty. She was surrounded by squalor. Her clothes, her sheets, her body – everything felt worn, threadbare and nasty. Life was not only unfair, she concluded, it was horrible.

She had drifted off to sleep, dozing until mid-afternoon, when she had finally woken but remained in her bed looking through the window. As she gazed, she became increasingly aware of the window itself, the glass pane and the metal frame surrounding it. There was something odd about it – something she could not quite place. A large brown seagull flew by, distracting her, and in that instant she realised what it was that had been puzzling her. There were no dead flies or moths on the windowsill. There were no tattered shreds of spiders' webs dangling from the frame. She glanced around the room, searched the corners of the ceiling, and again there was nothing. No daddy-longlegs resting in the corners where the walls met the ceiling.

She got up from her bed and, kneeling on the floor, bent down, searching beneath the bed for anything that might signal life. In her bedroom back home she might have found a fly or a moth or even the occasional weta but here, in this room, there was nothing at all. There were bits of fluff, black felted slugs of wool, but nothing else. The room was devoid of life. She was its only breathing creature.

Towards evening a man had made a call from the phone outside her room. She could hear him, though she didn't recognise the voice. However, he was clearly married with children. She listened as he laughed and said, 'All kids get lice, it's no big deal.' She heard him say, 'It's not too bad. The people are okay, we've had a few laughs,' and then she registered the softness in his voice as he said, 'Love you,' the slight pause before he repeated, 'Love you, love you … see you, yep, okay, love you, bye.'

The receiver had barely been replaced before she heard the same voice call out, 'Hey, Phil, want a beer before dinner?' A second voice had replied and then, again, the man's voice broke the silence, saying, 'Fucking kids have got lice and Gaylene's crashed the car into the garage door. Glad I'm out of it.' Then she had heard the swing of the double doors, a lisped dripping tap of a noise that grew gradually slower and quieter, until everything fell quiet.

As she lay on her bed waiting in vain for the light in her room to diminish, the shadows across the snow to lengthen, she felt weighed down; as if, since leaving New Zealand, she had been trapped within a single, endless day. Although the hands on the clock indicated the passing of time, there was nothing to suggest any change from morning to night. It had been dawn when she'd flown out of Christchurch, she thought, but there was no sign of sunset. Just slow repetitiveness, a rotating conveyor belt of hours, incessant daylight. She turned her head, watched as another brown gull flew past her window. How did the birds adapt to continuous daylight? In the absence of dawn and dusk, how did they know when to sleep, when to wake?

She'd thought she was hungry but in the end she'd had trouble finishing her meal. There'd been too many people looking at her and she'd felt claustrophobic, imprisoned by their stares. It had been a relief to know she had the evening off and could go for a walk. She would climb Observation Hill, the low cone that loomed above the road to McMurdo. At least she could spend an evening on her own. She wouldn't talk to anyone. Yet, as she sat by the door, lacing her boots, she heard a voice and, looking up, saw Tobin smiling down at her. His navy T-shirt, she noticed, was streaked with soap powder, broad bands partly obscuring the image of a woman screen-printed across its front. It looked as if she had been baking and had wiped the back of a flour-dusted hand across her cheek.

'Are you looking at my T-shirt?'

Marilyn started. She'd forgotten about the man inside the clothes.

'I couldn't be bothered dissolving the soap powder before I chucked everything into the machine,' Tobin laughed, 'so everything's munted, eh?' Despite herself, Marilyn had smiled. If Andrea hadn't warned her about the quality of the water she might have made a similar mistake.

She hadn't seen Tobin, she realised, for almost a week. In fact, the last time she had seen him was the night he had hugged her. The memory made her blush. She heard Tobin ask, 'What's wrong?' and she shook her head, focusing on the zip of her padded jacket. She felt flustered. Tobin had a way of talking that appeared relaxed, almost playful, while at the same time it pushed her towards some destination she found difficult to identify. She heard herself mumble, 'I'm just going for a walk,' and then she was outside, the cold wind striking her face, causing her to gasp.

She followed the road that led over the saddle to McMurdo. As she walked, her mind drifted back to her grandmother, whom she had not thought about for years. Her grandmother had grown up in Lancashire, and although Marilyn had never bothered to find it on a map, she could remember a photograph, a picture of a ploughed English field covered in a fine crust of snow. Standing in the middle of the field had been a blackened figure. As a young child she'd thought she was looking at a scarecrow, but later she'd learnt that the figure was human – it was her great-grandfather. 'Oh, those winter mornings,' her grandmother used to say. 'It was still dark when we left for school, my older sister and myself, and we'd trudge across the fields, our eyes streaming from the wind, my hand in hers as I tried to keep the chill from my bones. It was a devil, that cold.'

The words had meant little to Marilyn. Her grandmother was far too old to have an older sister. She was red-faced and sunburnt from days spent in the garden at her home in Amberley. Her grandmother had pulled off her sandals and socks and stood at the edge of the sea laughing as waves soaked the hem of her skirt. She was the woman who had died early one summer's morning and been buried in Kaiapoi cemetery on a day when the thermometer had climbed to thirty-four degrees. And yet, her grandmother had also trudged across frozen ground, following blackened furrows cut through fields of white, just as Marilyn was doing now. Marilyn trudged.

She heard an engine behind her and, looking around, saw a large orange truck approach Scott Base. It pulled up near the helicopter pad and she watched as four people climbed out and one climbed in. She turned her back, aware now of the noise of the truck's engine as it trailed slowly behind her. As she walked she listened to the sound of its wheels skidding on the ice, and the grind of its gears as it negotiated the hill. The vehicle drew nearer, gaining on her, the smell of diesel and a trail of blue-grey smoke engulfing her as it continued up the hill. There was a moment's lull, then a voice behind her said, 'Thanks, mate,' and she heard a door being slammed. She stood to one side, watching as the truck pulled past, and then glanced back to see Tobin jogging up to meet her.

They walked in silence, continuing along the road towards the saddle before veering left up the conical hill. As they walked, Marilyn searched her head for something to say but she could think of nothing. She felt uncomfortable, embarrassed by the fact that she was no good at conversation. A bird flew by and she suddenly felt grateful. 'What are those brown seagulls?' she said, watching the bird as she caught her breath. 'Skuas,' Tobin replied. 'They're beautiful birds but you have to watch them. There was a pair of them nesting by the tank stand last year and they dive-bombed anyone who went too close. They're quite vicious – more like hawks than seagulls.' Marilyn nodded.

When they reached the top of the hill they sought shelter from the wind and sat down. A few minutes later they were joined by two people in nylon jogging suits. The runners, a man and a woman, said 'Hi' and then jogged on the spot, talking to each other in breathless gulps while checking the time on their watches. Then they turned and ran back down the hill. Their brightly coloured outfits made a sharp contrast with the volcanic stones, and as they grew smaller they took on the appearance of a couple of tennis balls bouncing across an asphalt court.

After several minutes Tobin asked, 'Have you been down to McMurdo?' Marilyn shook her head. She had intended to go but hadn't been sure of what to do once she got there. 'I'll take you, if you like,' said Tobin. 'It's a pretty weird place but it's got this really cool recycling thing going, called the skua bin. If you're lucky you can find all sorts of stuff in it, like clothing or skis – stuff that people can't be bothered taking home.' He stood up, stretched, then added, 'It's better towards the end of the season, though. Last summer Andrea scored a snowboard. It was practically new.'

At the mention of Andrea's name Marilyn sat up. Her physical discomfort at sitting on the stony ground was mirrored by an emotional one as she imagined her roommate making love on her bed. Having spotted Andrea with the carpenter, she felt sure that he was the owner of the condom wrapper. She wondered how long they had been going out together and just how many more times they would make use of her bed for their rendezvous. With luck, she thought, the relationship might be short-lived.

'How well do you know Andrea?' she asked Tobin. She had begun to feel cold and in order to keep warm she started walking again – over to a large wooden cross that stood at the summit of the hill. She looked at the words on it, five names carved into the wood: Scott, Oates, Wilson, Evans and Bowers. Then she read, 'To strive, to seek, to find, and not to yield.' Whatever it meant was lost on her.

She'd forgotten her question and was startled to hear Tobin say, 'Pretty well, but I don't have much to do with her, really.' It took Marilyn a second to remember who Tobin was talking about, but before she could say anything he was saying, 'You're a lesbian, aren't you?' The remark so surprised Marilyn that she felt her chin drop; her mouth, she guessed, was gaping. 'It's just ...' He suddenly laughed, then looked awkward. 'You probably know this already, but in case you don't, there's a lot of lesbians over at McMurdo, so you might be able to make some friends, or whatever ...' Tobin fell silent and readjusted his hat over his eyes. It seemed to Marilyn that he was trying to hide his face.

In the silence that followed, Marilyn was aware of the sound of the wind blowing against her jacket and the noise of heavy machinery rising up from the station below. She felt almost too embarrassed to reply. Never in her life had she had reason to talk about lesbians. She had no idea why anyone would think she was one. In fact, she had thought that everyone in the base knew about Chris and practically everything else there was to know about her life back in Christchurch.

'I'm not,' she began. 'I'm not, you know, like that.' She turned back to the cross, tracing her fingers over the words 'And not to yield'. She couldn't look at Tobin; she felt too uncomfortable.

'Oh, I'm sorry,' he said airily. 'I thought I heard someone say you were. I'm sorry. That's the problem with living in a place like this. People are always passing on bits of information and most of it isn't true. You know how it is? It wouldn't matter if you were a lesbian, of course, I'm not saying that ...'

Marilyn shook her head.

'Let's change the subject, then. We'll talk about something nice.' Tobin paused, thought for a moment and then said, 'I heard your newsreading last night. I was instructing a group out on field training and we tuned in. It was really great, professional ...'

Marilyn swung around. He must be making fun of her. She expected to see him laughing but his expression was sincere. She shook her head. 'I can't believe you'd say that. It was terrible. It was probably the worst news bulletin ever.'

Tobin laughed, 'No, honestly, it was great. There were a few stops and starts when those phone calls came through – and then that longer one, but no, it was great. Except for one thing.'

Marilyn smiled. She knew there would have to be a 'but'.

'You forgot to tell a joke.'

'A joke?'

Tobin explained that at the end of every news bulletin the reader always told a joke or a funny story. They were always terrible, he went on – in fact they were often so bad they made you groan rather than laugh. But that was the tradition: the news wasn't complete without a joke.

Despite herself, Marilyn had smiled. She didn't know any jokes. No one had ever mentioned anything to her about funny stories. Christine, her supervisor, had kept that bit of information to herself. Then, as if recounting a bad dream, she began to explain to Tobin how she had felt. She told him how she had felt queasy all day, how when the phone had rung she hadn't known what to do. She described the moment when she had suddenly imagined the faces of all the listeners watching her and how she had felt so sick that she'd had to go and vomit before the bulletin was finished.

'I know I probably sound mental,' she'd finished, 'but I just don't feel confident enough to do it. Everything always seems so rushed. You know, there's always people calling in, wanting stuff, and I seem to spend so much time chasing my tail. I don't know...' she trailed off. 'There's just so much pressure ...'

Her voice slowed to a standstill. She suddenly had so many things she wanted to say that she was scared to continue.

If she got started she might not be able to stop and then she'd never be able to face him again. Eventually, he would tell the others and she couldn't bear the thought of everyone making fun of her behind her back. It was bad enough that there was already a rumour going around that she was a lesbian. What else was being said about her?

She hadn't known what she expected Tobin to say. In a way, she'd convinced herself that he'd remain silent. In her mind, he played the part of a listener or some object like a tape recorder – a machine she could talk into without getting a response. She'd been surprised, therefore, when he had spoken. He'd talked very calmly. Bit by bit he summed up everything she had said, and little by little he made each problem diminish.

He told her she didn't need to worry about the news bulletin, it had been fine. As to the lesbian thing: she shouldn't worry about that, either. Rumours were always going around the station and they never meant anything. Last season, he'd told her, there'd been a rumour going around that he was sleeping with Andrea, but he had been living with a girl back in New Zealand at the time. His voice suddenly trailed off, as if detained by some memory. It took a minute before he was able to continue. His girlfriend, he frowned, coming out of his dream, had recently dumped him. In fact, he added, he had hoped that being in the Antarctic, having a change of scene, would have helped him get over her but so far there had been no improvement. He still missed her terribly. What was worse, he admitted, was that the break-up had been his fault. And then, to top it off, his roommate Brent, another climbing instructor, was also getting over a relationship. It was harder for Brent, because his girlfriend had been killed in a skiing accident. Whenever the two of them got together, which wasn't that often, fortunately, they'd end up chatting about love and death and stuff like that and, to tell the truth, it tended to bring them both down. Brent was a great guy, but they didn't make for a very happy twosome. It was almost inevitable that sooner or later they'd wind up drunk or depressed or both.

Tobin laughed. 'It's not that bad, really. It will pass.' He smiled at Marilyn, held her glance for an instant, and then, pulling the hat from his head, passed it to her. 'Put this on. Your ears are turning blue.' As she pulled on the hat she was surprised to hear Tobin observe, 'I love this hill – all the colours.' Marilyn didn't understand what he was talking about. Only a few minutes before, she had been thinking how ugly the place was. Although on a larger scale, it reminded her of the mounds of shingle that were dumped beside roadworks. 'Sometimes, when the light's good,' Tobin continued, 'the volcanic rocks catch the sun and the whole hillside glows with purples and reds and yellows ... kind of like a flower garden.'

Marilyn couldn't believe her ears. There was no way the hill could look anything other than grey and black. She realised Tobin must be having her on and smiled, embarrassed to be caught out. 'Yeah, right.'

She saw Tobin smile, then shrug and shake his head, 'You don't believe me, but it's true,' he countered. 'It can be really beautiful.'

They'd remained on the top of Observation Hill for only a few more minutes. Given what Tobin had just told her, Marilyn half expected the hillside to come alive with colour, but soon it became clear that it would remain as dull and unattractive as a grey school uniform V-necked jumper. As they began to walk down, she found herself thinking not about the colour of her surroundings but about what Tobin had said about Andrea. She'd been so wound up when he was talking that she wasn't sure now whether he'd slept with her or not. As she walked, a question formed in her head, one that she couldn't shake, until finally she blurted, 'Can I ask you a personal question?'

Tobin stopped and turned to face her. 'If you want.'

Marilyn blushed. She felt embarrassed now. 'Have you slept with Andrea?'

Tobin watched her for a minute, and then smiled and shook his head. 'No. I haven't.' He must have seen something in Marilyn's expression that invited a fuller explanation because he added, quietly, 'I'm pretty sure she wanted to, but ...' He looked at his feet, unsure what to say. Then he said, 'She *did* want to ...'

'But you didn't?' The words were out of Marilyn's mouth before she could stop them.

'No, I didn't. I had a girlfriend, and anyway ...'

It seemed to Marilyn that he was reluctant to talk about what had happened the previous year.

'I don't want to make a big deal about it,' he suddenly said. 'Andrea's a nice person but she's just not my type, you know?'

Marilyn nodded but Tobin didn't notice. He was striding ahead, following the path over the broken rocks, which tipped and knocked against their boots as they walked. 'I feel bad about Andrea,' he suddenly called back. 'I think I might have humiliated her somehow. It certainly wasn't my intention but that's what I think happened. The problem is, I'm not very good with emotions so I tend to run a mile when things start getting awkward that way. Either that or I'm so embarrassed that I make a joke of what's going on. And in Andrea's case I think I've done both those things. She's pretty pissed off with me, as you've probably noticed.

'What's worse,' he added, 'I tend to wind her up. I don't mean to but it's the only way I can handle the situation.'

The wind prevented Marilyn from hearing everything Tobin said. She heard him mention emotions but her mind had attached itself to an earlier remark: 'She's not my type'. She repeated the words to herself as she followed him down the hill. 'Andrea's a nice person,' Tobin had said, 'but she's not my type.' Marilyn smiled. She didn't know why, but she felt relieved.

There was a knock on the door and a voice called, 'Honey, are you okay in there?' Marilyn glanced at her watch. Shit, she'd been sitting in the toilet for more than twenty minutes. No wonder the crew had started to hammer on the door. 'Can you answer the question?' There were two of them. 'Hey in there!' She could tell from the tone of their voices that they were standing very close to the door, their mouths almost pressed against it. Why couldn't they just leave her in peace? In a few more hours she had to face Chris, drive with him through the streets of Christchurch all the way back to her house in Woodend. She could imagine what he'd say. He'd be so keen to hear about her summer that he wouldn't be able to keep quiet. He would try to anticipate all her news, speak for her, and yet he would have no inkling of what it was she wanted to tell him. In a few more hours she would mention the name Tobin and everything in her life would change.

'Please answer ...'

'What?' She shuddered, then repeated, 'What? What do you want? I'm not well. Go away!' She mustn't cry. Not here. Not on some revolting toilet in some disgusting plane. She wiped her eyes, noticing as she did so a trail of vomit on the underside of her sleeve. It looked like part of a muesli slice: the sultana was intact but the rest resembled porridge. At least it didn't smell any more. She leaned back, her head resting against the wall as she tried to work out what she would say to Chris. It was hopeless. She'd already had plenty of time to come up with a story and she'd got nowhere. What had happened still didn't make complete sense, so how could she hope to explain it to someone else?

She hadn't intended to sleep with Tobin that night. But whenever she went over what had happened all she could picture was water rushing towards a drain and her body, small and inconsequential – like a tea-leaf – being carried with it. And, like a tea-leaf, or some other food scrap caught in the flow, she had done nothing to fight the current.

It had been after eleven when she'd let herself into her room. The first thing she'd noticed was that although the shutters were closed, the room was not really dark. For one peaceful moment the filtered light had reminded her of her childhood: the summer nights spent in bed watching as the colours in her room drained away, the objects merging with shadow. But then she had glanced from the shutters to her bed and in that instant she had registered the outline of a stooped body, a man's back swaying rhythmically above someone she couldn't see. Like a twisted version of *Goldilocks and the Three Bears*, there was some stranger trying out her bed. Doing 'it', despite the fact that he had to keep his head tilted awkwardly to one side so as to avoid hitting the base of the bunk above. It wasn't until she stepped quietly back into the hall, however, that she allowed herself to feel startled, her body shaking as she tried to calm down and think straight.

Then, instead of knocking loudly on her door, calling out and then waiting a minute, like any sensible person would have done, she had wandered off, dazed, walking the length of the main corridor several times before finally settling on the library as her destination. Somewhere in the back of her mind she'd suddenly got hold of the idea that now might be a good time to hunt down a joke in one of the books shelved there. The fact that she hated jokes and, at that moment, felt herself to be the victim of a particularly nasty one, had done nothing to deter her. In fact, she recalled, her decision seemed all the more appropriate given the circumstances she had found herself in. Her sense of despondency had intensified when, on entering the library, she received an electric shock, the abruptness and force of which caused her to cry out. Continuing into the room she'd suddenly noticed there was someone already there, watching her. But for some reason she hadn't felt startled by her discovery. She lacked the energy to register surprise. It hadn't even entered her mind to wonder what Tobin was doing in the library at that time of night. He was simply there, that was all. She took in only that he smiled before extending his hand, saying, 'Thanks. I was missing it.'

Those few words had thrown her. They'd jolted her from her trance, forcing her to search her thoughts for a hint as to what he was talking about. She had completely forgotten about his hat; had even forgotten what it looked like. It wasn't until she was holding it in her hand, looking at it, that she was able to say that it was grey with a black and white zigzag pattern. Not that any of that mattered, because Tobin hadn't appeared to notice. He appeared more concerned about the shock she had received, explaining that the dry air in the base caused a build-up of static electricity. Despite the fact that he knew to expect the occasional shock, he said he was always disconcerted by receiving a 'zap'. In a way, it wasn't so bad, because it reminded him of home – the dry nor'westers, and the electric shocks he got from his car. It was enough to make you feel homesick – if you let it, he added.

He probably hadn't intended to sound funny but Marilyn had smiled all the same. She liked hearing references to New Zealand. It brought the country closer, rescued her thoughts from the unpleasantness of their present surroundings. 'I was just looking at those clouds,' Tobin said, pointing towards Mt Erebus. 'They're just like the hogbacks you see over the hills in Canterbury, aren't they?' She'd looked in the direction he was indicating and recognised the smooth, off-white curved clouds that reminded her of the seashells that littered her beach near Woodend. It hadn't occurred to her to look for them in the Antarctic. Briefly, she wondered what else she might have missed, but, glancing through the small window towards the frozen sea, she realised there was nothing else out there to remind her of home. She was completely cut off, isolated.

For the first time since her arrival at Scott Base she understood, then, that it would take somebody other than herself, someone more capable than she was, to bring home within reach. It would be only through the company of that person that she could create something habitable out of such intimidating surroundings. She had felt alone – even more so since discovering that her roommate had a boyfriend. And so, because she felt at ease with Tobin, had already confided her feelings to him – and because he had understood and offered friendship – she had turned to him. It was Tobin who had brought her South Island clouds to the Antarctic. With her prompting, he might be encouraged to create more: a 'homescape'. They could talk about New Zealand and, through their conversations, she could construct a normal life. Through him, she could return home.

'You decided – just like that – to sleep with the guy? You went to bed with him because he reminded you of home? But you know I love you – couldn't you have talked to me? What's wrong with you?' That's how it would look to Chris, and she couldn't blame him for being angry. But it hadn't been like that. She hadn't been that calculating. She had been homesick and had felt trapped in a situation that scared her. Though it struck her as all screwed up and crazy now, what she had done had made sense at the time. In Tobin she had found a substitute for Chris. Not only that, but in her confusion she had transformed him into Chris. And though it was difficult to comprehend – and she had not guessed it at the time – there was another reason why she had turned to Tobin and not Chris. Simply, it was because it was not possible for Chris to understand. He had created for himself an image of the Antarctic that was not real, that didn't even exist. It was to that place that he imagined she had journeyed. His Antarctic was complete fantasy: a storybook adventure in which men shared dreams while wandering around in blizzards looking for a Pole on which to attach a pole.

The place she had found herself in, however, was closer to some creepy institution. People drifted around as they tried to convince themselves that what they were doing was important. The fact was, however, that nobody belonged in the Antarctic. Nobody was needed. It was like the artist had said, they were all No-men – but No-men with too great a sense of their own worth. Instead of having the sense to leave the place to the penguins, they wandered around with test-tubes and drills and stuff so that one day, when they returned home, they could talk to other people – people exactly like themselves – about all the valuable things they had achieved.

And it was meaningless. It was completely meaningless, and realising that, at last, made her angry. She felt tricked, identifying herself with those men who had gone to war and then returned home unable to speak to their wives and families about what they had experienced. Like her, she thought, they couldn't confide in the people back home because they had been stripped of the language of certainty. They didn't know how or where to begin. They could be sure of only two things: that they were completely baffled by what had happened, and that only someone who had been caught in their world, who had experienced, at times, their confusion, could understand – and accept without judgement – the decisions they had made.

From her seat on the aircraft toilet, Marilyn replayed fragments of her conversations with Tobin. Sitting with him in the library she had listened as he told her tales about the years he had spent as a student in Dunedin. She had absorbed every word and then mentioned something she had noticed about the town. Every time she'd visited Dunedin, she said, she'd seen someone – a student, she guessed – walking down the street carrying what appeared to be a brand-new red vacuum cleaner. The first time it had happened she hadn't taken too much notice, but because, since then, she'd seen at least eight people wandering around with vacuum cleaners, she'd been forced to conclude that within the whole university area there was only one functioning vacuum cleaner and that there must be some kind of roster dictating that it be passed from flat to flat. Retelling the story had made her laugh. It was so absurd – yet it was true!

Tobin had laughed, too, but said he'd never seen it. All he knew was that he had never used a brand-new red vacuum cleaner in the four years he'd spent flatting, but then he had lived out on the peninsula so he was hardly in a position to comment on what took place in the city. Marilyn had smiled, replying that she had never lived in Dunedin but had spent a bit of time there on account of her boyfriend's parents living in Mosgiel. It hadn't even occurred to her, she realised now, to avoid a reference to her boyfriend. He was a part of her life; it had been natural to talk about him.

In case she had insulted Tobin, however, she had made it clear that she loved Dunedin. She loved the fact that when you walked beside the one-way systems you would always be passed by several stock trucks, and the smell of sheep was always stronger than the smell of car fumes. She liked that about the place. Tobin had responded that he liked the people. During his first week in town he had had to catch a bus in a suburb he didn't know and so had asked the driver, 'Does this bus go to the Octagon?' The driver, he remembered, had looked at him as if he was mad, before replying, 'All buses go to the Octagon, mate. That's why they're buses.' For some reason, Tobin continued, the comment had struck him as hysterically funny and he had spent the entire day laughing whenever he recalled it. But the very next time he travelled on a bus – which was weeks later – he heard another bus driver say exactly the same thing to another passenger. It was as if all Dunedin's bus drivers were living in a state of anticipation, waiting for the opportunity to repeat, time and time again, a remark that wasn't, in reality, really all that funny.

It had been relaxing, sitting in the library. She'd forgotten all about wanting to find a joke and had been content to chat with Tobin. After a while he had brought up the subject of his girlfriend, telling her that she was a medical student – very bright but somehow able to carry her intelligence lightly, if that made sense. He'd fallen silent for a while, then yawned and stood up abruptly, saying it was time for bed. Only then did things suddenly become awkward. Marilyn hadn't known what to say. She must have hesitated or looked lost or something, because Tobin had asked what was up and she'd ended up telling him about Andrea and the fact that she felt she couldn't go back to her room.

She'd followed Tobin, then, to his room. His roommate, Brent, he'd explained, was climbing Mt Erebus with the search and rescue team from McMurdo, so she could have his bed. It was the top bunk, he said, adding that he couldn't vouch for the condition of the sheets. They should be okay, though, he'd assured her. Brent was a very tidy guy – the type of man who would actually *buy* a vacuum cleaner.

She'd been lying on the bed for an hour when she had heard Tobin's voice below, asking, 'Are you still awake?' Her heart had started beating, thudding, as she wondered whether or not to respond. Seconds passed before she said yes. In retrospect, she should have remained silent, pretended to be asleep, but she had said yes and there had been a long silence, filled only by the sound of her heart in her chest. Then she had heard Tobin's voice. 'There's room on my bed, next to me, if you don't mind a squeeze.' And she had felt sick, unable to decide what to say or do, yet feeling that she had somehow already made her intentions clear through the simple fact of being in his room. 'Marilyn?' She heard his voice once more and then, feeling anxious and excited, she climbed down from her bunk and sat on the edge of his bed, her back to him, passively waiting for his hand to reach out and turn her around.

There was another knock on the toilet door. 'Marilyn? Marilyn!' She recognised Sally's voice. 'Marilyn, are you okay?' She sat silently, her thoughts swinging from Tobin's room to a place that she had not thought about for many years. A place where shouting had been accepted as both normal and necessary. It was the way people communicated.

One summer, before her final year at school, she had found work in a nursing home in Rangiora. She had loved the job. Listening to the old people's stories about the past had fascinated her. With few exceptions, all of the residents had made do with so little and had achieved so much. There was one man, James, whom she had liked more than all the rest. He was more self-contained than the others; he wasn't interested in the gossip or rumours that circulated around the home. He could spend all day in his room reading and writing, or looking through the window, and whenever he saw Marilyn he would smile and ask how her day had been. Unlike the others he didn't grumble; he was content. He was also deaf, so it was almost impossible to talk to him. Every word had to be shouted and she had found that embarrassing.

There was one nurse aide, Lorraine, who had appeared to

enjoy shouting the most personal of questions at James. She would stand in the doorway to his room and yell, for everyone to hear, 'Did Dr Black have a bowel movement this morning?' Not only did she shout, Marilyn recalled with a cringe, but she made a point of addressing him in the third person, and always by his full name, Dr Black. It was demeaning.

Standing next to Lorraine, Marilyn had felt ashamed, yet she had done nothing about it. She had never found the courage to confront the nurse aide. She simply looked at the ground, avoiding James's glance, until she was sure Lorraine had stopped speaking. Then, once she had gone, she would smile and yell, 'Tell me what you're reading, James,' and sit down with her friend and carry out a shouted conversation until she was called away to help with afternoon tea or dinner.

Hearing Sally's voice now, straining above the noise of the engines, reminded her of those shouted conversations. She hadn't thought about James for years. When that summer had ended she had promised to visit him often. She had planned to return once a week – not because she felt she ought to, but because she had enjoyed hearing his stories; his memories of being a doctor on the West Coast during the 1930s and '40s. They were memories that should have been handed down like precious keepsakes, or heirlooms, to members of his family, but, as far as she knew, James had only one surviving relative, a granddaughter, who had not visited him in all the time he had been in the nursing home.

Sitting with James, Marilyn had sometimes found herself thinking about this granddaughter, wondering what kind of person she was to stay away from such an interesting, lovely old man. It was a question she should have liked to ask the woman herself, but of course the opportunity to do so had never arisen. Once the summer was over, Marilyn discovered that her own plans to visit were disrupted. Through her brother she'd met Chris and before long she had found herself tagging along on their weekend surfing trips. Weeks of Sundays had passed without her once having set foot inside the nursing home.

It was Lorraine, she remembered, who, passing her in the corridor during one Sunday visit, announced bluntly, 'If you're looking for Dr Black, don't bother, he's dead.' Marilyn recalled the way in which Lorraine appeared almost to take pleasure in breaking the news. 'I wasn't sure which would go first: my voice or him,' she had continued. 'Luckily for me,' she'd added, 'it wasn't my voice.' Marilyn recalled the expression of triumph in Lorraine's eyes – a look that gave the impression she really believed she had won a battle with the old man. As Lorraine continued down the corridor, she called back, 'He left you something but don't get your hopes up – it feels like it's just one of his rocks. It's in the office, wrapped up in newspaper – I guess he was too tight to buy proper wrapping paper.' Even then Marilyn hadn't responded. She hadn't spoken up for James but had simply allowed the final insult to burn into her – a mixture of anger and guilt she still felt, even now.

'Marilyn!' Sally's voice was almost shrill. Shouting, thought Marilyn, must be unfamiliar territory for her. She can't have had a lot of a practice. Unlocking the door, she saw three people standing there. Within seconds, Sally had her arm around her, smiling, yelling, 'They've swapped our seats with the Distinguished Visitors' so we could have more room. If you need to dash to the bathroom it will be much easier now. Are you all right? You look pretty pale.' Marilyn nodded and, catching Sally's eye, frowned. 'I think I might have got some vomit on my seat.' She glanced to where she had been sitting and caught sight of the black jacket of the richest man in New Zealand. She faced Sally who, in return, smiled, shouting: 'Let's hope so.'

WILLIAM

William stepped aside as the two women passed in front of him. He watched as they shuffled towards their seats, the arm of the woman called Sally draped around Marilyn's shoulders. He felt sorry for the younger girl. She'd flown out to Cape Royds once and he'd spent a few minutes in her company, talking to her as several boxes of supplies were unloaded and his poorly colleague, Trevor, had climbed aboard the helicopter for the journey back to Scott Base.

He remembered the way she had smiled when she caught sight of the open sea and how, over the noise of the helicopter, she had shouted, 'Waves! Look, waves.'

He had been touched by her voice: the tone of relief, it seemed to him, as she made her observation. She had also asked him a question, one that appeared to embarrass her, as if she was unsure of its validity. He would have replied immediately had it not been for the fact that she was suddenly recalled to the helicopter. He smiled at the memory. In truth, it was a question he had heard many times before, and yet one he had been asked only by people who had found themselves in the Antarctic. 'When do the birds sleep?'

He glanced once more in her direction, registering her hunched shoulders and pale face. It was obvious, even back then, before all this other business, that she had been homesick. In all his years' experience, no one else had ever visited Cape Royds without immediately mentioning Shackleton's hut and the penguin colony. She was the only person who had been first drawn to the sea, who had looked at it as if being reunited with a friend. He frowned. She should never have come to the Antarctic. Not her.

She was also, he thought, one of the worst newsreaders he had ever heard. He remembered her Christmas Day bulletin and cringed, embarrassed by the memory. Christmas was something he preferred to avoid. He felt cornered by the notion of having to celebrate the birth of Christ. In fact, anything to do with Christ or the church made him uncomfortable. In previous years he had gone to church on Christmas Day simply so that he might keep Alice company. She appreciated the music and drama of the church, and although he respected her opinion he nevertheless felt trapped by the church's hypocrisy. Sitting beside his wife on a hard pew, listening to the drivel spouting from the minister's mouth, made him both impatient and angry.

He hated having to sit still for any length of time; it was a character flaw, he supposed, but one he had had for as long as he could remember. He only felt comfortable standing and, more than that, he craved movement. For him, the depths of misery resulted from having to sit in one place, listening to people he had not chosen to be with speak about things he had no interest in. In many ways, that accurately described the Christmas just past.

He had been watching a skua chick, the first of the season, when he had heard a helicopter approaching from the south. The sound had carried on the wind; he had listened to the heavy drone of its engines for several minutes before finally catching sight of the machine off Cape Barne. 'Museum conservators,' he mumbled to himself. Although forewarned of their visit, he found their arrival too abrupt, too intrusive.

He watched as four people approached the wanigan, their arms laden with bags, which they dumped outside the small building before returning to the heli-pad for another load. His assistant, Trevor, joined them, walking alongside as they carried bag after bag to the hut. An area that had looked almost spacious an hour earlier had suddenly appeared cramped as five tents were erected next to the wanigan. His own tent disappeared from sight, hidden behind the larger teepee shape of a polar tent. So much for his view. Instead of looking out over the roof of Shackleton's hut, towards the glowing, guano-encrusted penguin colony on the far side of Pony Lake, he would now be within touching distance of his neighbour's flapping yellow tent. It was as if a subdivision had suddenly sprung up in a wilderness.

He listened and heard the muffled sound of voices, followed shortly after by the sound of a portable drill and hammer. He could clearly make out the figures of two bright-blue-suited men against the side of the wanigan where the toilet buckets had been set up. As he watched, they began to construct a low fence, fully enclosing the buckets, obscuring them from view. Within minutes the construction was complete. The men swung the new, chest-high gate on its hinges a few times and then, picking up their tools, walked back to the wanigan and disappeared inside. A few seconds later the entire group came out, walked around the building and stood looking at the now fenced-in toilet. He heard laughter as someone stepped forward, opened the gate and went inside, his head, shoulders and chest still clearly visible from where William stood, looking.

William frowned. It seemed to him that this group had taken over the place. Not that he had any more right or claim to it than they did. It was just that there were too many of them. He felt uncomfortable, painfully aware of their intrusion.

He turned his attention back to the chick. It was a day old, its grey-white feathers dry and fluffy, a dandelion gone to seed. Although he had been standing watching the nest for more than an hour, he had caught only rare glimpses of the chick. For most of the time its small body had been protected by the adult bird, sheltered from the chill wind that blew from the south. More chicks would soon be hatching. Only that morning he had heard cheeping from inside several eggs, and cracks had begun to appear on some of the shells. It was a good sign. Occasionally the shells were so thick and strong that the young couldn't break free. But that didn't seem to be the case now. Within the next twenty-four hours there should be several hatchings.

William smiled. Despite the cold and the long hours of inactivity, he felt something close to excitement. The colony was on the brink of change: the chicks would soon appear and with their arrival his research would gather momentum. He remembered back to his first season at Cape Royds – how little he had known back then about South Polar skuas. He had read accounts by Edward Wilson which had described the disappearance of one skua chick from a nest, but, like Wilson, he had not been able to account for the loss. It was only after weeks of observation that he had understood that the older of two chicks often attacked the younger chick, driving it from the nest, so that it either starved or fell victim to an adult predator. It had pleased him to solve a problem first identified more than fifty years before. More than at any other time in his life he had experienced a sense of history, connection, as if he was continuing the work of Wilson himself.

So many things had changed since that first season. The presence of the museum conservators' team reminded him of that. Whereas he had once lived in Shackleton's hut – had tidied the clutter, shifted furniture, even eaten tinned food taken from the explorer's stores – the door was now locked and only those with a permit were allowed to set foot in the place. He knew that resting on a table inside the hut was a visitors' book, its pages filled with the banal observations of those fortunate enough to enter. He could imagine the comments without having to see them: from people who 'stepped back in history' to a place 'frozen in time'. No longer a shelter from the weather or a simple work shed, the hut had been redefined as a monument, taken over and catalogued by people whose job it was to preserve the past. The hut's history, its clutter and equipment, would soon be processed into a museum display, a replica of something that was once real, alive.

He realised, then, that he felt a sense of loss. In his heart he knew that he belonged to a different generation, one whose time was passing far more quickly now than it had thirty years ago. This would be his final season at Cape Royds. What he would be doing next year he didn't know. Once the summer season was over, his notes written up, he had no plans. For the first time in his life his future was undefined. His logical, focused life of science was about to be replaced by the vague, meandering world of retirement. In the past, he had felt slightly dismissive towards people who had labelled him a world authority on skuas, but now, as a future of uncertainty presented itself to him, he felt a desire to hold on to the security of that label. In a few more years, he realised, his name would slip from view. Some people might remember him with admiration but others, those of a younger generation, would take his findings, his years of research, for granted. To them he might well appear as some dressing-gown-clad 'former' scientist, a crank who had spent most of his life fixated on skuas. He frowned. Never before had he given any thought to how others might perceive him. As long as his research was recognised he didn't care how people saw him. What they had thought was their own business.

For the first time in many years he found himself thinking about his wife's career. It had taken a long time, but now she was as well known in her field as he was in his; indeed, her works were performed on a regular basis before audiences throughout the world. And despite the fact that she was well into her sixties, she didn't have to face the prospect of being 'finished'. Concerts were booked in advance, recordings made, guest lectureships offered. She still had a future. Every time an audience applauded she could feel reassured that she had achieved something. More than that, she would be remembered. A wave of bitterness passed over him. He knew, however, that he had no right to feel bitter. His life, by anyone's standards, had been remarkable.

He shuddered. The cold had seeped through his gloves, stinging his fingers, making them ache. His joints felt sore; the simple task of holding his pencil was becoming uncomfortable, almost painful. His entire body, he noticed, felt chilled. If he didn't move soon, his legs would stiffen, his hips and knees seize up. Although, in general, he felt as healthy now as he ever had, he had noticed that he wasn't as agile as he used to be. Climbing out from his tent, finding his feet in the mornings was something he achieved now only with effort. And the cold – it had become part of him.

The sound of footsteps caught his attention. Turning, he saw a small group of Adélie penguins. There were six of them, walking in single file, their flippers held out stiffly. As they came closer they hesitated, huddling together as each individual bird looked at him. He stood still, watching them. After several minutes one of the birds broke free from the group and ran past him. Smiling at the sight, he was reminded of something he had heard at the start of the season.

He had come out to Cape Royds in November. Because he had been to the Antarctic within the past three years he hadn't been required to undertake field training, but one of the instructors, a climber named Brent, had been assigned to help him set up camp. Like William, Brent had kept to himself, but whereas William had felt excited at being back at Cape Royds, he had got the impression that Brent didn't really care where he was – as long as it wasn't New Zealand. It was as if he was cut off from his surroundings, his attention held by some conflict that seemed to be playing out in the privacy of his thoughts. The only time William came close to glimpsing that conflict was during Brent's last evening at the camp. The two of them had stepped outside for some fresh air because Trevor, William's colleague, had had problems lighting the stoves for dinner and as a result the wanigan had filled with kerosene fumes.

They had been standing in the cold for only a few seconds when their attention had been caught by the noise of footsteps. As they turned to face the sound, an Adélie, William heard Brent ask, 'Does it ever piss you off when people describe penguins as comic?' William had smiled. It didn't really bother him one way or the other, he'd replied. After all, people had to use some image, no matter how inappropriate, to describe what they saw. In his experience, most people simply resorted to the most clichéd description, regardless of how misleading it was. Skuas, for example, were nearly always described as vicious, when in fact they were no different from any other bird of prey – no better or worse than hawks or eagles.

Brent had kept his eyes on the penguin as William spoke, but a faint smile had crossed his face as he replied, 'It looks like a walking pillow to me.' William had nodded in agreement, and had already begun to walk back to the hut when he thought he heard Brent add, 'I wish Alice could have seen this place.'

The unexpected mention of the name had made him turn, puzzled. 'Alice, my wife?'

Brent looked at him in incomprehension. 'Your wife? No, I meant my girlfriend. Ellis. She died …' His voice trailed off and then quickly – too quickly, William thought – he had manoeuvred the conversation back to birds. 'Skuas are nasty, though. You've got to admit that.'

Watching the penguins run past him now, William thought Brent's walking-pillow description remarkably accurate. His thoughts lingered on the climber. He was younger than either of William's own sons. Ralph was somewhere around forty and Hector was in his thirties – thirty-seven, perhaps. William frowned. He couldn't remember the ages of either of his sons with any certainty. Not only that, but he couldn't be sure of the dates of their births. He knew Ralph had been born premature, and that Hector had been born in summer – January some time – but other than that, he had no idea. He tried to picture a birthday party, a present, or some other thing that might spark a memory of a celebration, but the truth was, he had no recollection of any of their birthdays. His mind grew more and more restless as he searched for some hint that might lead him to an actual date and eventually, after several more minutes, he found what he was looking for. His son Hector's sixth birthday.

It had been thirty, thirty-one – or two – years ago. It was the summer Alice's father had died. She had returned to Canada to nurse him through his final weeks and for some reason – perhaps because it was summer in New Zealand and lectures had come to an end – it was decided that the boys would remain at home with William. He hadn't planned a trip down south that year so there was no reason why he couldn't take care of them. It was, he realised, the first time he had been left alone with his sons and he had a clear memory of waving goodbye to Alice at the airport before turning to face both Ralph and Hector and wondering, as he took in their tear-stained faces, what on earth he was going to *do* with them during the weeks ahead. Neither boy spoke; all three had walked in silence and once they were in the car, he had sat with his hands on the steering wheel, the engine running, as he tried to think of where to go, what to do. He had a vague idea that he ought to try to cheer them up and had suggested that they go to the library. They had smiled, he recalled, and replied, 'It's all right.' So, in the end, they had gone home where, from memory, he had left the boys to get on with whatever it was they were doing while he had gone to his study to work.

For the first week of Alice's absence it had appeared to him that the boys spent vast amounts of time simply moping around the house. Whenever he had made some suggestion they had given their by now familiar reply of 'It's all right', and wandered off to another room where they could be left in peace. They seemed only to come to life when Alice phoned. As they spoke with her, their faces had lit up, their expressions becoming alive with excitement. In his company, they appeared inward looking, almost dull, and for a time he had wondered if perhaps there was something backward about them – an intellectual disability of some kind that he had failed to notice before. Eventually their lack of purpose had begun to annoy him and, feeling increasingly irritated, he had taken them out of the house and driven to a car yard, where, in a rush of impatience, he had traded in his Triumph 2000 for a Bedford van. They would, he decided, take a holiday.

They were living in Christchurch at the time. William had recently been promoted to senior lecturer and Alice had started studying part time towards a music degree. Her decision to go to university had pleased him. She was exceptionally bright and he had felt proud of her, relieved that she wasn't like the wives of his colleagues: women who went to coffee mornings or joined groups called The Friends of … the Art Gallery, or the Museum, or the Cathedral.

He had decided to take the boys on a tour of the South Island. He had no interest in going north – the North Island was overcrowded, while the area around Nelson only reminded him of his childhood and all the seasons he had spent helping out on his uncle's tobacco farm. So he had decided they would start by going west. It had been years since he had been to the coast; even longer since he had travelled south past the glaciers and over the Haast Pass.

Their first night, he recalled, had been spent at Mt White – a few kilometres east of Arthur's Pass. They'd parked in a camping area beside a stream and immediately upon stepping out of the van had been set upon by sandflies. There were thousands of them, attaching themselves to their heads like speech bubbles to comic-book characters. The shrill whirring of wings as the insects became entangled in their hair remained an irritation that refused to abate, no matter how much insect repellent was applied.

They had walked upstream, he remembered, searching each deep pool for fish. The afternoon had started well, but after only a few hours Ralph had started to complain of hunger and Hector had become increasingly silent. William hadn't thought to carry food with them; it was neither lunch nor dinner time so the idea that food might be important had not entered his mind. It annoyed him to think that they might have to turn back, but after only half an hour more it had become clear that Ralph was not going to let the matter of his hunger drop – so they had returned to camp.

On arriving back he had discovered that the van was full of sandflies. In his excitement to explore the creek, Hector had forgotten to close the passenger window and now the inside of the van was thick with the insects. To add to William's annoyance, neither child removed his boots before entering the van, and by the time he had noticed, it was too late: the floor was already covered in a fine layer of silt and mud.

The three of them had sat in silence, munching on bread and ginger marmalade, while William tried not to think about all the hours of research and writing lost through being on holiday. After fifteen minutes or so he had turned to say something to Hector and been surprised to find the boy looking pale and shivery. He was actually shaking. For a fleeting moment a lurch of panic had passed through William as he imagined his younger son struck down by some fast-acting virus. Even now, thirty-odd years later, the harsh tone of his voice as he demanded, 'What's wrong?' still embarrassed him. He remembered, too, that it had not been Hector who had replied but the older, Ralph. Speaking on his brother's behalf he had said, 'He's cold from falling in the creek.' William had neither seen his son fall into the water nor noticed that he was wet. It was obvious now, however, that the boy was soaked through.

Recalling his guilt after all these years, he remembered, too, that he had not packed clothing for the boys. He had gathered together his own clothes, sleeping bags, food and books, but had assumed the boys would take care of their own needs. It was only as he searched through the van for their packs that it suddenly occurred to him that he could not remember having placed any bags in the van before leaving. They had nothing but the clothes they were wearing.

He had felt ashamed of himself. Worse than that, he had felt annoyed with the boys for failing to speak up. He recalled asking, 'Why didn't you say you had no clothes?' And the long silence that followed echoed in his ears. Eventually, after almost a minute had passed, Ralph replied, 'We were scared you'd be mad at us. We thought if we kept quiet you wouldn't notice.' The truth contained in his son's remark had caught him off guard. Again, he had felt ashamed, but more than that – he felt lost. He didn't know what to do and for the first time in his life he missed Alice.

If he'd been a better father, he thought, they might have made a game of drying Hector's clothes over the fire. They could have pretended they were explorers or cowboys – or even shipwrecked sailors. But instead he had yanked the clothes from his son's small shivering body and pulled one of his own large sweaters down over the boy's head. He had been so frustrated, he recalled, that he hadn't even bothered to turn the cuffs back on the sleeves and for the rest of the evening Hector had had to flap his arms in order to make his tiny hands visible beyond the white knitted arms of the jumper. The clothes, once dry, smelt of smoke and a brown scorch mark stained the right leg of Hector's corduroy pants.

William had wanted to make it up to the boys – to say or do something to cheer them up – but, in truth, he had felt so sick with himself that he'd been unable to break free of his ill-temper. He spent the evening in sullen silence, watching as his sons, both miserable with uncertainty, huddled together on a mattress, too scared even to protect themselves against the mosquitoes that had arrived with the night.

The next morning he had woken early and prepared

breakfast for the boys. Bacon, tomatoes, eggs and sausages. It had been a feast. Immediately the boys' spirits had lifted and by the time they reached Greymouth they were all talking happily, laughing with delight as he described his previous summer, when he had travelled by dog-sled from Scott Base to Cape Royds. He recalled that they had been far more interested in the dogs than in either the skuas or the penguins. They had wanted to know the dogs' names, what they ate, where they slept at night and, most of all, how fast they could run. He had answered all their questions, going so far as to invent names for the dogs when, in fact, he hadn't a clue what they were called.

At Greymouth they had bought fish and chips and sat on the wharf at the river mouth, watching as a fishing boat lurched and rolled, surfing into the harbour. The boys had new clothes: waterproofs and tramping boots – but more important than any of those things, they now had penknives. They had only been cheap knives – toys, really, small blades that folded into plastic handles printed with pictures of cowboys and Indians – but the boys had been delighted. And, seeing their delight, William had begun to relax. The holiday, he thought, might work out after all.

In fact they had had fun for several days, but as they drove towards Jackson's Bay, south of Haast, the mood changed. The boys' occasional bickering had developed into a constant squabble, and finally into a full-scale battle. Hector had wanted to draw a picture using Ralph's new pen – a souvenir bought at Franz Josef which, when tilted, showed the glacier advancing down the length of the pen's barrel – and, when Ralph had refused to share it, Hector had snatched it from his older brother, hurling it through the window of the moving van into the dense scrub at the side of the road.

William had had to stop the vehicle so that they might search for the pen, but after half an hour it became obvious the pen was lost for good. At that point a fight had broken out between the brothers. Although older and stronger than his brother, Ralph had thrown himself at Hector, kicking and biting as he rammed the small boy's body against the side of the van. The attack had erupted so suddenly that both Hector and William had been taken by surprise. Even now, William could recall the look of complete incomprehension on Hector's face as the back of his head knocked against the sliding door, before catching against the edge of the hard metal doorstep as he fell to the ground. So taken aback was the boy that he had not had time to call out in either surprise or pain, but had simply cowered on the side of the road, staring mutely up at his brother, anticipating the next blow.

Without pausing, Ralph had then flung himself on top of Hector, beating him with his fists and crying, 'You bloody, bloody, bloody ...' He hadn't known what to say next. Bloody was the worst word he knew, and what came after such an expletive was beyond the range of his vocabulary. 'You bloody, bloody ... *boy*!' he had cried, giving Hector one more kick before William dragged him away from the smaller boy's crouching body. After what seemed an age but was really no more than several seconds, Hector had managed to get to his feet and run away, disappearing into the bush at the side of the road. Fearing that he might get lost, William had managed, somehow, to jostle Ralph into the van before taking off on foot after his younger son.

The boy, he now recalled, could not be persuaded to return. He sat mutely, staring into the middle distance, his hands over his ears as William tried to reassure him that he would be safe. Fifteen minutes passed, then half an hour and then an hour, and only then did the boy reluctantly stand up and follow his father back to the van. On seeing Ralph, Hector began to whimper. It was apparent that he was terrified of his older brother – and that he felt betrayed by his father.

For the rest of the day they journeyed in near silence. One boy sat in the front of the van, beside William, the other in the back, stretched out on the sleeping mattresses, gazing towards the rear window. Hector would not eat, and he was afraid to sleep unless William sat between him and Ralph. Even then, he would wake in the night and call out for his mother, his small hand reaching out, crawling insect-like over his father's body until it found his beard and stopped.

For his own part, William had felt increasingly disconcerted by his own response to Ralph's attack. It was little wonder Hector had felt betrayed; he had done nothing to prevent Ralph from striking the boy, but had watched, disengaged, like some bystander at a pub brawl. Again and again he tried to make sense of his own behaviour and it was only on the morning of Hector's birthday, two days later, that he suddenly realised what had happened. He understood, then, that he hadn't been emotionally detached at all but had spent the first few minutes of the fight standing by because he was so interested – he had wanted to see how the fight would develop. He had observed one son attack the other as if watching the elder of two skua chicks attack the younger, weaker one. Much as it now appalled him, he had treated his sons not as human beings, his own flesh and blood, but as case studies in a research project.

William frowned, shaking his head at the memory. That was all he could recall about Hector's sixth birthday – that it had fallen two days after the fight. What he had bought for his son, what they had eaten or where they had spent the night was lost to him. Between his two sons there must have been at least seventy-five years of birthdays, he thought, but that was the only one he could remember.

As he approached the wanigan he was aware of laughter coming from inside. It was Trevor's voice. He recognised it instantly, although it had been a long time since he had heard his colleague laugh aloud. He hesitated before entering, conscious that his unannounced arrival might be unwelcome but, because he was feeling cold, he pulled the heavy door open and stepped inside to meet five faces looking at him.

'William. Nice to meet you. We've just been hearing about your research. Please excuse our mess – just push our things out of your way. Here, have a Swiss Miss. It's ghastly, I know, but at least one can say it's hot.' William stood stunned, inundated by the flow of words that gushed towards his body. He looked at the man who had spoken but his face was obscured by a navy blue balaclava. Only his eyes and a small dark hole that was his mouth were visible. 'Please, please come in and get warm. This cold is so beastly I'm still wearing my balaclava!'

The cup of steaming chocolate was thrust into his hand and as he took a sip he was aware that the faces of several men were focused on him, as if anticipating his reaction. 'Thank you,' he nodded, embarrassed by all the attention.

'Right then, food!' It was the balaclava man who spoke, and William guessed that he was the leader of the group, though it was difficult to gauge any indication of the man's age. He stood, sipping from his cup as the man pulled food from a red wooden box. He was surprised at how quickly he worked, how easily he lit the stoves, ladling cup after cup of crushed ice into the large pots for water.

From listening to the conversation he learned that the man's name was Nicholas and that he lived in a cottage somewhere in Wales. It was clear, too, from the way his colleagues addressed him, that most of them had met him only recently, on the flight down from Christchurch. With one exception, they seemed slightly uncomfortable in his presence, as if unsure of what was expected of them, or how they should behave in his company. Only one of the men, a carpenter named Calum, had worked with Nicholas, and from what William could tell, they had worked together in Laos the previous year.

There were too many people in the hut. Whenever one person moved, three others would have to shift, in order to create enough room for movement to take place. Unaccustomed to sharing the hut with anyone other than Trevor, William found himself feeling increasingly claustrophobic. He was also irritated by Nicholas's constant chatter. He was telling the others about Shackleton's hut, the work that needed doing, but there was something annoying about the sheer number of words he used. He couldn't be quiet.

After a while, William edged through the door in search of the peace he knew awaited him outside. Much to his annoyance, Nicholas followed, joining him where he stood watching a whale cruising back and forth along a channel cut through the ice. Following a short silence, he was surprised to hear Nicholas observe, 'It's a minke, I think.'

William nodded, said, 'Yes,' but, not wishing to encourage further dialogue, said nothing more. Without turning his head, he was vaguely conscious of movement to his side, the sound of clothing being rearranged. Through the corner of his eye he took in that Nicholas had removed his balaclava and was running his hands over his head.

'Calum's the real whale expert. He spent several seasons at Rothera Station – with the Brits.'

Something in the tone of Nicholas's voice caught William's attention. He turned and, catching full sight of the other man, gasped.

Nicholas gave no indication of having noticed. 'I was fascinated to learn of your work. I was just telling Trevor that I once spent several months on the Falklands. It was a remarkable place. When I first arrived I was struck by the wildlife – coming from Britain, you see. It was marvellous …

that is, until the war destroyed everything.' His thoughts and words appeared to have become entangled, his voice trailed off – choked, it seemed to William, by anger. After a while he composed himself. 'I remember the Falkland skuas. They were wonderful, incredible on the wing – slightly smaller than your birds, I think. I could have watched them all day.' He paused, lost in thought, then said, 'I wonder how that water's coming along. You will join us for a bite, won't you?'

William shuffled awkwardly, aware that he was unable to meet his companion's gaze. Nicholas's face was so badly disfigured that it had reminded him of a chicken he'd once tried to roast. Believing it to have come packaged in a roasting bag, he had placed it in the hot oven only to be alerted several minutes later by the smell of burning plastic. Removing the chicken he had encountered the still creamy-white raw carcass encased in a film of wrinkled, melted plastic. He knew that if he did look at Nicholas he would have to stare. There was something so remarkable about the man's lack of features, the remnant nose and ear, the left eye staring out from a barely protected socket and the mouth with only the faintest suggestion of lips, that despite his desire to act naturally, he couldn't. His options seemed to be either to stare, or to cut the conversation short and avoid looking at Nicholas's face altogether. He chose the latter.

'I'll take your silence as a yes,' Nicholas laughed.

William flinched, aware of how rude he had been. Turning to Nicholas, his gaze fixed somewhere around the man's collar, he forced a smile as he replied, 'Yes, thank you.'

As Nicholas entered the hut, he turned, saying, 'We're very lucky, aren't we? To find ourselves amid such breathtaking beauty.' William nodded and turned his attention back to the whale. As he watched, his thoughts drifted to Nicholas, wondering what had happened to leave him so badly burnt. It wasn't only his face that was disfigured; his body, too, appeared almost lopsided, his left hand hanging limp like a penguin caught by a leopard seal. It occurred to him that Nicholas had followed him outside for a reason, that he had been acting out of kindness. Anticipating William's involuntary gasp, he had afforded him a private space in which to come to terms with his appearance. It had been a simple gesture but one of such selflessness that William felt touched and embarrassed.

As lunch progressed, Nicholas had spoken less and less frequently. At first William had assumed he had nothing left to say, that he had been talking so much earlier that he had run out of energy. But he noticed, too, that as the food disappeared, the other men appeared more at ease in Nicholas's company. They had stopped shuffling about and moving whenever he came close. As he watched, it occurred to William that perhaps Nicholas talked as a way of diverting attention from his appearance, and that now the men had had time to grow accustomed to it, he was able to relax a little. Previous experience must have made him see some benefit in being so extraordinarily sensitive to other people's feelings. Day after day, William mused, Nicholas must put aside his own feelings, channelling all his strength and will into ensuring that others saw him as a normal, intelligent man. To live like that must be tiring, thought William. He knew that if he was in Nicholas's shoes he would not be so generous. He would make no allowances for other people's feelings and he certainly wouldn't go out of his way to make things easy for them. It was a wonder Nicholas showed no signs of bitterness, that he hadn't simply given up.

It was after seven when William returned from his birdwatch. As he expected, no more eggs had hatched, although a second chick had cracked its shell, making a small hole through which its cheeping could be heard. As he walked back to the camp he decided, on the spur of the moment, to pass Shackleton's hut. He hadn't looked inside the hut for years but there was something about the evening, the presence of the conservators' team, that had made him feel a sadness, a longing almost, for the past.

Although the hut caught the sun, he knew from previous summers spent in the building that the inside would be cold, too well insulated to permit heat to either enter or escape.

As he approached, he was surprised to hear a voice ask, 'Would you care to see inside? I'm just locking up ... sounds absurd, doesn't it?' Turning, he was taken aback to see Nicholas. 'I was watching you; I hope you don't mind. There was something very peaceful, very lovely about the careful way you moved around the penguin colony. You seemed very deep in thought.'

William smiled. 'I was just trying to avoid standing on any eggs.'

'Oh, I see. It reminded me of those images of Christ one used to encounter in children's books. Do you remember? An image of Jesus standing amid a group of children, his hands resting gently on their upturned heads.'

William nodded. 'My father,' he replied, 'was a religious man. We didn't get along – for that reason. Fortunately, he lived in Scotland, on Islay, so I rarely had to see him.'

The two men stood in silence, their eyes focused on the sea. Large slabs of ice dotted the bay like tables draped in creased white cloths, and as they watched, small groups of penguins leapt from the water, landing on the ice. Eventually Nicholas took up the conversation. 'I didn't get on with my father either. He was a commander in the navy and something of a bully, I'm afraid. It was because of him, I suppose, that I ended up flying jets. It was only through a rather remarkable twist of fate that I was able – eventually – to return to my first love, art. Still, they say every cloud has a silver lining.'

He paused, then, stepping up to the door of Shackleton's hut, asked, 'Shall we go in?'

William stood still as his eyes grew accustomed to the gloom. Many years had passed since he had spent a summer in the hut, and yet everything seemed so familiar that he almost expected to see his socks hanging from a line strung across the ceiling.

'Trevor said you spent a season here?'

William nodded. 'The summer of '59–60.' He hesitated, then added, 'Long before your time.'

After only a few minutes he was ready to leave. He had felt certain that being in the hut would reignite memories of that first season, but nothing of the sort had happened. The interior was familiar, but nothing more. Little caught or held his attention. It belonged to another time, a different life, one he could not re-enter. As he was about to leave, however, his gaze fell on something Nicholas was examining. He stepped closer and recognised, immediately, his own jersey. He reached out to claim it but, aware of the white gloves Nicholas was wearing, hesitated. Feeling uncertain, he listened as Nicholas explained, 'I was rummaging around outside a little earlier when I happened across this sweater caught between some boulders over that little rise. It's rather curious – you see, the right elbow is quite badly damaged but the left appears in almost perfect condition. Odd, don't you think?'

Although he recognised the jersey, had worn it on an almost daily basis, William found himself looking at the elbow as if seeing it for the first time. He started, aware that he felt guilty, still, for not having patched the hole. The hole itself was easily explained: whenever he had to handle a skua he held it firmly under his left arm while working with his right hand. As his hand crossed over the bird it would struggle, its head extended, its sharp beak worrying a spot at his elbow, tugging at the wool until, after only a short while, a hole had formed, and grew in size with each bird examined.

'It's beautifully made,' Nicholas observed. 'My mother was a great one for knitting, but socks were her thing.'

As William watched Nicholas turn the jersey about in his hands he was overcome by a desire to reach out and snatch it from him. He couldn't account for the strength of his feelings. It was as if he needed to tell Nicholas the history of the jersey, draw his attention to the too-short sleeves, the stains incurred by weeks of wear, and, most important, about the woman who knitted it. Alice. He wanted to explain his marriage to Nicholas so that he might understand what had happened. How that had also been lost.

He opened his mouth and made a sound, but found he didn't know where to begin. Never before had he experienced anything like the lurch in his stomach that he felt now, on watching Nicholas fold the jersey carefully and push it aside. Then he heard Nicholas's voice announce, 'I expect dinner's almost ready,' and jumped, confused by the sudden intrusion into his thoughts.

'What will you do with the sweater?' he asked. He was aware of Nicholas's eyes on him, but could read no expression on his companion's face.

Nicholas shook his head. 'I'm not sure.' William had the uneasy feeling he was being studied, his reaction monitored as Nicholas concluded, 'Maybe I should put it back where I found it.'

The image of the jersey, folded on Shackleton's table, remained with William throughout dinner. He was aware of voices around him, conversations circling the room, but he was so engrossed in his memories that he paid little attention. Occasionally he would hear his name and he would look up in a daze as a glass of champagne or a plate of Christmas dinner was passed his way. But he was barely able to utter the words 'Thank you', so preoccupied was he with what he had seen in Shackleton's hut and, moreover, his own puzzling silence.

A bowl of Christmas pudding was thrust into his hand and he smiled, nodded his head, and for several minutes tried to focus on the conversation. He heard someone ask, 'What's your fucking opinion, William?' and realised that, despite his best intentions, he hadn't heard a thing. 'The fucking road to the fucking Pole. What do you think?'

He turned to the man who had spoken, a builder named Roy. 'Road to the Pole,' William repeated, unsure of where the conversation was going. A silence followed before Roy took up the conversation once more. 'Americans. Building a fucking road all the way to the fucking Pole. Fuck fucking nature – let's put a fucking road in. Fuck, how the fuck do they get away with it? Someone should fucking remind them that the Antarctic isn't the United fucking States of America.'

William shrugged, barely aware of the laughter that met Roy's outburst. Only the constant repetition of the word 'fuck' had caught his attention, reminding him of a musterer he had met during a summer on the Chatham Islands. Like Roy, the musterer had relied on the word 'fuck' as the mainstay of his vocabulary. Without it, he would have been left almost speechless, unable to articulate even the simplest of thoughts. And, like Roy, the musterer had appeared – in all other regards – a thoughtful, almost gentle man; someone who spoke quietly and only after much consideration.

He'd been sitting for too long. He needed to move about, get some fresh air. He glanced at his watch: nine-thirty-five. The news would be almost over. He hesitated, wondering if there would be anything worthwhile in the bulletin, but thought it unlikely. Nevertheless he reached for the radio, tuning in to Scott Base.

'Two lovers locked in passionate embrace…' It was

Marilyn. He knew then that it would be better to turn the radio off and conserve the battery but as he reached for the knob he heard Roy's voice request, 'Can you leave it on for a fucking minute, please, mate?' Everyone, he realised, was listening, waiting for the story to develop.

'A man and a woman were today rescued from the boot of a Holden Barina where they had locked themselves in accidentally while getting cosy in a passionate embrace, unaware of the fact that they were trapped …'

'Goodness,' Nicholas's voice broke into the reading, 'she's worse than that little man you have on television every night.' There was a shush from Trevor as Marilyn continued.

'Patrons at the Western Tavern heard the cry of despair from the pair and came to their assistance, freeing them from the vehicle boot, but less than thirty minutes later they were alerted once more by cries for help. The young lovebirds had once more locked themselves in the cramped confides – confines – of the car and had to be rescued yet again …'

The bulletin broke off. Everyone in the hut remained silent, waiting for it to resume. Several minutes passed before Nicholas remarked, 'What interesting lives you New Zealanders lead.' He was about to add something else when transmission resumed.

'And now for the joke. An Englishman, an Irishman and a Scotchman went into a pub in Sydney. "What will you have?" asked the barman. The Englishman replied, "I'll have …" '

The radio faltered, static obscuring Marilyn's words. For a moment no one spoke, each lost in the possibilities of where the joke might lead. It was Roy who broke the silence, his simple 'Fuck' filling the room as William stepped outside.

An announcement from the flight deck interrupted his train of thought, dragging him back to the present. 'Could I have your attention there, folks?' Glancing up, he could see the captain speaking into a microphone. 'We're expecting a little turbulence up ahead, so if any of you are moving around, we'd appreciate it if you could return to your seats and buckle up …'

The voice trailed away, to be replaced by another voice, that of a member of the flight crew who was standing next to him. Taking William by the arm, he said, 'Take a seat, please, sir.' William felt himself being directed to where Sally and Marilyn sat, and then the hand on his shoulder became firmer, pushing him down. 'Make room there, gals. You've got company.'

As he sat down he noticed that Sally was holding his seat-belt buckle, waiting to pass it to him. He nodded 'thanks' but said nothing. He wanted to be left alone, to think. Hearing Sally speak, however, he turned towards her as she said, 'It's hot, isn't it?' Once more he nodded. 'Sorry,' he heard Sally continue, 'I've already said that, haven't I? About the heat, I mean.'

He leaned back against the webbing, his eyes closed, but despite his attempt to discourage conversation he was dismayed to hear Sally say, 'I like your jersey. It reminds me of one I used to have, years ago, when I was living in Scotland.'

At that moment the aircraft lurched, throwing William against Sally. Almost immediately the aeroplane jolted and dropped, before jerking upwards like a ball kicked into the air.

'My flatmates' mother knitted it for me.'

For a second, William couldn't recall what Sally was talking about. He hesitated, then asked, 'What? The jumper?'

'Yes. My flatmates' mother came to visit and she brought a jersey she'd knitted. It was an Aran one, just like yours. It was meant for her eldest son but he'd put on quite a bit of weight since she'd last seen him ... so, you know ... Ralph's loss, my gain, I suppose.'

William frowned. Sally had a tendency to speak increasingly quietly as her sentences progressed. Her voice would trail off and he found it almost impossible to hear what she was saying. It didn't matter. She was only talking about a jersey. Still, in order to appear polite, he replied, 'My wife knitted this one for me.'

'Your wife?' He heard Sally shout more loudly than before. 'Well, she's a very talented knitter.'

'Yes, she is, I suppose.'

'You should ask her to mend the elbow for you!'

'No, I don't think so. She's got better things to do with her time.'

'Why? What does she do?' The aeroplane gave another tremendous jolt, causing Sally to fall heavily onto Marilyn. William registered a gasp but had already turned away, terminating the conversation and Sally's seemingly endless questions. He slumped into his seat, closing his eyes. As soon as the all clear was given he would stand up again, but in the meantime he would try to sleep – or at least pretend to sleep.

He had sat in his tent for almost two hours, laughter from the hut reaching him in waves, blending with the birdcalls from the colony. Occasionally he would hear the door to the wanigan open and steps would sound outside his tent. He would freeze then, anticipating a voice calling out to him, but although the footsteps would appear close enough to be almost on top of him, he would register, instead, the swing of the new toilet door and the shuffling steps of a man trying to position himself so as to urinate into the opening of the piss-pot's funnel.

At midnight he realised that the voices inside the wanigan were not getting any quieter and, unable to sleep or relax, he had dressed and left his tent, walking away from the campsite in the direction of the heli-pad before circling back towards the coast where he hoped, at last, he might find peace. As he scrambled up a low, wall-like cluster of rocks, he was neither surprised nor concerned to discover Nicholas already ahead of him, standing alone and watching a skua as it circled out to sea. Not wishing to disturb him, he hesitated, then turned to retrace his steps. He was too late, however. Nicholas's voice called him back.

They stood next to each other in silence, watching the bird, its body appearing almost black against the bright off-white sky. Eventually Nicholas broke the silence. 'When I was in the Falklands,' he said, 'one of our helicopters was brought down by a bird. Not a skua; an albatross. At least that's what we all presumed had happened. Feathers were found floating on the sea at the crash site.' He paused before adding, 'It's a terrible thing to say, but I remember feeling sorry for the bird.' He laughed, a hollow sound that brought to mind the cries from the penguin colony.

'I like your jacket, by the way,' Nicholas continued. 'It's not one of ours, is it?' The sudden change of topic took William by surprise. For an instant he didn't know what Nicholas was referring to but then, remembering that he was wearing his red coat, he replied, 'It's American. I found it in the skua bin at McMurdo a few weeks ago.'

'The skua bin! How delightful. I've heard so much about it.'

William felt embarrassed. It was an old jacket; most of the lining was torn away but from the outside it looked almost new. It had been too good to leave for someone else.

'And the sweater I found today,' Nicholas said. 'That belongs to you, too, doesn't it?'

William flinched.

'I was looking at it again and I discovered some words

sewn into it. I hope you don't mind but I read the message. I hadn't realised it was yours.'

William felt a sudden chill go through him. He had no idea what Nicholas was talking about. Although he had worn the jersey every day for weeks he had never discovered anything remotely resembling a message on it.

'I've got it here, as a matter of fact. It's stuffed down the front of my coat – keeping me warm. I was going to give it back to you in the morning but you should take it now.' Unzipping his jacket he reached for the jersey, exposing it little by little until it was a bundle in his gloved hands.

William didn't know what to say. He would have been no more surprised had Nicholas pulled a white rabbit from a top hat. He took the jersey and turned it about in his hands, wondering where on earth to look. He was acutely aware of Nicholas's eyes on him and he felt flustered, embarrassed by the absurdity of the situation.

'Here. Allow me.'

He felt almost helpless as Nicholas took the sweater, turned it inside out and indicated some fine chain-stitching circling an area around the heart. 'Dear Bill – Happy Skua-ing. Summer 1959–60. Keep safe. Alice.' He felt his eyes prick as the shame of his ignorance caught him; the fact that for years he had overlooked something so close to his heart. Lost for words, he looked up to see Nicholas's bright blue eyes focused on the bird that flew overhead.

They had stood peacefully for several more minutes. Neither man spoke and William could remember feeling grateful for the space between them. Revolving in his head, in endless, unforgiving motion, was the thought that it had taken Nicholas only minutes to find something that he himself had not noticed in decades. He knew that he was often inattentive, failing to register new clothing or furniture or whatever else Alice had bought over the past years, but this was different. It was as if he was suddenly being called to account. In the back of his mind he could hear the words, 'Look at what you missed.' A dull ache of sadness seeped through him. All his life, he realised, he had been able to concentrate on only one thing at a time and, as long as he was focused on his research, it was not possible for him to pay close attention to his wife or children.

But, more than that, he had not even *tried* to find time for them. That would have required more effort, greater organisation and sacrifice than he had been prepared to make. He had lived a selfish life, had missed seeing his sons grow to adulthood, had fallen out of step with his wife. Yet something inside told him that things couldn't have been any different. He had made the right decision. Not for them, but for himself. He loved his work. And, despite his regrets, he knew that his life would have been empty and meaningless without it.

A sound – a faint splash – reached him and he turned in time to see a group of penguins diving into the sea.

'It's a very peaceful sound, isn't it? I don't suppose you would ever tire of hearing it?'

William faced Nicholas and found himself searching the man's face for a trace of expression. There was none. The face, like bark on a tree, needed to be touched in order to be read. He raised his hand, watched mesmerised as it moved gently towards the other man's face before it swung away, towards the safety of his own pocket.

'I discovered,' continued Nicholas, showing no sign of having noticed, 'that I carry very clear memories of sound. Once, when I was flying, I was forced to ditch into the sea. My plane had been hit, you see, and the cockpit was on fire and things were pretty hopeless, to tell the truth. I'd thought I'd make it back to the carrier but the fire became too intense and I had to eject just short of the runway. The one thing that sticks in my mind is the sound made by my body hitting the water. I am absolutely certain that as my body entered the sea I heard a sizzle – like water splashed against a hot frying pan. I tell myself constantly that I must be mistaken, that my memory is playing tricks on me, that I couldn't have heard that noise above the other sounds around me, and yet I swear to you, that is the sound I remember. A short "t-se" as my flesh touched the sea.'

William watched, lost for words, as Nicholas looked at his watch. He wanted to say something, but he realised his words wouldn't make sense. His desire to thank Nicholas would, he thought, appear meaningless. And yet there were no other words he could use to convey the gratitude he felt for being reintroduced to his past, to his wife and even, he thought, to the people around him. He felt more aware of others than he had for many years, and yet it was impossible to communicate that connection. He was out of practice. He tried to think of what he might say to Nicholas but already it was too late; the other man had begun to walk away, back towards the wanigan and his colleagues, his team who would, no doubt, keep talking and laughing well into the night.

William would not join them; he preferred to be solitary – it was how he felt most comfortable.

'Tell me,' he heard Nicholas suddenly call out, 'how would you describe the sound made by all those penguins? It's got me stumped.'

William watched as Nicholas raised his hand in a slight wave. Slowly, hesitantly, he waved back, then listened as Nicholas's boots skittered across the loose stones before fading away, to be replaced once more by the cries of thousands of penguins.

The plane shuddered, the passengers opposite him swaying like bamboo flagpoles caught in the wind. He felt the weight of Sally's body against his own but his attention was focused on the woman across from him. She had unzipped her jacket and he could make out her T-shirt, the words printed across her chest reading 'HOW ABOUT A GREAT BIG CUP OF SHUT THE F**K UP?' William smiled. So that was how people communicated.

Sally's shoulder suddenly bumped against him and, turning, he noticed that her expression was tense, her fingers clenched into tight fists.

'Are you feeling all right?' He saw her nod and felt relieved. If she vomited he might not be able to get out of the way.

'It's a bit bumpy!' she shouted. She opened her fingers and he glimpsed a pitted black stone, the size of a small egg, in her palm. It was polished, almost glossy, and she began to roll it in her hand as if it was a ball of plasticine. She must have seen him looking because she suddenly said, 'It's a stone.' She laughed. 'I picked it up on Bratina Island.'

Nodding in response, William asked, 'What were you doing there? Are you a geologist?'

'No,' she shouted, 'a composer!'

William started. He had assumed when he'd met her that she was a scientist. It had never crossed his mind that she might be a composer. He opened his mouth, was about to say, 'My wife's a composer,' but thought better of it. He didn't want to be dragged into a discussion about composers or music. He knew nothing about either and, if Sally was anything like himself, she wouldn't welcome the conversation. There was nothing worse than having to talk about your profession to someone who was clearly ignorant – and in all likelihood indifferent – to what you had to say. And anyway, what could he say without it sounding self-congratulatory? Something like: 'My wife's a composer. Her name is Alice Glenton – perhaps you've heard of her? Yes? No? Well, she's very highly regarded. Her works are performed all over the world.' No, it was better to keep quiet. It would do neither of them any favours to bring up the subject of his wife. Instead, indicating the stone, he said, 'May I look?'

SALLY

Sally watched as William turned the stone in his fingers. She felt a pang of concern, as if fearing he might drop it, or, worse, pocket it and refuse to return it. The truth was, she hadn't picked it up. It was a stone Craig had passed to her one evening and, simply by keeping it, she had made it precious. It was hers and she didn't want anyone else to handle it.

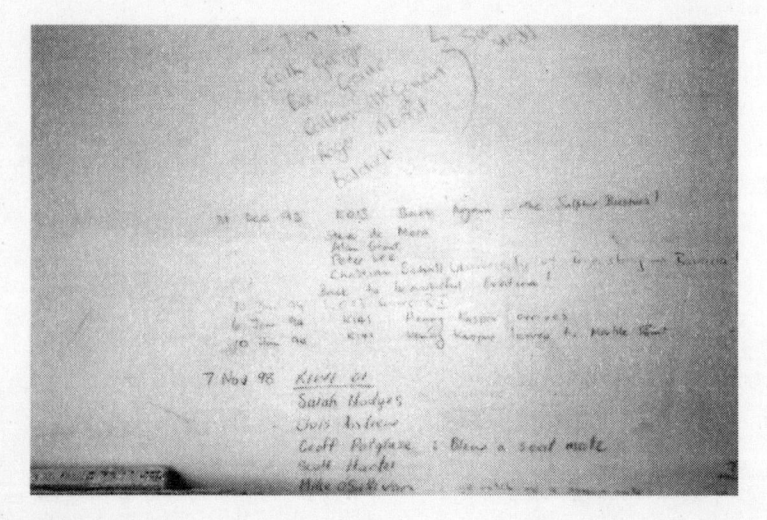

The day, she remembered, had begun like the others – with a hot drink. Only this time, as she'd stood outside Craig's tent, the steaming mug in her hand, she'd heard him ask, 'If you've got nothing special planned for the day, could you give me a hand with some stones?' She hadn't responded immediately but had stood silently, waiting to see if he would come to the door of his tent. 'If you've got other plans, though, it's all right. I can manage on my own.'

She'd remained standing, gazing towards a shingle bank and a skua that was circling above. The night before she had gone for a walk, taking her recording equipment with her. She had inadvertently wandered too close to the bird's nest and had been attacked. As she'd crouched low to the ground, protecting her head, the bird's attacks had become increasingly frenzied: instead of making wide circling movements and flying towards her at a low angle, it had begun to jerk up and down above her head, like a twist of paper tied to a string held by someone teasing a kitten.

They'd walked towards the southern end of the island, to an area where small coloured pebbles of granite lay scattered across hummocks of black, angular stones. The ponds in this area were larger than elsewhere, lakes with patches of ice glinting like steel on their surface. Her attention was caught almost immediately by a round, pale pink stone. It was the colour of the skin on the palm of her hand, and as she turned it in her fingers she could feel its abrasive surface. It was a beautiful stone and she felt proud for having spotted it. Holding it up for Craig to see, she asked, 'What do you think?'

He'd turned, looked at it, then reached out. 'Ah, that's nice, isn't it?'

Sally had blushed, pleased that he'd noticed. Although she'd wanted it for herself, she'd offered it to him. 'Do you want it?' Even as she spoke, she could feel her hand reaching out, as if uncertain of making a gift of such a perfect object.

Something unexpected had happened then. Instead of

returning the stone, Craig had laughed. 'Nah, it's rubbish!' he said, and tossed the stone away. Sally stood speechless, watching as it curved gently in the air before landing on a piece of ice and skittering into a pond with a plop.

'So,' Craig asked, 'have you found inspiration yet?' She'd laughed then, told him she'd done hours of recording but was having trouble determining what direction to take. She felt overwhelmed by the scale of her surroundings on the one hand, and yet unsettled by the fact that there was so little in the way of natural, environmental sound. The more she thought about it, the more impossible it seemed. She'd smiled, hoping Craig might say something helpful, but he'd simply murmured, 'Tough, eh?'

She was not dismayed. She had grown accustomed to his teasing, but now she detected a slight undercurrent, a shift — not so much in what he said — but in his expression. It was as if he was now genuinely interested in what she was doing but was unsure of how to say so. He didn't know how to manoeuvre the conversation away from the jokey banter they had both grown comfortable with. She noticed, too, that he now often held her gaze.

Yet, despite her desire to encourage him to have a serious discussion, she felt self-conscious, fearful that she might be mistaken — that his interest in her was no more than an attempt to be polite. There was something both sweet and sad about the situation. Had she been younger and single, she might not have felt so hesitant in his company. She could imagine herself challenging him in some way, even flirting in order to ascertain just where she stood. In her twenties she wouldn't have given so much thought to the consequence of her actions, the possibility of rejection or humiliation. She would have revealed something of herself and, had he rejected her, still had the optimism to pick herself up and move on.

Not any more. Although she might match him, step for step, she would not expend the energy to make the first move, not unless she could predict the result. A sigh of frustration escaped her. Suddenly irritated, she said, 'I thought we came out here to measure bits of gravel.'

It took only a few minutes for Craig to collect five bags of stones. From what Sally could tell, he selected them at random, his hand moving quickly as if picking up loose coins or keys from a kitchen bench. She noticed, however, that he ignored both the largest and smallest rocks; his stones were all similar in size.

'Right,' he said, once they had found a sheltered place to sit. 'So, each bag has fifty stones and the first thing we have to do – before we measure them – is sort them. We'll call these ones,' he said, holding up a polished, black, pitted stone from the first bag, 'bubbly lava.'

Sally laughed. 'That's not its real name, is it?'

Craig shook his head, frowning at the interruption. 'No, it's not,' he said, without offering any further explanation. 'These ones,' he continued, indicating several dark grey, gravelly-looking stones, 'are fine-grained volcanics – they're basalt; these are granite – like the stone you found just now, and these,' he said, indicating some slightly greenish-grey stones, 'are Transantarctic mountains metasediments.' He looked up. 'That's their real name. Right, got that?'

Sally nodded.

'So, I measure the stones, and you write down what I say. Is that okay? The important thing is that you tell me if you miss something. Don't, whatever you do, make it up. It's important to get it right.'

Sally found herself nodding again, but the more he said, the more she began to feel on edge. A doubt formed in her mind as it occurred to her that he might be having her on. Even as he held a pair of callipers in his hand and measured the longest axis on the first stone, she half expected him to stop, look up and say, 'You didn't really think someone would pay me to come to the Antarctic just to measure bits of gravel, did you?'

She suddenly started as she realised she'd missed the first measurements completely. Feeling embarrassed, and conscious of the delay, she struggled to hold the pencil stub in her gloved hand. The fingers on her right glove were too long and the tips had caught under the pencil lead. She'd have to take it off. She was becoming flustered. Out of the corner of her eye she could see Craig still holding on to the first stone, watching and waiting for her to get organised. She was struck by her ineptitude and she blushed.

At last she was ready and she looked up, catching Craig's eye, as if he was a conductor drawing an orchestra to him in the split-second before the first note fell. They could begin.

Instead of hearing the first note, however, she heard Craig say, 'That pencil needs sharpening.' She recalled the way she had watched, silent yet horrified, as shards of wood had flicked across the space between their two bodies; red flakes landed, helter skelter, on the ground. He can't do that, she remembered thinking. He's breaking the rules. As she took the sharpened pencil from his outstretched hand she looked around furtively, anticipating that someone – a member of the pencil police, perhaps – would step out from behind a hummock and announce, 'Not so fast; you're nicked!'

'Okay.' Craig's voice broke into the emptiness of their surroundings. 'Let's crack on.' He spoke slowly, softly, and once again she began to relax, lulled by the sound of his voice and the repetitiveness of what he said. 'Bubbly lava. 45.6, 36.9, 18.4. Sub-angular – no, make that sub-rounded. 33.2, 24.5, 12.1. Sub-rounded.'

Sally listened for several readings, then interrupted. 'What does sub-rounded mean?'

Craig had explained to her that, as well as measuring each stone, he needed to describe how round it was. By examining the roundness of the corners on each stone he could scale them from very angular to well rounded. As he spoke he traced his finger around the outline of the stone in his hand, remarking casually, 'Basically, it just helps us look better.' He laughed. 'It's more professional than writing "This stone looks a bit like Greenland". '

As he finished with each stone he threw it away, sometimes laughing as he did so. 'Last three. Transantarctic mountains metasediments: TMM. Okay. 16.5, 14.4, 11.'

Sally looked up as he tossed the rock over his shoulder. 'What was it?' she asked.

'What?' Craig frowned.

'The stone. You didn't say what it was.'

'Shit, didn't I?'

'No.'

He turned to where he had thrown the stone, his eyes scanning the shingle bank before turning back to her. 'It was sub-angular, wasn't it?'

Sally laughed. 'I don't know. I didn't even see it until it whistled past my head.'

Craig turned once more to face the low hummock. 'I think it was sub-angular. That will do, won't it?'

'Are you asking me?'

Craig shrugged. 'Sub-angular, then.'

'Are you sure?'

'Nope.'

Sally laughed. 'I could always put down that it was shaped like Greenland.'

It was a small thing but she felt happy, as if, for once, she had got the upper hand in the conversation. Taking advantage of the situation, she said, 'It's a shame it's not music – then we could invent anything we liked.'

Craig smiled, his eyes fixed on hers. 'If it was anything like your music we'd probably be sitting around waiting for the stones to measure us.'

Sally could think of nothing to say.

Sally sighed, shifting in her seat. Looking around, she was aware of the faces of her travelling companions, eyes staring blankly ahead, almost too dulled by boredom to flicker. Even Marilyn appeared to be in some sort of daze. Yet there was also a restlessness in Marilyn's body. Although her eyes stared straight ahead, her hands were constantly moving, her fingers grasping and releasing each other, the fingers of one hand tugging and twisting at the gold signet ring that adorned her little finger. Sally half expected to see a length of worry-beads appear, a further testimony to the conflict that seemed to be playing through her companion's mind.

Touching Marilyn gently on the shoulder, she shouted, 'Almost there.' She saw Marilyn nod, but she appeared too absorbed by her own thoughts to respond.

Several seconds passed, then she saw Marilyn look at her watch. 'There's still two hours?'

As Sally checked her own watch and nodded, she felt suddenly restless. She glanced down the length of the plane, taking in the faces of the other passengers, creating imaginary lives for each of them. It was difficult because, with few exceptions, everyone looked stony-faced and bored. The expressions they wore were the same as those of the commuters travelling to and from work in Glasgow all those years ago. Back then, she had seen the same faces over and over again, of people who had become familiar to her and yet had bristled with non-communicative hostility whenever she had approached too close to where they were sitting. The only people who had not felt her intrusion were the drunks with whom she shared the small underground train most Friday evenings. Joking and talkative, they would reach beneath their jackets to reveal can after can of lager, bringing them to their lips and draining them before placing the empty tins on the floor, where they would roll from one end of the carriage to the other with every stop and start of the train.

Only once in the entire year had she had a conversation with another passenger. She had been sitting by the door when an elderly man had boarded. He had hesitated for a second and was glancing around for a free seat when the train had suddenly started to move, throwing him onto Sally. As he righted himself he'd apologised and tipped his hat in a gesture that had reminded her immediately of her grandfather, a man well into his seventies who lived alone in a small house in Rangiora. She hadn't thought about him for months, but seeing the man on the train made her feel a sudden pang, a mixture of guilt and remorse, as she imagined James sitting alone in his front room, the volume on his radio turned to its maximum setting as he tried to make sense of the music played on Concert FM.

They'd talked for several minutes and there had been nothing out of the ordinary in their conversation. From memory they'd talked about the weather, the length of the winter, the lateness of spring. At some point she'd mentioned that she was from New Zealand and he'd nodded, saying he'd met a woman from New Zealand once, many years before, in a hotel in Trieste. They had spent three evenings together and then parted, promising to meet up again once she arrived in Britain. Although he had given her his address, he had never heard from her again. He had sighed then, murmuring, 'Oh well,' and shaken his head as if still carrying around his disappointment from all those years ago.

Watching him leave the train, Sally had promised herself that she would write to her grandfather that evening. From that moment on, she would keep in touch with him, and would visit as soon as she returned to New Zealand. It was a promise she had almost kept. She had visited him upon her arrival back in the country, but shortly afterwards she had moved to Dunedin, married, given birth to her daughter, divorced and taken up her position at the university. Trips to Christchurch had become less and less frequent and, in the end, she had renegotiated the promise she had made herself, rewording it until it stated that she would ensure that James was always looked after and that she would write to him as often as she could.

She had been relieved, she remembered, when James had decided to move into a rest-home. The establishment was less than a kilometre from his home and he had been pleased to remain within reach of his familiar surroundings. And, as far as she knew, he had been happy with his decision. Although she had visited him only once or twice, she had continued to write to him. His letters, she remembered, often made her laugh. He'd describe how he was constantly plagued by well-meaning staff members — women who, mistaking his desire to sit alone for loneliness, often sat with him for long periods of time throughout the day. He'd learnt, he said, that given his loss of hearing, it was far easier to talk than listen, and, as a result, he was often completely hoarse by the end of the day. The visits were becoming so frequent, he'd laughed, that he could barely sleep at night through trying to concoct some new tale with which to entertain them the following day. Thank God, he'd finished, that the worst culprit, a lovely girl, a teenager, was due to leave at the end of the summer. He just hoped his voice and his memory would last until then!

Just before he'd died, Sally had been touched to receive a large bundle of school exercise books which, an accompanying letter apologised, documented incidents from his past — events he might not have remembered had it not been for the perseverance of certain rest-home staff members wheedling the information out of him. He was grateful for her correspondence; her letters, he wrote, had given him much pleasure. He hoped she would not feel obliged to wade through any of his journals – he had merely wished to save the nurse aides the trouble of disposing of them once he was gone.

The truth was, he'd stated matter-of-factly, he had not been feeling the best and had decided it was time to tidy his affairs. He had made only one request: that she should not organise a funeral or hold a service of any kind on his behalf. His life, he'd said, had been wonderful and he felt it would be bad manners to gloat about the fact in front of his less fortunate acquaintances. His letter had finished with the words: 'A fond farewell! James.'

Sally smiled at the memory. Of all the things she possessed, James's exercise books were among the most precious. She had brought one of them with her, reading it in her tent each night. His descriptions of travelling over the Otira Pass by stagecoach brought to mind a former age and a physical environment that belonged to a distant past – one that was wet and lush with bush-clad hillsides coloured with flowering rata, clumps of daisies and yellow buttercups. Imagining his journey from the West Coast – and others, such as cycle trips through the Haast Pass in the 1930s – she was impressed by the sense of exploration and adventure in his travels and, by contrast, its absence in her own.

The topic of hardship had often entered her thoughts while she was on Bratina Island. Watching Brent prepare the evening meal, pulling packet after packet of dehydrated food from the well-stocked food box, she had found herself thinking not how awful the food was but how remarkable it was that they should have so much of it, so easily. It was almost as if there was something inherently lazy about the way they lived. Every task had been simplified and for a time she couldn't decide whether she felt glad or discomforted by that fact. Never before, she realised, had the label 'tourist' fitted her so well.

They had been sitting around the small table in the wanigan one evening when Brent had suddenly broken the silence with a question. 'You know what I really hate?' Everyone, Sally recalled, had stopped eating dinner and looked up, waiting for him to supply the answer. 'The Teletubbies. I can't stand the Teletubbies.' No one had responded; they had simply nodded and gone back to eating. Several more minutes had passed before Craig had glanced up again. 'If you were going to invite three people to dinner tonight, who would they be?'

The question had struck Sally as impossible to answer. Her mind had swum with possibilities – dead family members, famous composers, writers, world leaders – before settling on the most simple reply: 'You three.' Immediately her response was met with cries of mock horror.

'What about you, Karen? Who would you invite?' And, as if it was already decided that whatever Karen had to say was worth listening to, they had sat quietly, waiting for her to open her mouth. Her answer had come surprisingly quickly: 'No one. I hate dinner parties.' An 'Oh,' rose from the table, as everyone turned back to their plates.

'Well, I'd invite Jesus Christ, Mohammed and ...' Brent hesitated, and several seconds passed. Sally could remember glancing at Craig, mouthing the name 'Gandhi', then shrugging at his softly whispered 'Nelson Mandela'. The seconds continued to tick by and for a time it seemed that Brent's third seat might remain empty. The pan of sweet and sour pork was passed once more around the table and forkfuls of instant noodles were hoisted from their sticky tangle at the bottom of the billy.

'Jesus Christ, Mohammed and …' Brent smiled suddenly. 'Michael Palin!'

'Michael Palin?' Like extras in a crowd scene, they turned to one another and shook their heads in amazement. Then Karen said, 'What are you going to talk to them about?'

For a second Brent looked uncertain, as if he was having regrets about his choice. 'I don't know – the weather, the usual things: food, travel …' His voice trailed off as he glanced around the small room as if searching for inspiration.

'Where they like to spend their holidays?' Karen suggested. Brent shrugged, smiling slightly.

'Well,' said Craig, reaching across the table for the salt, 'they're not going to be too happy about travelling all the way to the Antarctic just to be served a plate of pork, are they?'

Everyone looked unenthusiastically down at their plates, registering the mound of food swimming in a pool of soy sauce.

'Yeah, I wondered about that,' said Brent, jabbing at some noodles, which rose out of the billy in a large clump. 'I thought I'd just tell them it was chicken.' Like the others, Brent was beginning to laugh.

'You'd invite Jesus, Mohammed –' Karen began.

'And Michael Palin – don't forget Michael Palin,' added Craig.

'And Michael Palin. Heap a huge pile of pork onto their plates and then make out it was chicken? You mean you'd actually lie to Jesus?'

'Well, they could always pick the meat out of the vegetables if they didn't like it, couldn't they?' said Brent.

Craig glanced from Karen to Sally. 'I reckon Michael Palin's going to be wondering what the hell he's let himself in for …'

The mood had changed with that conversation. Suddenly, it had seemed to Sally, the group had drawn closer. It was almost as if the air in the wanigan had suddenly become warmer, gentler, protecting them from the cold outside. They'd talked on into the night, their conversations becoming more intimate as the hour advanced. It was after eleven when Brent raised the subject of his girlfriend's death. Looking back, Sally realised, she had been anticipating its mention all evening, but had still been startled to discover how uncomfortable it made her feel. She couldn't say why she felt so uneasy. She'd wished she could simply relax and let him talk, but a voice within her was urging him to stop, to save himself from exposing too much and regretting it later. As Brent talked, she found herself increasingly reluctant to listen to what he had to say. Every nerve in her body was on guard, anticipating the moment when she would have to step in and say, 'Stop. Don't say any more. You're making yourself vulnerable and you might feel differently in the morning.'

But then it dawned on her that everyone else was just letting him talk. There were no questions demanding details. No one was exclaiming, 'Oh, that's terrible,' or 'And then what happened?' While she was sitting upright, tense, the others were relaxed, sipping from their red plastic mugs, listening and waiting as Brent's story unfolded. And when it had finally come to an end, she could remember watching as Karen stood up, touched Brent lightly on the shoulder and said, 'I think I'll go to bed.'

Sally had been afraid, then, of appearing heartless. She'd already admitted, once, to not knowing what to say to Brent. She recalled the last time she had visited James; the memory of his smiling face watching her from the window was still vivid.

'Do have a very strong image of the last time you saw Ellis. Is it, you know, imprinted in your mind?' She saw, with relief, that her question made Brent smile. She smiled back, encouraging him to answer.

'She had just finished fastening her skis onto the roof-rack and was getting into the car when she looked up at me and asked, "Are you sure you won't come?" I said no, I wanted to stay home, read the paper, tidy up, wash some clothes – and make marmalade. And she said, "Fuck you, then," and drove off.' Brent stood up and stretched. 'And those,' he said, smiling ruefully, 'were her last words to me.'

After he'd left the wanigan, Sally and Craig had sat in silence, each lost in thought. Eventually Craig had looked up. 'Are you going to bed, then?'

Sally shook her head. She felt tired but she couldn't be bothered to move, and besides, she wanted to stay up a little longer in order to retain the memory of the day. 'No,' she said, 'I don't feel very tired yet.' She yawned and laughed, rubbing her neck with her hand.

'Me neither,' she heard Craig reply.

They fell silent once more and Sally found herself listening to an unfamiliar sound, a whining hum. As she listened she became aware that the entire hut was vibrating; the wind had picked up, not much but enough to cause the cables that anchored the hut to the ground to whine and the hut itself to drone like an idling engine.

'Can you hear that?' she asked Craig.

He glanced up, nodded and turned to the bench. 'Shall we make a start on the dishes?'

They continued to sit, without speaking, happy, it seemed, to have a break from the conversations of the evening. Occasionally the hut would catch a particularly strong gust of wind and the vibration would give way to a sudden jolt, as if the building might break free from the ground and rise, weightless, into the clear blue sky. Then the wind would stop and a silence, a deep hole cut into the air, would engulf them, to be replaced moments later by a hum as the cable outside began to vibrate in the wind once more.

'Brent's a good guy, isn't he?'

Sally nodded in response but said nothing.

Then, indicating several bags of stones stacked on the table, Craig said, 'I don't suppose you'd like to give me a hand measuring those, would you? If you're not too tired.'

A thin stream of sunlight entered the hut, sending a bright slash of light across the surface of the table in front of her. Sally sat quietly, listening to the scratch made by Craig's pencil on the open page of his notebook. It was well past midnight. Her thoughts wandered to her home in Dunedin, imagining the glow of the orange street-light outside her bedroom window, a light that somehow managed to edge its way into the bedroom, despite the curtains she had made the previous winter. She wondered what Manu would be doing – would he be working at his desk? Or perhaps slumped on the couch listening to music, or lost in some book? It was a Friday, she realised. Perhaps he'd be out with friends, drinking in some student bar and enjoying an evening away from the children. Far more likely, she thought, that her daughter would have gone out dancing with friends and Manu would have remained at home, the content father, cherishing each minute spent alone with his sons.

Heated by the stove, the hut grew warmer. Moreover, the drone of the primus filled the room, replacing the emptiness of the hut with something more hospitable. The sound made her feel safe, dulling the noise of the wind outside, as if offering protection from the frequent shuddering wind gusts. She felt more comfortable than she had for days, and she was beginning to find it difficult to concentrate. There was something mesmeric about the list of measurements; in her ears they became hypnotic, rhythmical and transcendental, and more than once she was startled by Craig asking, 'Are you all right? Do you want to stop?' She'd sit up then, straighten her back and shake her head, indicating soundlessly that she was fine, she wanted to continue. She'd watch as Craig shrugged. 'Granite: 17.3, 16.3, 10. Sub-rounded.'

As he finished the second bag he stood up, walked to the door and went outside. Standing by the window to see where he had gone she caught sight of him some distance away, scraping a slight hollow into the ground with the heel of his boot before urinating. Again, her mind filled with the protocols and rules set out in her field guide and she felt her hand edge forward as if, like some prying neighbour, she intended to tap a warning on the small pane of glass. Instead, she turned back to the room and sat down on the low bench-seat that ran the length of the table.

She expected Craig to return immediately but almost ten minutes passed before she heard his footsteps. Stepping inside, he removed his gloves and held out a black polished stone.

'Look.' She was aware of his eyes on her as she turned the stone in her hand. He continued to watch quietly, his body almost touching hers. 'It's nice, isn't it? I found it yesterday near the top of the island – where all the polygons are.'

She smiled, uncertain of what to say, then stated the obvious: 'Bubbly lava.' She looked up and saw that Craig had stopped smiling and was simply looking at her, studying her, as she warmed the stone in the palm of her hand. She waited, expecting him to say something more, or to sit down and resume his work, but instead he remained standing, his eyes fixed now on the stone as if, perhaps, it was his own hand she was warming.

Sally had the impression that the air in the room became very still, very calm, and as Craig looked on she closed her hand around the stone and raised its smooth surface to her face. She continued to sit quietly, motionless, the stone pressed gently against her skin, its rounded form nestled in the softness of her cheek. Fearing, then, that her own tiredness might be making her misinterpret things and yet conscious of his nearness, she found herself willing Craig to erase the space between them so that his body might somehow, of its own accord, simply touch her own. She lowered her head and closed her eyes.

He didn't move.

Sally waited, then glanced up, faced him. As she watched, she had the impression that, although it was barely discernible, his body was swaying. His eyes had not lifted from the stone in her hand and, although she tried to read his expression, his thoughts remained unfathomable. As she continued to search his face for some sign, some invitation, she remained silent. Suddenly she felt tired; she wanted only to leave the room and fall into the solitude of her tent, yet still she continued to sit and wait. She was conscious, then, that he had raised his glance and was watching her. His gaze didn't falter and, in that fraction of time, she felt as if she had been stripped of sight. What passed between them could not be seen.

It was not until some time later that she was able to look back and fully comprehend how she had felt during the minutes that followed. Although Craig hadn't turned away, her sense of relief had remained intact no longer than a snowflake falling onto a pool of water. But, unexpectedly, it was not a feeling of hopelessness that followed, but a bittersweet recognition; one barely able to support the weightlessness of acceptance it carried. Frail and delicate, it descended slowly, settling upon her in a flimsy layer of understanding. Although she was certain now that he shared her feelings, his reluctance to step forward, to narrow the distance between them, confirmed what she, too, felt: they didn't need to do anything. It was all right the way things were.

Craig's voice, quiet, dreamlike, broke the silence. 'I thought you might like it – the stone. It could replace the one I threw into the pond this morning.' There was something resigned in his tone: a hint of regret that acknowledged his feelings towards her, but also determined that only the most neutral of statements could fill the space between them. And despite the fact that she knew what he was doing, even agreed with his decision to steer things back to the visible, the tangible, she felt empty, too drained to respond. She saw him hesitate, as if drawing breath, and then he reached across the table and took the third bag of stones. He sat down on the bench, his leg brushing hers as he edged forward on the seat. They sat together, side by side, each aware of the proximity and warmth of the other and the hollowness within themselves.

'It's all right,' Craig said. 'I won't tell anyone if you take it home.' She nodded, willing herself to smile but taking comfort only in the nearness of his body and the weight of his leg, which remained pressed gently against her own.

A voice interrupted her thoughts, jolting her back to the present. 'Folks, it looks like we've gotten through the worst of the bumps. If you need to stand up and stretch your legs momentarily, you go right ahead, but don't stray far from your seats, as unforeseen turbulent incidents may recur at any moment without warning.' The moment the handset was replaced, many of the passengers unbuckled their belts, some standing or climbing onto their seats so that they might find some room in which to stretch their cramped limbs. William was among those passengers, pushing himself up, manoeuvring himself to a standing position. Sally watched absentmindedly, her thoughts still contained in the memory of the hut on Bratina Island, when she suddenly felt a sharp tug back to the present. William, she realised, had not returned her stone. He must have seen her daydreaming and thought she was asleep. He mustn't have wanted to disturb her, or perhaps he had slipped the stone back into her coat pocket without her noticing. Even as she tried to calm herself, her hand fumbled through her pockets, her fingers edging into the deep, padded folds, walking through the furthest corners as she willed the stone to be there. As her fingers found nothing, a feeling of dread swept through her, a sense of anxiety she had not experienced for years.

It puzzled her that she should recall an incident that happened so long ago – one, moreover, that she had all but forgotten. And yet she had been gripped by a similar fear the morning she had seen her daughter waltz into the kitchen wearing the necklace gifted to her by Manu only the day before. Then, like now, she had felt sick. The necklace had no real value – it wasn't, after all, made from gold or diamonds – but it was precious because it had been entrusted to her. It belonged to her – and no one else. Seeing it around her daughter's neck had been upsetting not because it had been borrowed, or stolen, but because the necklace represented a moment of intimacy, an experience shared by Manu and herself. It was disturbing, too, because she felt she had failed to look after it properly. She hadn't protected it.

Although others might have seen no more than a few shells strung together on a length of plaited flax, the necklace was much more that that: it was a private message from Manu to herself. It was also the first thing he had ever given her. She had watched him make it as they sat side by side on the sand at Boulder Beach, waiting for yellow-eyed penguins to return from their day at sea. Though almost autumn, the evening, she remembered, had been mild, the sea in front of them satiny, rippling occasionally in the wind like the flank of a horse touched by a fly. She had known Manu only a few months; he was one of her students, but already she had discovered that in his company the sense of bitterness she had carried since leaving her husband had diminished, replaced by something gentler, more forgiving. Even so, she had not felt entirely comfortable. Not only was he her student and almost fifteen years younger than her, but he also appeared so relaxed and uncomplicated that although he made her feel more carefree than she had for years, she was nevertheless watchful in his presence, careful to maintain control.

They had sat for over an hour before the first penguin appeared, tottering up from the sea as if its legs were tied loosely together at the ankles. It moved quickly towards the rocks and then paused, its neck stretching like a caterpillar on the end of a branch as it turned back to face the water. They had watched it jump from boulder to boulder as it began its ascent of the hill, and then its body had become lost to view, hidden in the undergrowth.

She had turned her attention to Manu then, and watched as he selected each shell carefully from those scattered around him. There was nothing casual in his selection; even though most of the pieces were no more than broken fragments, he inspected each one, keeping only those that were the right size and shape. They had been sitting in silence when he had asked her to name her favourite composer. It had taken her several minutes to respond and even then she'd felt it necessary to qualify her answer. 'It changes all the time but at the moment it's Arvo Pärt.' She'd smiled hesitantly, unsure of the impression her selection might make, adding, 'Oh, and a Canadian woman I met years ago called Alice Glenton. She made a huge impression on me and a lot of my early work was very derivative …' Her voice faded as she recalled her flat in Glasgow and the wonderful long conversations she had had with Alice all those years before. 'I even named my daughter after her,' she continued, laughing.

She had waited, expecting Manu to question her, but instead he had replied, 'Mine's Jimi Hendrix.'

She had laughed again, turning her attention back to the necklace which, she noticed, now had six pieces of shell attached to it. She heard him murmur, 'Just one more,' and, smiling in her direction, he asked her to select the next piece. She looked at the small pile balanced on his knee and indicated a fragment of paua, a purple-pink disc no bigger than the nail on her little finger. As she watched him position it next to the others, she was astounded to hear him say, casually, 'When we have kids we'll call them Arvo and Jimi.' Then, before she had time to respond, he had held up the necklace. 'What do you think?' before singing through the seven notes of the scale: 'Doh, ray, me, fah, soh, la, ti …'

She'd been too amazed to say anything. She had sat dumbstruck as he tied the threads of flax around her neck and then, as she raised her hand towards the shells, she had felt his lips brush against her, just below her ear, and she had scrambled to her feet, bewildered by the rapid and unpredictable turn of events.

She smiled now as she recalled her state of shock, which had remained with her as she drove home from the peninsula, Manu beside her in the passenger seat, humming a tune she thought might have been 'Hey Joe'. Refusing his invitation to join him for a drink, she had dropped him off in the Octagon, barely pausing long enough for him to step clear of the car before driving off towards her own house in Opoho. Once home, she had remained in a state of disbelief, moving restlessly from room to room until Alice had told her to cut it out; she was trying to watch a video and the pacing was driving her crazy.

It was only later, when she was standing in the bathroom waiting for the bath to fill, that she had allowed herself to relax. Naked, except for the necklace, she had gazed at her reflection in the mirror and watched herself trace a path from the spot where he had kissed her, over the necklace and between her breasts, her ribs and down her belly to the long horizontal scar that marked the place from which her only child had been scooped into the world. She could remember mouthing the words 'Arvo and Jimi' before looking away, embarrassed, her fingers fumbling with the knotted flax as she untied the necklace and placed it on the vanity unit beside her daughter's nailpolish.

She had been standing at the kitchen bench the following morning when Alice had entered and said, 'What do you think?' She had looked up then and noticed that Alice was wearing her necklace. Immediately a tight knot had formed in her stomach and she had not been able to stop herself from snapping, 'That's mine, take it off.'

Her voice had been shrill and for a minute Alice had stared back at her, her eyes narrowing with spite as she sneered, 'Why? Did your new boyfriend give it to you?' Then she had laughed. 'Finders, keepers!'

A powerful rage, animal-like in its rawness and unlike anything she had felt before, had surged up in Sally then, and she had lurched forward, intent on snatching, if need be, the necklace from her daughter's neck. Only the look of sheer amazement on Alice's face had stopped her from reaching out and grabbing her by the throat.

Then, just as suddenly, she had snapped out of it and calmed down enough to speak. 'Could you give it to me, please? I need to wear it.' Even so, her heart had been racing as Alice yanked the necklace from around her neck, flinging it onto the table, yelling, 'Keep your piece of hippy shit – I wouldn't be seen dead in it anyway!'

Although she had been relieved to get the necklace back, she had also felt embarrassed and guilty about her overreaction. As a sign of her remorse, she had offered to take Alice into town, where, in a gallery specialising in contemporary jewellery, she had allowed her daughter to select her own necklace and had paid for it silently, without complaint. Still fuming over the price, and vowing to send the bill to her ex-husband, she had then followed Alice to a café, where, amidst a crowd of high-school pupils, her daughter had quizzed her about her relationship with Manu. As she listened, she had guessed that behind her daughter's sweet-natured curiosity lurked an unspoken insecurity and uncertainty.

She remembered her daughter's voice, noticing that as the conversation progressed and Alice began to feel more in control, her tone shifted from that of a confused young girl to that of a best friend sharing gossip; from a middle-aged mother advising an adult daughter, to an adult daughter talking to a befuddled, elderly parent. 'I know it's hard at your age, Mum. I understand that you're lonely,' her daughter said. 'And I can handle it if you want to go out with men. I mean, it's not like you're *that* old …' Sally had nodded, aware that if she said the wrong thing her daughter might snap. So she listened silently as Alice meandered on, nodding appreciatively as one snippet of adolescent wisdom followed another.

Forty minutes slipped by before she heard her daughter finish: 'You need to accept that I'm a teenager now and stop treating me like a child.' Sally had nodded once more, grateful that the lecture had finally come to an end. But just as she thought it was safe to suggest leaving, Alice had started again. 'Things are different now. I'm more mature than you were at my age. I would like you to be able to come to me and tell me straight off if you're serious about this Manu guy. I need to know where I stand.' Then, twisting the thread from her new necklace in her fingers, she had stared hard across the table. 'Remember, I'm always here for you.'

Manu's necklace was in her bag, rolled into a pair of polypropylene longjohns and stuffed into one of her shoes. She had brought it with her, wearing it during her first few days at Scott Base, but then, for no reason she could think of, she had removed it and packed it away. It was as if it didn't belong in the Antarctic. She hadn't wanted to be reminded of home, or of her identity as lecturer, partner and mother.

She had felt, very keenly, that she wanted to distance herself from all that clutter, that *stuff*.

Shuffling in her seat, Sally continued her search for the stone, lifting first one leg, then the other, in case it had somehow slipped beneath her. She realised that all her fidgeting had disturbed Marilyn, who was now regarding her with a look of mild irritation. 'I can't find my stone,' she yelled by way of explanation. Then she got to her feet, tugging at William's coat as she did so. 'Have you got my stone?' she yelled as he turned to face her. 'The stone. The bubbly lava!' she repeated, aware that she was shouting louder than necessary and had attracted the attention of some of the other passengers. 'My stone?'

She felt flustered and reached for his sleeve, and suddenly the stone jumped out of his hand and fell to the floor. Fearing that it was lost, she tried to crouch and search but discovered, to her dismay, that the boots and bags of her fellow passengers made it impossible. Embarrassed though she was, she had no option but to drape herself across the knees of her neighbours while groping through the gloom at their feet. It was a ludicrous situation. Visions of schoolboys bent over the knees of headmasters further increasing her humiliation.

She could feel the blood rushing to her head as she lowered herself into the small gap between the legs of two army personnel. She knew that everyone was watching her, and yet she had to find that stone. A voice in her head tried to reason with her, urging her to calm down and wait until the plane had landed and all the passengers had disembarked. But a louder voice encouraged her to keep looking, not to give up. She had to find it.

Then 'Honey, honey …' Yanked upwards by several pairs of hands she suddenly found herself face to face with a US servicewoman. 'Honey,' she frowned, 'You looking for this?'

As she returned to her seat, her cheeks burning with shame, Sally recalled Craig's parting words. 'Remember, you don't have a permit for that stone,' he'd said, 'so take care of it and keep it hidden.' He'd smiled and, unable to read anything in his expression, she'd felt disconcerted – as if everything that had happened only two nights before had been a figment of her imagination. She'd tried to return his smile but had been too unsettled by her imminent departure to muster up the strength to appear happy. She had been suddenly conscious of the helicopter pilot signalling her to board and, flustered by the urgency of the moment, she had become inarticulate, unable to source the words she needed to tell Craig. Helpless, she remained silent, a construction of her parting words floating through her mind, iceberg-like – a casual farewell visible above the surface while deep below, submerged, the weight of meaning: words that would somehow enter Craig and become part of him. Instead, she managed only a choked, 'Keep in touch, eh?' as she joined the pilot and watched, through the bubble of the cockpit, as Craig crouched low and ran back to join the others. It wasn't particularly significant, but his hands, she noticed, were thrust deep into his pockets. Then, as the helicopter lifted off, she thought she saw him mouth – and then repeat – something, but she couldn't get it and by then it was too late, and it didn't matter anyway.

Looking down from her seat in the helicopter she had been able to see where she had spent the previous day, her last on Bratina Island. It had been a strange day, one in which the hours had passed slowly but time itself quickly, bringing to mind the actions of an overeager waitress clearing plates from a table after a long, relaxed meal. She had woken late, still feeling tired from the night before and she had stayed in her sleeping bag, a line from a poem she could barely recall weaving through her thoughts: 'I wake to sleep, and take my waking slow.' Then she had closed her eyes, allowing the warmth of the tent to lull her back into a dreamless, drifting doze.

Although she hadn't been fully conscious of the feeling at first, she realised that as she dozed, she had been waiting. It would only be a matter of minutes, she convinced herself, before she would hear the sound of approaching footsteps, a warning cough, or perhaps simply the rustle of fabric as a hand reached out for the zip of her tent, unfastening it with a cheerful, 'Good morning. I've brought you some coffee.' She sat up, anticipating the wake-up call, her enquiry about the weather already planned.

Several more minutes passed and she rested back on one elbow, her eyes gazing at the wall of her tent as she tried to see through its fine fabric for the shadow of a person approaching. Counting backwards from a hundred, she lay down at seventy, her head resting on her hands as she watched the fabric flutter in the wind, the circled glow of the sun strengthening then weakening as each cloud passed before it. Glancing at her watch, she noted that it was almost nine. No one was coming and she needed to pee – she would have to get up.

The camp was deserted. She had known that the minute she climbed out of her tent. There was no reason why she should have felt the emptiness of her surroundings so keenly, but she had. She felt abandoned.

She glanced through the window of the wanigan as she walked by but knew, from the lack of sound, that no one was inside. Approaching the port-a-loo, she kicked the long warratah wedged against the door to the ground, allowing the door to swing open, revealing two translucent containers positioned on the floor. Both were more than half full. She pulled the lid off the shit bucket and noted, with only passing interest, that implanted in the most recent pile were small chunks of carrot. She focused then on the orange funnel inserted into the pee barrel as she willed herself to use her personal urinary device.

There was something bleak about having to piss through a funnel while standing. She took no comfort in emptying her bladder and she realised then that the experience reminded her of all the times she had had to provide urine samples while pregnant with the boys. She recalled visits to the doctors that began with her going to a tiny toilet cubicle and urinating into a small plastic beaker, a cup so fragile and thin that the heat from her urine could be felt through its skin. Then, like now, there had always been some hesitation, a tension that prevented her from being able to do anything other than stare helplessly at the walls of the cubicle for minutes on end. She remembered the stickiness on the occasions when she had not directed the flow accurately, yet she recalled, too, the comfort of being able to wash her hands whenever she wanted. Here, all she had at her disposal was antiseptic gel – an odourless slime that seemed to wash and dry her hands at the same time.

It was strange, she realised, to be in the Antarctic, an area defined by the actions of heroes and adventurers – a place where men raced towards the Pole, slipped off mountains, got stranded on icebergs and crawled out of crevasses – and yet find herself consumed, at that moment, only by the coordination required to pee through a small opening into a plastic bucket. She wasn't like one of those television celebrities who travel to a Third World country and then spend the entire trip bitching about the lack of proper sanitation, but she did care about accidentally pissing on her trouser legs or shoes. That was her Antarctic challenge – to pee straight and not get splashed.

As she walked back to the wanigan, her impression of being abandoned returned more forcibly. Plates from the night before remained where they had been left, piled up on the bench beside the primus. Cups containing the dregs of tea and Milo littered the table. As she glanced around, her eye was drawn to a green mug – the one that, despite belonging to none of them, had, in all their minds, become *her* mug. Now filled to the brim with black coffee, it suggested that the person who had made it had been vaporised before being able to deliver it to her tent. She took a sip and sat down, her body assuming the position she had taken the night before, elbows propped on the table, legs drawn back beneath the bench. Trying to recall the warmth of Craig's leg bumping against her own, she closed her eyes and sat very still, aware of her solitude and the space around her.

Within minutes she was back walking beside Craig, listening as he described his desire to share his trip to the Antarctic with his wife. She recalled how, unlike him, she had wanted to keep everything about the visit to herself. She had felt everything so intensely she could not trust anyone else with what she had seen or felt. Moreover, she could not risk her response to the environment being diluted through hearing – and therefore having to acknowledge – that others had responded as strongly as herself. It was vanity, she supposed, but she needed the security of privacy – a condition that allowed her to believe that her impressions of the Antarctic were unique, and also more profound, than those of anyone else. It would be discouraging, even slightly humiliating, to discover that what she felt was simply the 'norm'.

Sipping from her mug, she looked around, once more taking in the names and comments pencilled onto the wall by the people who had inhabited the hut before her. Her own name, like those of the others in her group, was absent. None of them had thought to make themselves visible to future visitors. Perhaps in a way they all sought the privacy she held on to: the belief that their own visit was too exceptional to be scrawled onto a thin white wall where it would have to share space with people called Jacko, Spud and Zippy.

Once more she began to revisit the hours she had spent with Craig, and as her thoughts shifted from one memory to another she became increasingly aware that she had been mistaken in thinking she wanted to safeguard her experience of the location from everyone. For the first time in her life, she realised, she had found herself in the company of someone – one person – with whom she believed she could share her visit. More than that: she had wanted to engage in a wordless dialogue with him, so that just as he might inhabit the world she was discovering, she might enter his.

She recollected something she had read once: a brief passage in an anthology of travel writing which at the time had struck her as sentimental, yet somehow simple and moving. The author had been describing a journey through the Swiss Alps, and as he walked he had allowed his thoughts to drift, imagining his pleasure increased through sharing it with a companion. In his daydream, such was his desire to transmit his feelings of utter contentment, he had wanted to draw his companion's attention to everything: the smallest of details such as the alpine flowers, the insects – even the colour of the dust on his boots – as much as the magnificence of the alpine scene opening up before them. He imagined the joy to be had from putting into words, making visible, everything before them, and then he realised that all he really wanted to do was walk through the place he loved with the person he loved. The real pleasure would be peaceful, it would come from knowing that the woman walking beside him knew and understood everything about him without the need for description, explanation – or even words. It would be more than a comfortable silence, however; rather, soundless communication, like prayer, or touch – one hand nestled in the palm of another.

Sally sighed, and the sound of her sigh echoed around the

room. Hearing a noise, she glanced towards the door. The thought that Craig might be outside entered her mind and she smiled, hopeful, imagining his hesitation as he tried to justify his arrival back at the hut, his reason for leaving the others and returning to her. Even as she pictured him standing in front of her, her delight at seeing him, she knew he was not there. Hers was the illusory hope of someone buying a lottery ticket, nothing more. She felt at once foolish and melancholy, unable even then to dismiss all thought of him, the chance, however slight, that he might appear. She waited a moment longer, her eyes resting on the door. It remained closed. 'Sally,' she heard herself say then, 'don't think about it any more.' She waited, her ears straining for a sound, the crunch of gravel or the heavy thud of a pack lowered to the ground. 'It's not worth it,' she continued, hoping the words might give her strength. Then, shaking her head, she smiled again, embarrassed now by the intensity of her feelings, and the knowledge that although she had found her comfortable silence – had even, in the writer's words 'walked through a place she loved with a person she loved' – she had not permitted herself to believe it.

A gesture, wave-like, caught her eye and, looking through the small window, she noticed that a skua had landed outside the hut. It stood still, its eyes fixed on the building as if willing it to become edible. There was something pitiable about the bird, the fact that it had chosen to nest on this island, so far from open sea and, she guessed, any source of food. With the exception of that single bird and its chicks, she had seen no other sign of life, had not even seen the bird's partner which must, she thought, be somewhere nearby, scavenging for scraps.

Watching the bird reminded her that she was hungry. Glancing around, she found an opened packet of chocolate biscuits and took three before searching though the piles of paper and boxes on the table for a note, something that would tell her where the others had gone. There was nothing – they had simply disappeared. Her feeling of disappointment became one of dejection when she noticed that the water container was empty. The freshwater supply was a good ten-minute walk away, and then it took a further ten minutes to chip enough ice to fill the box. Taking into account the walk back to the hut and the melting and boiling, it would be at least an hour before she could enjoy a fresh cup of tea. Feeling resigned to the task, however, she murmured, 'You don't know how lucky you are!' and stood up.

As she walked towards the freshwater pond her thoughts drifted, swinging from one topic to the next like the red wooden box bumping against her knees. Her footsteps beat out a shuffling rhythm and she caught herself talking aloud, chatting to Manu about the direction her work would take. Although she had not missed him, she had, at times, felt the absence of their conversations – the awareness that in him she had found someone with whom she could talk about her music; someone, moreover, who would understand the challenges confronting her: the gulf between the sounds she had expected to record and what she found. She could imagine him encouraging her, reassuring her that the proposed sound map would not be the disaster she predicted, that it would all be okay and that she was not to worry. In the past, their discussions had often filled her with wonder. Whereas she often felt under an obligation to compose – it was something she had to do in order to ward off the remnants of guilt that had remained embedded in her from the time of her marriage – Manu appeared refreshed by his work. An unlimited source of pleasure, music was something he carried lightly, lovingly, as if cradling a sleepy child in his arms at the close of day.

Reaching the place where she expected to find fresh water, she hesitated, confused by the number of ponds around her.

Only a few days earlier she had helped Brent collect ice, but she had not paid a great deal of attention to where she was going and had simply followed him. Now all the ponds looked both familiar and unfamiliar – any one of them could have been the right one. The others were filled with salt or brackish water – only one contained fresh water. She sat down, irritated with herself and equally annoyed with the location. Why were there no footprints leading to the water's edge? She had been sure she was following a trail of steps but now, looking around, she could see nothing at all resembling a path. In fact, she realised, she wasn't sure where she was.

She grimaced, comforted only by the fact that she was on her own – there was no one waiting for her, no one growing impatient at the length of her absence. At least she had privacy. She smiled foolishly but relaxed a little. The stones beneath her were warm, and the sun on the water sparkled, giving the impression of heat. Resting with her head in her hands, her back propped against the box, she gazed around, listening. Silence. She coughed, reassuring herself that all sound had not been sucked from the atmosphere, leaving only a vacuum around her. After a few more minutes she thought she could make out a faint noise, a trickle of stones falling into water, but too quickly the sound was replaced by the absoluteness of silence. It was as if she was dead, she thought. As if someone had allowed her to experience the end of all noise, all sound. She had been gifted the finality of nothingness.

She remembered something Brent had described the previous evening. He had been talking about his girlfriend – about her death – when he had happened to mention that once he himself had been buried in an avalanche. He described the weight of the snow pressed against his body, the sensation of being unable to move or even tell up from down. He said he had felt buried not so much by snow but by silence, a weight of soundlessness, and he had found himself disorientated by it. Relieved to discover he was alive, he had become quickly confused – unsure of whether he was actually alive, or merely remembering what it was to be alive. It had taken all his willpower, he said, to persuade himself that he was present, and not some kind of human residue. Thinking back later on the experience of being buried, he knew his surroundings couldn't have been completely silent. He had been under the snow for only a matter of minutes; there had been the faintest echo of human voices above him, and his own voice calling out in reply. What's more, he said, there had been the beating of his heart. The steady thud, thud, thud so loud, he contended, it had been like torture.

He remembered hearing his heart beat again the instant he heard his friend's voice over the phone the day Ellis was killed. He had been making marmalade – of all things – and had been standing at the stove when the phone rang. For a minute he had considered ignoring it – he didn't feel like talking to anyone and he was enjoying what he was doing. The smell of oranges had filled the kitchen and made it seem warm and summery, despite the fading light outside. He recalled that as he listened to his friend, even as the news of his girlfriend's death was broken to him, he continued to stir the boiling mixture, never lifting his eyes from the circle traced by the wooden spoon round and round the saucepan. He remembered hanging up, returning the receiver to the kitchen bench, and feeling as if someone had yanked a plug out of his body: his soul had flowed into his arm, through his hand, the spoon it held, and into the pan of boiling marmalade, where it caught in the whirlpool of bubbling liquid and was drawn down and held under, suffocating and drowning amidst the strands of orange rind. He had stood dragging the spoon round and round the pan for a further fifteen minutes.

'Ellis and I had always spent a lot of time bickering,' Brent had told them. 'We argued about everything. The way she used to place rubbish in the kitchen bin used to drive me mad. She would never put anything inside the plastic bag I had placed in the bin, but would somehow manage to drop stuff onto the top of the bag, down the sides, so you could never remove the bag neatly from the bin once it was full. We had huge arguments about stuff like that. I just couldn't see why it was so hard to put rubbish inside a bag – and she couldn't understand why anyone would get so upset over something so stupid. We seemed to spend all our time bickering: the apple core left in the car's ashtray, the supermarket dockets stuffed with the vegetables into the fridge, the way she would tear a hole in a plastic bag to get at the bread rolls rather than making the effort to open it – all that stuff. And then she was killed and everything became very, very quiet. It was as if we had spent all those years arguing over silly, inconsequential things so that when the one big, life-changing thing happened, we would know how to be silent. We would know how to be very still and very calm and very quiet. We would just "be".'

Brent had paused then and looked away, past them at something that had caught his attention outside the hut. 'I think about her all the time and I often wonder if she heard her heart beat when she was buried. I wonder whether it sounded really loud and whether it annoyed her the way it did me. And I try to imagine what it must be like to hear the noise fade away – whether at any point it occurs to you that the things that irritate you most are also the things that give your life meaning … that keep you breathing and alive.'

Sally started and looked around, shocked to find herself alone. Why hadn't she paid more attention to Brent's words? Why had her concern for him, her desire to protect him from the response of the others, made her so insensitive to what he actually said? Had she paid attention more fully, she wouldn't have felt the need to ask him about the last words Ellis had said to him. Instead of trying to control the conversation, to rush things, she should have taken her cue from him and simply allowed things to be.

She wondered why, in everyday life, she found it so hard to feel peaceful – why, even when happy, she seldom relaxed but found herself worrying about the future, second-guessing events she felt no real interest in. Her relationship with Manu had developed in a series of reluctant steps. Whereas he had made it clear that he believed in their being together, she could not shake from her head the suspicion that she had been forewarned: the residue of her failed marriage was still firmly implanted in her mind. The speed with which Manu had fallen in love with her, the joy with which he displayed his love had, at times, pained her. No one, she had thought, could fall in love that quickly. He barely knew her and already he was talking about children, the future, and using the word 'we' to describe a relationship that should have been defined by the words 'you' and 'I'. And yet there was nothing frantic or desperate in his emotional language. He was not needy. His love was born of a generosity: he believed it was the most natural thing in the world to love her. He loved her and, in return, she adored him. And nothing would ever change that fact.

Turning to Marilyn, Sally smiled, pointing to her watch. 'Not long to go now,' she shouted. Marilyn nodded then shrugged, a gesture Sally found disconcerting. She remembered what she had heard earlier that day in the cafeteria, and said conversationally, 'Your cat will be pleased to see you.'

Marilyn turned towards her, her face frowning with concentration. 'Cats?' she said. 'Who told you about my cats?'

'No one. I heard you talking about them at breakfast …'

Marilyn nodded. 'I hope they'll be happy to see me …' She glanced away. 'You never know, though, with cats.'

A few minutes passed before Marilyn spoke again. 'You found your stone, then?'

Blushing, Sally said, 'Yeah, sorry about that.'

'Special, is it?'

Sally nodded.

'I knew a man once,' continued Marilyn, 'an old guy when I knew him, but when he was young he used to collect rocks – greenstone mostly. He left me an adze when he died – my lucky adze.' She smiled ruefully. 'I'd show it to you but I've hidden it in case MAF try to take it off me – you know, it might be a special Maori thing.'

Sally thought about her grandfather. While he'd lived in Westport James had often visited a place near Cape Foulwind called Okari Lagoon. At low tide he had sidled around the estuary picking up greenstone fragments and adzes on an almost weekly basis. He had such sharp eyes, and nothing escaped his notice. Through his eyes these objects glinted like a mirror in the sunlight, beckoning him to stoop down and take a closer look.

'He was such a nice old guy, really generous,' Marilyn continued. 'He was a resident in the nursing home where I worked one summer. It sounds stupid but I loved him, like he was my own grandfather or something.' She looked thoughtful. 'He had a granddaughter but she never visited. I don't know why – she probably couldn't be bothered.' There was anger in Marilyn's voice.

'I guess people can be selfish and cruel sometimes,' Sally agreed.

'I suppose so.'

During her last evening on Bratina Island Sally had recorded Marilyn's news bulletin. Although she had been interested primarily in collecting sound, she had found herself drawn by its content – a fact that caused her discomfort now that she had met Marilyn. As the bulletin had got under way, Sally recalled, she had become fixated on the awkwardness of Marilyn's delivery. Although in content the bulletin was similar to any other, in Marilyn's presentation even the most straightforward item became mangled as her monotonous voice drifted from one word to the next without pause or punctuation. It was clear to Sally that Marilyn suffered from a kind of stage fright, and listening to her she felt embarrassed and guilty. In fact so excruciating was the experience that Sally had found herself hoping against hope that someone – anyone – would come along and rescue the girl: simply drag her away from the microphone.

She recalled the long pause that followed the last item of news. She remembered, too, the deep breath as Marilyn prepared for what must have seemed like the final torment: 'the joke'. A faint cough sounded over the radio, a prelude to speech, but instead of a voice there was once more silence: an uncomfortable, squirming hesitation that struck Sally as foreboding. She waited, willing Marilyn to resume while at the same time entreating the transmission to end. It was all she could do not to murmur, 'Forget the joke. Do it another night – once I'm gone. Wait until I've left, so I don't have to hear it.'

'And now for the joke,' said Marilyn, her voice flat, barely audible. Again, a long pause followed, the pink noise from the radio engulfing the wanigan in a blizzard of static. 'It has been reported that in Britain there are 50,000 dogs per tree instead of watching their P's and Q's they now have to queue for their pees.' Nothing filled the gap left at the end of the sentence. The bulletin was over. Sally leaned forward, relief flooding through. In a few minutes she would be outside, standing in the fresh air, surrounded by space and light. But as she reached forward to stop the recording, her hand was stopped by a cough and the words, 'One more thing ...' Sally wavered. She had her recording, she didn't need to tape any more and yet she couldn't move. Engulfed with dread, she slumped back, her head resting in her hand.

'Tonight I have another joke for you, a special joke – one that I dedicate to Tobin because he was the one who first told me that it was important to end the news bulletin with a joke.'

Sally froze. She didn't know Marilyn, let alone Tobin, and yet she had the impression that she was about to be drawn into their private lives. She felt convinced that she was about to be told something she had no desire to hear.

'Tobin, I'm pregnant. I tried to tell you but you wouldn't let me, so I had to do it this way …'

Like a hospital patient finally informed of her test results, Sally felt swamped by a wave of relief. She no longer had to guess – to anticipate – what was about to be said. She knew. And even though the news was disconcerting, it was no longer threatening. A mirthless snigger caught in her throat, a grin of horror settled on her face as she tried to imagine why anyone would do such a thing. It was too awful, too humiliating. Why didn't she just send the man a note if he wouldn't listen to her?

She shrugged. What did it matter? She didn't even know Marilyn. She was nothing more than a faceless voice transmitted over the radio, that was all.

Sliding her recorder across the table towards her, she was about to switch it off when she heard a sound, a kind of a squeak, and then Marilyn's voice, faint and uneven, returned. 'I don't know what to do.'

The words stopped Sally in her tracks. Once before, years earlier, she had watched a documentary about a sailing regatta. En route from New Zealand to Tonga, many of the yachts had been hit by a force twelve storm and had capsized or sunk. The programme had been compelling, the descriptions of the storm terrifying and those of the various rescue operations heroic. But what had stuck in her mind, stayed with her all these years, was one small sentence – a cry that had chilled her. Making a mayday call to the station in Kerikeri, one of the crew members of the yacht *Quartermaster* had finished with the words: 'I don't know what to do!'

The anguish in the man's voice had stunned her. Never before had she heard such despair. It had seemed to her that the voice belonged to someone who was, in every sense of the word, lost. Here was someone who, despite all his experience, all his skill and level-headedness, was helpless. His future, and that of his crew, was out of his hands. And no matter where he looked, he knew that there was no one in the entire world who at that moment could offer assistance. His voice betrayed the fact that he knew he was going to drown. Even now, Sally could not recall his desperate cry without choking back tears. Never before and never since had she been so affected by a human voice. In the minutes that followed his call there had been a deathly hush. An unbroken silence that erased hope and created images of its own, horrific images, but ones that could not compete with the cry of that voice – the voice of a man who had reached the end.

And now a woman called Marilyn was uttering those same words, that same helpless plea. Sally sat with her eyes fixed on the dials on her recorder as she waited for Marilyn's voice to return. Her headphones still in place, she felt disorientated by the sudden roar of static, her ears playing tricks as she conjured up the sound of a voice, faint in the distance, in conversation with someone too far away to be heard. She imagined a laugh, a playful cry of 'Good joke, eh! Did you fall for it? I bet I had you worried there for a minute!' A voice that subsided into unrestrained laughter, a joyous giggle as the speaker repeated her joke – the words that must have stopped Tobin in his tracks, if only for a minute. Sally willed the voice to reach her, straining in her attempt to hear beyond the noise distorting the dead air of the radio. She waited and as she sat she became increasingly aware of other noises – sounds that, until several minutes before, had gone barely noticed: the plaintive squeak of the windsock as it hung listlessly in the breeze, the crunch of gravel beneath the boots of her friends waiting outside, and the distant thud of the toilet door, banging as it swung against the flimsy wall of the port-a-loo.

Sally suddenly felt engulfed by the sounds of her immediate environment, a sense of unease verging on panic taking hold of her as they gained in number and volume, preventing her from hearing the voice she was waiting for. No voice returned and, too anxious to wait any longer, she turned the radio off, not caring to know what happened next, whose words would ease into the empty space vacated by Marilyn.

Standing up, she suddenly heard laughter coming from outside. She walked to the door and caught sight of the others, grouped loosely a short distance away, sharing a story she was unable to decipher. For an instant she felt alone, set apart from her friends by what she had heard on the radio. It dawned on her then that she would probably never learn the conclusion to Marilyn's story. Although she might replay the bulletin many times in the forthcoming months, the drama would remain, for her at least, unresolved. And then, from being only a partial story it would eventually fade away to become a forgotten one.

Watching her three companions, she wondered how long it would take for her to forget them, too. She imagined parting and how, in saying goodbye, she would make a cheerful promise to keep in touch. Yet she knew she wouldn't. She hadn't managed to keep up visits to her beloved grandfather so why would she communicate with these people? Removed from the intimacy of their shared environment, they might have nothing to say to one another. Inevitably, they'd become like one of those couples who, when eating together in a restaurant, spend several minutes summing up the service and the décor before looking at each other helplessly, aware that all conversation, like their meal, has solidified in their gut, leaving them uncomfortable and miserable, waiting only for the relief of being able to stand up and leave.

As time passed, her memory of the place would fade, the details would become obscured, the only honest answer left to the question 'Do you remember what it was like?' being 'No, I don't.' Despite the fact that the Antarctic was 'memorable', she would forget it. Picturing the place would become as difficult as trying to recall her own face as a teenager. If anything, she might retain only the memory of the memory.

She suddenly recalled an incident that had taken place years before, to which she had given no thought for many years. Selected to participate in a collaborative arts festival in Oamaru, she had been invited to create a site-specific work within the region. She had found herself paired with a sculptor from Auckland and travelling around the countryside, searching for a location that might provide the setting for their combined piece. It had been a tense day. Right from the start it had been clear that she had nothing in common with her companion. Their pairing – a result of their names being pulled from a hat – clearly displeased her partner and, rather than making the most of the situation, he had spent the day driving from one small settlement to another, the music on the car stereo uncomfortably loud, stifling any attempt on her part to strike up conversation.

Towards evening they had driven into the southern town of Palmerston. The sun was low in the sky, casting long shadows from the macrocarpa shelterbelts that dotted the farmland around them. She had spent the day on edge but now the softness of the light fading from the sky soothed her, replacing her tension with a sensation of subdued melancholy. Passing a sign indicating the cemetery, she happened to glance across the road and notice a wrought-iron gateway at its entrance. Arched high above the gate, and fashioned from the same wrought iron, were the words 'Lest we forget'. Feeling weary, yet moved by the sign, she had pointed it out to her partner, who had surprised her by stopping the car.

Without getting out of the vehicle, he had leaned across the front seat for his camera and taken several photographs, sneering as he did, 'Fucking hypocrites.'

Although common sense had urged her to remain quiet, not to question him, tiredness and irritation had clouded her judgement and she had erupted, 'What do you mean, "fucking hypocrites"?'

She recalled the way he had looked at her, his obvious contempt as he replied, 'Well, it's obvious, isn't it?' She had been forced to wait as he considered whether it was worth his while to explain. Yawning, he looked at her for what seemed to be several minutes before replying, 'Well, it's clearly a case of "Lest we forget our own", isn't it? I mean, no one gives a fuck about anyone outside their own family or circle of friends, do they?' He had hesitated, she remembered, as if wanting to confirm what he already suspected: that she was too stupid to understand. Eventually he continued. 'I know how to fuck them off, though.' He had smiled at Sally for the first time that day. 'I'll change the sign.' Then he scrawled in the air in front of her, mocking: 'Let's forget!'

By some strange coincidence – one that could only happen in New Zealand – Sally had learned that he, too, had been awarded an arts fellowship to the Antarctic that summer. She had read a brief description of his project and had been dismayed to discover that despite the intervening years, he was still congratulating himself on his ability to transform one simple phrase into another. 'Let's forget!' she had read, groaning. So much for practising what you preach, she had thought, hastily checking the dates of his trip, comforting herself that she would miss him entirely.

Looking at Marilyn, Sally was taken by how young she looked; her face reminded her of her own daughter's. Behind Alice's façade of self-assurance she was prone to introspection, hours of soul-searching and anxiety, which, Sally hoped, would subside as she grew older. Having made a connection between Marilyn and Alice, she found herself feeling increasingly concerned for her travelling partner's well-being. She continued to look at Marilyn, willing her to read her thoughts and respond. But she also felt dishonest – suddenly suspicious of her own motives; worried that her need or, rather, desire to hear the conclusion to Marilyn's story was stronger than her concern for its principal character. Nevertheless, she felt somewhat disconcerted by the girl's continued silence. Embarrassed, and finding herself on the verge of blurting out 'I'm worried about you!', she forced herself to look away. On the other side of her, William had returned to his seat and was writing in a small black notebook. She registered the words 'penguins' and 'kookaburra' but nothing else.

Minutes passed and there was still no word from Marilyn. Sally frowned. She felt she owed it to the girl to offer support, but, despite clearing her throat several times, she found she couldn't broach the subject. It was too private, too personal. Despite the fact that one day she might make Marilyn's words public before an audience, Sally now found herself incapable of referring to them in the presence of the one person who could claim ownership of them. Was she really prepared to sacrifice the girl's right to privacy for her own creative needs? The fact that Marilyn was unlikely to ever hear the finished composition – might never even hear of its existence – did little to ease Sally's conscience. So much for creativity, she thought bitterly. Creativity was as destructive as anything else.

'Is anyone meeting you at the airport?'

Sally started, surprised to hear Marilyn speak. 'No,' she replied. 'I don't have any friends in Christchurch.' Not wanting, however, to be thought friendless, she said, 'My grandfather used to live in Rangiora but he died ...' Her voice trailed away, detained by an image of James. How happy he would have been to know that she travelled to the Antarctic. She could imagine him sitting in his armchair, listening intently as she shouted descriptions of Bratina Island across the room, his fingers turning her sample of lava as he peered at its surface through the small hand lens held to his misted eye. Until now, she had never really understood his love of stones. Perhaps, she thought, every piece in his collection was a reminder of an important event in his life: his history written in stone. She smiled sadly; her desire for his company surprised her. A sense of loneliness – the hollow, fragile feeling she had experienced that morning – returned and once again she found herself hugging her body, protecting herself from that empty, drained sensation.

James would have understood, she thought. Of all the people she knew, he was the one who would have appreciated her desire to retain some memory of the Antarctic; the ache she felt now, as she anticipated its clearly defined outline blurring, disappearing.

'What about you?' she asked Marilyn. 'Is anyone meeting you?'

Marilyn's mouth quivered before revealing a wobbly smile. 'My boyfriend.' She looked down, twisting a ring on her finger. 'Chris,' she shouted. 'Chris will be waiting.'

MARILYN

Marilyn sighed. It was true, Chris would be waiting. She could picture him now, roaming the airport, entering the various small shops, loitering in front of a book or magazine display as if in a daze before deciding to go upstairs to the observation deck to watch her aeroplane land. With less than an hour of the flight remaining, he would be waiting already, his camera poised to take a photograph of the Starlifter and the queue of disembarking passengers.

She hadn't been able to tell him why she was returning early. Somewhere in the back of her mind she had almost persuaded herself that there was no need — not because he would guess but because she imagined that once she left the Antarctic, the baby might, somehow, fade away. The change in environment would prove too much for it. Like a microscopic bug that could survive only in polar conditions, it would find it impossible to adapt to its new, hostile surroundings. The unfamiliar warmth, the dark sky at night, the sound of birdcall, the smell of earth or the sudden, unexpected movement of trees blowing in the wind would prove too much for it. After the Antarctic it would find it impossible to cope with so much life. It would shrivel up and her life would return to normal.

Marilyn glanced back at Sally. At least, she thought, she was no longer frowning. A short while ago she had looked so angry that Marilyn had been afraid to speak for fear of being yelled at. The silly thing was, just a few minutes before that she had considered the possibility of confiding in her neighbour. She didn't know why she thought Sally might be able to help. Perhaps she felt protected by the fact that they were strangers, or maybe it was because Sally reminded her of the women from support services who used to come into the rest-home every now and again to chat to the residents who were having trouble adapting to their new lives. However, seeing the look on Sally's face had been enough to dissuade her from opening her mouth. She'd rather have spoken to William about her problems. But he already knew too much.

Things had gone wrong almost from the start, she remembered. No, it wasn't that things had gone wrong, exactly — that was too definite a word for what had happened. It was more like everything had become fuzzy, unclear and, as a result, she'd felt isolated and uncertain.

She recalled the morning after she slept with Tobin. She'd

woken early and had looked at the slats of the bunk above, silently counting them, one by one, as Tobin continued to sleep peacefully beside her. Whereas she had covered herself in a T-shirt before falling asleep the night before, he had remained naked, oblivious to his own vulnerability and the sense of protection afforded by clothes. She had felt the weight of his body, his damp warmth, impressing itself against her own, forcing her to take a position hard up against the wall, where she remained rigid, unable to move for fear of waking him.

At first she hadn't known what to think. It was as if she couldn't think – so many things forced themselves into her head that she was unable to sort them, or make sense of them. Feeling lost, she had tried to conjure up some fact, something definite, concrete, that she could hold on to until her mind cleared sufficiently to sort the emotional jumble that tossed through her head like clothes in a dryer. At last, after almost an hour, she struck upon something and clung to it, beginning the slow calculation of how many days had passed since her last period. She wanted to reassure herself she was not mid-cycle, at her most fertile, but the task was too difficult. In normal circumstances she would have used a pen and paper, or at least her fingers, to match the dates of her menstrual cycle against the days on the calendar. Moreover, without her diary before her, she couldn't be certain when her last period had started, guessing only that it had been around the time of her mother's birthday, a date that seemed so distant it bore almost no relationship to her life now. Giving up her calculations, she nevertheless had a sinking feeling that she was somewhere around the middle of her cycle, and she began to admonish herself with the fact that she had been too shy to suggest Tobin use a condom. Despite the fact that she had known she was taking a chance where pregnancy was concerned, she had allowed things to progress, reassuring herself only with the knowledge that everyone who travelled to Scott Base had been tested for various diseases, including HIV.

Watching as Tobin stirred in his sleep, she felt sick with herself. So full of self-loathing was she that she couldn't be bothered averting her face when he turned to her, smiling, asking how she was feeling. The question struck her as irrelevant. It didn't matter how she felt. She didn't deserve to have feelings. She was in bed with him – that, in itself, should satisfy his need for an answer. What did surprise her, however, was that she had found herself reaching out for him. That as he turned to climb out of bed she had pulled him back and tried to kiss him, her lips missing his mouth and crashing instead onto his jaw, so that her teeth ached with the impact. He looked stunned but then, stroking her face gently with the gesture of a mother about to leave her child, he had stood up and walked to the window, where the early morning light formed a golden frame around the closed shutters. 'The sun's up,' he joked, before opening the shutters and glancing out towards the radio masts that stood starkly like winter trees against the white ground.

Instead of leaving then, while his back was turned, she came and stood behind him, her body against his, her head between his shoulderblades as she listened to the rhythm of his breathing and the persistent drone of a distant machine which, like tinnitus, could not be shaken free from her head. As she clung to him, she noticed that his body was like Chris's. They were a similar height and Tobin's back, as she ran her hand over it, felt bony like Chris's, with no hint of softness around his waist. As long as she stayed still, her face clothed in the warmth of his skin, she could create for herself a breathing space, a retreat in which she could experience a moment's peace.

She felt Tobin speak, his words entering her ears through

his ribs, and the momentary calm evaporated. 'I don't know how to say this without sounding arrogant – and I don't want you to think I'm a bastard, because I'm not ...'

Marilyn froze; her ears, however, were seeking and hoping to hear the cadences of another voice, one more familiar, less hesitant. She wanted to hear the voice that occasionally sang out, teasing: 'Hey, Mari! Marry me!' Stupid stuff that was safe and didn't frighten her. What she was about to hear now she couldn't predict. It could have been anything and for that reason alone she felt fearful.

'I really fancy you ...' Tobin said, then laughed, embarrassed. 'Stupid teenage word. Sorry ...' He fell quiet as if trawling his mind's vocabulary for another, more mature word. 'I like you and I want to spend time with you – you know, find out more about you and how you think ...' He laughed again, self-consciously she thought, as if mirroring the way she felt on hearing his small speech. 'But the thing is – and I hope you won't think of me badly when I say this – but the thing is, I'm going to be wintering over here and even though I like you, I don't think it's possible to have, you know, anything other than, you know ...' She listened, anticipating the next word but heard instead, 'Don't expect too much, eh?'

She remained unmoving, thinking over what he had said, her face protected from view and smothered by his skin. His arm moved, reached behind his back, groping for her hand as if he was searching for a light switch in a darkened room. She didn't move, made no attempt to reach out and eventually he turned, shuffling his body around so that he could look down at her.

'You're all right with that, aren't you?' His voice was anxious, as if he found her silence disconcerting. Perhaps, she thought, he might be scared that it was a prelude to a sudden outburst, the type seen on television, where the man hits the wall with his fist and the woman covers her ears with her hands as she screams, 'Get out! Leave me alone!' She didn't feel like one of those people, however. She didn't even understand them. She felt more like an animal in a documentary about zoos. She imagined herself as a chimpanzee, sitting in the corner of the cage watching as a man with a banana approached. A chimpanzee who was wise enough to know, nevertheless, that it was not the banana she wanted but the key that swung unobtrusively from the man's belt.

She didn't want to talk. Only the day before she had spoken to him easily, the words flowing from her mouth like water squeezed from a wet cloth. But overnight the cloth had dried and now she would have to twist it more and more tightly in order to squeeze even a few drops, and she lacked both the strength and the will to make the effort. She had messed up, and no matter how she viewed the situation she could see no way out. All she wanted to do was go back to New Zealand. Like a child stranded at a school camp, she could almost hear herself wail: 'I want to go home!'

Hope, like a mirage, suddenly came into sight as she wondered if, perhaps, she could just leave. Maybe it wasn't out of the question. She could go and talk to Christine, who might agree to let her go. Even as she visualised packing her bags, however, she knew she would never have the guts to approach Christine – or anyone else, for that matter. The thought of everyone looking at her, watching as she walked through the building and murmuring, 'There's Marilyn. She's the girl who couldn't hack it,' was too shameful, too humiliating. She would have to stay.

'Say something, eh?'

Tobin's voice broke into her thoughts, drawing her back into the room, the sparseness of its walls reminded her of one of the rooms in the rest-home. It was the room where any residents who had passed away in the night were taken before being collected by the funeral director. She had seen her first and only dead body in that room. Laid out on a white sheet on a narrow bed, the woman had looked no more human to her than a mannequin in a shop window. She recalled how she had touched the woman's cheek, stroking her fingers gently over her skin. Glancing at her fingers, she had been appalled to notice that they were discoloured by a kind of pink dust. For one horrible second she had thought it was the woman's skin coming away on her hand and it was only after she looked more closely that she had understood it wasn't skin but face powder that had rubbed off on her. She could depict a faint line across the woman's face, a track marking the caress.

Something about Tobin's nudity made her think of that corpse. His body was so pale compared to Chris's, his skin unblemished where Chris's was marked by freckles and moles. It was as if their bodies reflected their surroundings, she thought. Tobin's was bloodless, almost white, featureless and unfamiliar, whereas Chris's was a familiar landscape: a path her fingers could trace from the dusty, pinecone-littered ground beneath the windblown trees on the edge of the dunes to the tawny beach bisected by one endless spine of a motorbike track, disappearing into the distance.

Her thoughts lingered, gazing after the tyre tracks in the sand while nearby, bobbing in and out of the viewfinder of her imagination, she could make out Chris's stooped body, hopping crow-like as he yanked at his wetsuit, trying to free it from his foot. She heard him laugh and a moment later saw him fall to the beach, his foot still caught in its black neoprene trap as he lay panting, laughing, his body and hair coated in sand, grey like a baked potato pulled from the ashes of a glowing fire.

'You're not angry, are you? Come on, Marilyn, say something.'

She heard Tobin's voice and closed her eyes, seeking to

retain the voice that was so far away. She felt miserable. 'I want to go home,' she mumbled, too quiet to be heard.

'Sorry. What was that?'

'You smell nice,' she offered, though in reality she hadn't been conscious of any particular scent.

'Do I?' Tobin laughed. 'It must be my deodorant. My mother sent it to me – Pine Fresh or something.'

'Oh,' said Marilyn. 'That must be it. Pine.'

The smell of pine remained with her, lingering in her imagination as she dialled Chris's number. She had wanted to talk to him in private but had been unable to find a telephone away from other people. In the end she had returned to the library, where, in a room shared with two others, she had finally reached him, her voice choking the instant he came to the phone. He was at work, distracted by what was happening around him, but pleased nevertheless to be taking a call from Scott Base. She could hear him speaking to someone else in the room, saying excitedly, 'It's my girlfriend calling from the Antarctic. Cool, eh?' before turning his attention back to her. But so eager had he been to quiz her about life 'down there' that he had not paused long enough for her to answer. He had talked on and on, telling her about a documentary he had seen on television the night before, one that featured footage of emperor penguins, and she had listened quietly, nodding and biting her lip, conscious of the two men in the library with her who, despite staring at books, were listening to the conversation and every word she would say.

The call had lasted less than ten minutes. Chris had had to return to work and she had been unable to tell him anything, managing only, 'Everything's fine,' before hanging up, a sob catching in her throat, which she disguised as a cough.

She had spent the rest of the day avoiding people. Like someone who has spent many months in solitary isolation, she felt unnerved by the proximity of people, scared because she could not predict their actions or avoid their attempts to draw her into activities or situations she had no way of escaping. She was glad to be working nights once more. She felt relieved that she could spend the night alone, secure in the knowledge that she would be communicating chiefly with people who were miles away, minute specks in an inhabitable desert; people she felt some connection to, because surely they must have felt as lost and exposed as she did.

Towards midnight she had taken a call from William, the scientist at Cape Royds. She had spoken to him several times in the past and knew from experience that he only called when something was wrong – when he had no choice. She also knew that he usually called with some kind of request, and she hoped that this one would not be as complicated as some of his previous demands. Waiting for his message, she experienced dread. She knew the feeling well; it was similar to the sensation she felt back home whenever someone from a charity organisation called. Whereas people like Chris or her mother were able to firmly but politely end the call, she always found herself listening to the speaker, becoming more and more drawn into the conversation, her sense of apprehension and guilt increasing as each minute passed. Eventually she would find herself flustered by the speed at which they talked, their message so well rehearsed that there were no pauses to allow her to think. It was only a matter of time before she would agree to pledge money and she would hang up feeling sick with herself, annoyed at her inability to simply speak up and say what she wanted to say. Her passivity in such situations irritated her; she hated the unfairness of what had happened and the knowledge that once more she had been taken advantage of.

It came as a relief, therefore, when William reported only that his colleague, Trevor, had been taken ill with a stomach bug and needed to be evacuated to Scott base for a few days – 'before the toilet bucket overflows'.

She processed the request and thought nothing more about it, spending the remaining hours of her shift watching videos on the small television by her desk. As she watched she became increasingly aware that it wasn't so much the storyline of any of the films that held her attention but the vibrancy of the colour that filled the picture. All the images shared a cartoon-like quality: the grass was greener than a Granny Smith apple, the trees, buildings and cities vibrated like multi-coloured Christmas lights before a bright blue sky, and the sea was as turquoise as bottled window cleaner. For once, the map that had decorated a wall in her school classroom made perfect sense: the domination of pinks, browns, yellows and greens scattered across the world and then, along the foot of the map, as if the poster itself had been ripped, the torn strip of the Antarctic – the only piece of white on the entire map.

Watching a video about surfers, her thoughts shifted to Chris. She remembered a holiday they had had together, travelling south of his parents' house in Mosgiel to a crib in the Catlins. The beach, she remembered, was called Porpoise Bay and once, towards evening, while sitting on the grass in front of their hut, they had suddenly noticed the shadowy outline of several large fish cruising up and down the bay. They watched for a few minutes, observing the rounded back and short fins of the fish as they surfaced briefly before diving into the waves. 'Dolphins!' The word was barely out of Chris's mouth before he was dragging on his wetsuit and running with his surfboard to the water's edge. 'Come on, Mari!' he had called over his shoulder. 'You've got to come. Come on, quick!' He didn't wait for her, however; he was already paddling out in the direction of the dolphins before she had reached the tidemark.

Standing in the shallows, looking out to sea, she could see nothing but water. The waves, which had looked small from the crib, now threatened her, obscuring the calmer water behind and swallowing Chris's body as he paddled out. Even though she was only knee deep, she could feel the steady tug of the surf, as strong as a river, pulling her off balance and making her unsteady on her legs. Suddenly she had spotted Chris, upright on his board, his arms spread like a bird learning to fly as he cut across a wave. Behind him, chasing him, it seemed to Marilyn, was the finned shadow.

'It's not a dolphin,' she remembered mumbling. 'It's a shark.' Even as she uttered the words, and felt a surge of sickening panic sweep over her, she *knew*, deep down, somewhere, that it wasn't a shark. She was simply imagining the worst: that Chris would get attacked, she would be forced to swim out to save him and that in the process she would be swept away and drowned. She had it all figured out. Even though she had no doubt it was a dolphin, that Chris would be perfectly safe and that she ought to follow him and share the experience of swimming with dolphins with him, she couldn't do it. She preferred to face the certainty of his disappointment and his dull acceptance of her decision – even her own frustration – than risk swimming out. She had known then what she knew now: that she was her own worst enemy.

Thinking about Chris made her uneasy. Despite appearances and his skill at putting a happy face on things, she felt certain that, somewhere inside, he found her behaviour draining. He was patient with her, always encouraging her to push herself just a little harder; and yet time after time he would feel let down by her. There was something inside her that was scared – and no matter how much support she received, she could never quite overcome that fear.

What was worse, she realised, was that she expected others to recognise her fear. She expected Chris, her mother and anyone who knew her well to be able, somehow, to read her thoughts and help her whenever she was feeling particularly needy. She had such high expectations of others' abilities that often, when they didn't predict or anticipate what was on her mind, she felt let down and abandoned.

If she could only take more control, she thought. If only she could be stronger she would be a better, more likeable person. Few people, she knew, could tolerate her passivity, and when she found someone who could, she tended to cling to them. That was why she had agreed to marry Chris. She loved him, but more than anything, she recalled that his proposal had brought with it not a flood of joy but one of relief. But even as she relaxed, anticipating that her future would be secure, that she would be spending the rest of her life with someone who would keep her safe, she had felt let down by her own sense of helplessness. In the end, she concluded, her ability to conduct her own life was about as developed as her skill in foreshortening conversations with telephone canvassers.

As the night drew on she had become more and more engrossed in the videos. Her eyes fixed on the screen, she forgot where she was and found herself back in New Zealand, where, alone in her flat, she would often sit late into the night staring at whatever programme happened to be showing. And, as so often happened when she allowed herself to observe her own life from a distance, she adopted the viewpoint of someone walking past her home: a night-time stroller who, glancing across the dark shadows of the garden, sees a young woman sitting alone in a dimly lit room, a cat curled up on her knee. She could imagine the voices from the television escaping from the room, filtering through the trees and rose bushes where they would reach the ears of the walker, causing him to pause a moment before moving on.

Once, she recalled, she had been so preoccupied with the image of her home that the sound of a call coming through had made her jump. Amid her confusion she had glanced outside and been so bewildered by the strong sunlight that she had felt disorientated, and had spent several seconds apologising and mumbling into the telephone while her mind scrambled to reorientate itself.

The end of her shift offered no relief. As she was leaving her work station, ready to sleep, she was accosted by the programme manager, who informed her that a helicopter would shortly be leaving for Cape Royds and, because her name topped the list of staff members scheduled for an outing, she should join the rest of the group at the heli-pad in twenty minutes. It was a perk – she understood that – but she felt no desire to go. Having to rush; to hurry back to her room where she would have to gather up all her extreme-weather gear and then struggle into it required more energy than she could muster. What she most wanted was a hot shower and twelve hours' uninterrupted sleep. Yet, despite her reluctance, she found herself smiling and nodding, thanking her colleague for the opportunity. Then she ran, as fast as she could, towards her room, hoping all the while that she would not burst in on Andrea and the carpenter.

Her distress had increased when, walking towards the heli-pad, she had spotted Tobin ahead of her – waiting, it seemed, for the same flight. She had not spoken to him since leaving his room the previous day, and the sight of him unsettled her. Too embarrassed to acknowledge him, she had stood back and pretended to adjust her clothing, her fingers fumbling with the zips on her jacket as if working their way over a rosary.

It was only as the helicopter lifted off and she experienced the extraordinary sensation of being hoisted upwards that she allowed herself to relax. She had never been in a helicopter before, and sitting in the front seat next to the pilot she discovered that she could see not only in front of her, but below her as well. In the gap between her knees she watched as the bright green buildings of Scott Base shrank, becoming no more than frozen peas scattered across a serving dish. In her heart she experienced the joy of escape – a feeling she held on to, smiling excitedly as the helicopter veered away, following the coast to the north, towards Cape Royds.

The greatest pleasure of all, however, came when the short flight ended. Standing on the hard, stony ground at Cape Royds, the deafening noise of the helicopter's engine behind her, and knowing that she had only five minutes before the return flight, she had faced the sea and glimpsed, beyond the old wooden hut and the penguins strewn like windblown leaves on the opposite hill, the white caps of breaking waves. She watched, mesmerised, oblivious to the group of men who moved around her, carrying loads to and from the helicopter. She absorbed the sight: the jagged black silhouette of coastline, the dull grey of the sea, which brought to mind an overcast sky. Echoing the voice of a child gratified after a long day's journey she had heard herself cry, 'Waves! I can see waves!' Her gaze still on the sea, she had literally reached for someone, needing confirmation of what was before her. Her hand, she remembered, had caught William's sleeve, and she had pointed and repeated for him to hear. 'Waves!' She had felt such relief at seeing what seemed to her to be a 'living' sea, that she hadn't thought through her actions.

'Yes,' he had replied. 'They're good, aren't they?'

Later, sitting in the canteen, her blunt knife skidding across the plate as she attempted to cut through a chunk of steak, Marilyn had been enveloped by bitterness. When Tobin pulled up a chair next to her, she barely raised her eyes, allowing them to rest on her glass of water, which she turned in her fingers, watching as small waves crashed against its rim, spilling out onto the table. It was only when he reached out and pulled her hand away that she permitted herself to acknowledge the thoughts that were going through her head – the self-pity and misery that came from being first shown and then removed from a place that was familiar and habitable.

She'd left her food, not even bothered to take her plate to the sink, and followed Tobin back to the accommodation block, ignoring Andrea's greeting as they passed in the corridor. In his room, for twenty minutes she lay beside him on the floor, fully clothed and under the duvet, as he stroked her hair and talked to her about his life back in New Zealand and his plans for the future – trips he hoped to make with the money earned from his year on the ice. She listened intently, feeling the pounding in her chest slowly subside, become more manageable, less painful with every word he spoke. After he stood up, apologising and explaining that he had to get back to work, she remained on the floor, her thoughts drifting out to sea as she fell into a deep sleep. She did not wake for several hours, but when she did, she felt no more refreshed than she had that morning.

At first she did not recognise the change that had taken place in her roommate. Marilyn had popped into the bar, intending only to say hello before beginning her shift, but had been called over to a table and had sat down with Andrea and several other people, acquaintances from both Scott and McMurdo stations. They had spoken briefly about her trip to Cape Royds but had not been talking long when they were interrupted by the sound of laughter at the far end of the table. Marilyn heard, through Christine's giggles, the question, 'So, come on, Lisa, your turn. What's your worst pick-up line?' Drawn in by the question, Marilyn turned to Andrea and noted that she too was intent on learning the answer.

'Well,' began Lisa, 'a couple of years ago there was this guy, a philosophy student who used to work part time at the Salvation Army op shop down the road from my flat. Despite the fact that we'd only had a few conversations,' she said, 'I got it into my head that I fancied him and that he was interested in me. So I decided I was going to ask him out. I planned everything so that the meeting would appear completely spontaneous, even trying on all my clothes so that I could wear something that looked thrown together yet kind of sexy, too. I went so far as to buy a book – by that baldy philosopher Alain de Botton – so that I could be reading when I bumped into him ...'

Lisa laughed. 'But at closing time, when I did bump into him, I freaked. I accidentally dropped the Alain de Botton book which, to my horror, fell on top of some fresh dogshit by my foot, and all I could concentrate on was the title of the book: the words *Status Anxiety*, which were half buried in mustard-coloured poo. It was totally mortifying but eventually, after what seemed like hours, I managed to squeak: "Do you want a drink?" He looked at me, looked at the book – which was meant to impress him and which had cost me, like, thirty dollars or something, and replied, "Why?"'

There was more laughter, intensifying as Lisa went on to describe how she had attempted to salvage the situation, becoming more and more flustered as she tried, in equal – though contradictory – parts to both make her intentions clear and backtrack out of the situation.

Feeling better than she had all afternoon, Marilyn laughed with the others. For a moment she persuaded herself that things might not be so bad after all. While Tobin was not Chris, he was a nice person and, moreover, someone she could rely on. Clearly he cared about her. Even Andrea and the others seemed somehow more human, less intimidating than she'd thought. Perhaps, like her, Andrea was lonely. That would explain why she had gone with that carpenter guy – she needed someone to help her cope, just as Marilyn herself had.

They probably had more in common than she had previously thought. In fact she ought to suggest to Andrea that they go out together to McMurdo one day, make an afternoon of it, go bowling or to a film, or to a café – anything so long as they could sit and talk and have a bit of a laugh. It was time, she realised, for her to spread her wings and make a real effort to get to know her roommate.

She smiled in Andrea's direction and felt happy when she saw Andrea return her smile. It was as if Andrea had read her mind, she thought – had known what she was thinking and agreed wholeheartedly. She recalled the feeling of relief she had felt when Andrea shifted closer and draped her arm around her shoulder, pulling their two bodies together in a loose embrace, and how Andrea had smiled, almost laughed, as she turned to the others. It had been such a warm feeling, which had surprised her with its power, a sensation she thought of as sisterly friendship. She recalled, too, the sense of anticipation that swept through her body as, still smiling, Andrea cleared her throat. And then, as Andrea spoke, as her words seeped through her brain, her whole body froze, a numbing chill of disbelief paralysing her as she heard: 'Hey, Marilyn, why don't you tell everyone about the pick-up line Tobin used to get you into bed?'

Marilyn started, the memory of that betrayal echoing through her mind. So lost was she in the recollection of that statement that she hadn't noticed that Sally was talking to her, asking for a pen to write something down for William.

'What do you want?' she asked, and Sally repeated her request. 'William wants me to write down the name of my latest CD ... his pencil's just broken.' Sally spoke very slowly. 'He says his wife is interested in music and he'd like to buy a CD by a New Zealand composer as a late Christmas present.'

Sally smiled and raised her eyebrows, leaning closer and shouting, 'She'll probably hate it.' Then she added, 'At least the cover's cool: it's an old photo of me and some flatmates outside a tattoo parlour in Glasgow. The sign on the shopfront reads: "Terry's Tattoo Parlour: 10 000 sailors can't be wrong". It was a really funny day.'

Marilyn tried to smile but she didn't understand what Sally was talking about. 'You've got a tattoo?' she heard herself ask but Sally had already turned away, writing her name and that of several CDs on a page in William's notebook. She watched as Sally pointed to the last title, *Recordings for Fatherless Sons*, and felt a pang of envy. It must be wonderful, she thought, to be able to create something – something concrete that would outlive the life of the person responsible for it. To make something out of nothing must be a real skill. She would never be able to do anything like that. Not in a million years. The closest she would ever get to that kind of creativity was what she was doing now: sitting next to a composer on an aeroplane. Not much of a claim to fame.

'It must be wonderful to be creative!' Her voice not only startled herself but seemed to surprise Sally, too. Her neighbour looked puzzled, even slightly uncomfortable, so she added, 'I mean, where do people like you get your inspiration? Do you just make things up, or do you get your ideas from things that actually happened?' She registered a strange smile on Sally's face and realised that she was probably not used to talking about her work in front of other people. Trying to encourage her, she added, 'Next time you have a concert in Christchurch I'll try to come along. I'd like to hear your work – you know, your Antarctic stuff. What are you going to call it?'

Again, she got the feeling that Sally didn't want to talk about it. It was probably too soon, too fresh, and artists, she'd been told, often felt superstitious about discussing things before they were finished. She could understand that. It was probably quite private – and you'd be scared of putting a jinx on things by talking out loud.

'I'm going to call it *Bubbly Lava*.' It was a relief to hear Sally's reply. 'That's just a working title, though,' Sally continued. 'Just for fun ... I'll change it some time.'

The title struck Marilyn as weird but she guessed it must have something to do with the stone she had been holding earlier. Still, it was different, and it was certainly better than *Recordings for Fatherless Sons*. A question entered her mind as her gaze remained on Sally. She wondered if composers felt self-conscious when their work was performed. Even though they weren't dealing with words, she had a feeling that someone like Sally probably had some sort of story in her head when she wrote a piece of music – so it was possible she felt exposed when her work was played in public. She looked across to Sally who was talking to William. She could make out some of what he was saying: something about Sally's name being familiar from somewhere. But then he was shaking his head, suddenly silent, just looking at the words written on the paper before him.

Marilyn remembered the evening after Andrea's comment about pick-up lines. She had sat at her desk, unable to concentrate on any of the messages scrawled on the scraps of paper before her. It was her job to pass them on to the teams in the field and yet none of it seemed important. All her mind could take in was the fact that Andrea had seen her in the corridor with Tobin and from that tiny shred of evidence had been able to guess what was going on between them. She had been caught out – exposed.

She recalled the days that followed. They had passed in a kind of fug, everything seeming filtered through a deep pool of water. Voices which, the day before, had sounded clear and distinctive over the radio suddenly echoed and reverberated in her ears, each word entwined with the one before it, until the only sound in her head was a noisy thud, as if a hammer was pounding every message into her, syllable by syllable.

The noise in her head was matched, she recalled, by a perceived absence of her own physical self. She had tried to make herself invisible. So sure was she that everyone would know what had happened between her and Tobin that she couldn't bring herself to face her colleagues unless it was absolutely necessary. And even then she would barely look at the person who addressed her, preferring to keep her eyes on the floor, on a mark several inches in front of her feet – the very spot, she imagined, where someone found guilty of a crime might fix their gaze as the judge prepared to pass sentence.

The only person she felt comfortable with was Tobin. When he wasn't away from the base, caught up with field-training courses, she would spend as much time as possible in his company. Beside him, she was able to see and hear clearly once more. Things that became distorted and uncontrollable when she was alone were reclaimed and defined in his presence; an air of normalcy once more settled over her life. In that state, although she still did what she could to avoid Andrea, to maintain a distance between them and to stay away from the room they shared, she no longer saw her roommate as predatory but rather as someone with whom she might be able to co-exist, provided certain invisible boundaries were not crossed.

It had shocked her, she recalled, when one evening, walking with Tobin towards McMurdo Station, she had heard him defend Andrea. They had been apart for several days and were still catching up on each other's news when suddenly Tobin had become impatient, snapping, 'Stop going on about Andrea. She didn't do anything. Lighten up a bit, eh? She was probably just having a laugh.' The tone of his voice had been so unexpected that Marilyn hadn't known how to respond. Something about the way he had looked at her made her feel ashamed, as if it was she who had wronged Andrea and not the other way around. She remembered glancing up at Tobin, expecting to see him face her in return, but instead he was frowning, and when he spoke again he avoided her eyes.

They had walked on in silence, descending into McMurdo where the size – and even the ugliness of the place – had filled her with relief. The sight of the fuel depot, the orange shipping containers, warehouses and trucks that drove along roads draped either side with power lines raised her spirits, bringing to mind not a vision of a desolate emptiness such as she had experienced throughout the past week, but a sensation of having crossed a barrier separating herself from the rest of the world. McMurdo was a town. People did the same things as inhabitants of any other town: went to cafés, cinemas and bowling alleys when not at work. Although it was the ugliest town she had ever seen, it was ordered, it made sense to her – it was recognisable.

A skua flew overhead and she found herself watching it, smiling as it suddenly swooped to the ground, descending on a food wrapper that lay in the middle of the road. She recalled now the way she had kept her eyes on the wrapper, gazing upon the bright colours printed across it, as if looking at a particularly attractive flower in a neighbour's garden. She couldn't understand why the wrapper should have caught her attention and it made even less sense that she was looking at it as if it was some object from nature rather than a piece of litter left fluttering in the breeze. It took a moment to realise that it was the only piece of litter she had seen since arriving in the Antarctic, that even the presence of rubbish, which back home would have annoyed her, now soothed her, adding one more symbol to the reduced alphabet that reminded her of humanity.

'Christ, you forget what a shit-hole this place is, don't you?'

Although she heard Tobin clearly, and was aware of him

stooping to collect the wrapper, her attention was focused on several bicycles propped up against a shed. They brought to mind her local dairy, where, at any given time of the day, school kids would discard their bikes on the pavement as they rushed inside to buy food or softdrinks. So familiar was the sight that she half expected to see a group of boys in grey shorts and shirts appear, small paper bags pressed to their faces as they munched on pies. She waited a minute, falling behind Tobin, and suddenly saw one of the bikes clatter to the ground, where it lay like a skeleton on the blackened, frozen earth. But there aren't any kids, she recalled thinking, an emptiness taking hold of her as yet one more absence was added to her ever-increasing list.

A horn sounded and she stepped aside as a large orange truck swept by, splashing her legs with mud and slush. She looked after it but it was already turning the corner, only the music booming from its stereo lingering in the air.

'Do you want to have kids?' The words escaped before she could stop them and, as usual, she realised that they had come out wrong.

After only a second's thought Tobin replied, 'Listen, Marilyn, I like you – I really do – but don't, you know, don't go falling in love with me or anything.' He must have seen the look of incomprehension on her face because he went on. 'It's not you, honest. But, you know, I'm not ready for another relationship yet – you know – I'm still not over my last girlfriend …' His voice trailed away and he smiled at her but made no move to draw closer, instead turning back to the road and walking away, too rapidly to hear her call, 'I didn't mean I wanted kids with you – I meant with Chris.'

She felt the sob catch in her throat at the mention of Chris's name. At that moment she believed she had cheated him in so many ways: not just by sleeping with Tobin but, equally, by not liking the Antarctic, not appreciating it. She had not only failed to recognise the place but had failed to understand what it was she was looking for. On her return to New Zealand she would have to lie about every part of her experience; she would have to say what a great place 'down south' was and how Chris had been right all along – that he had been right to make her go.

As her thoughts lingered on Chris she found herself watching Tobin more closely. He walked slightly ahead of her, his pace quicker than she found comfortable. Up until now she had believed that she liked him, that she was attracted to him, but now she wasn't sure. Perhaps her relationship with him was not so much to do with wanting to be with him as not having a great deal of choice in the matter. She suspected she was misinterpreting the facts – after all, she did like him – but, nevertheless, a doubt had entered her mind.

During dinner a few nights earlier she had listened to two women, scientists who had flown in for a few days before planning to return to Cape Adare. She hadn't intended to eavesdrop but she had heard them talking about the relationships formed between people out in the field. One of the women had admitted to sleeping with a guy she hadn't liked. She'd been sharing a tent with him over a period of weeks and they'd wound up having a brief relationship. 'The strange thing,' Marilyn had heard, 'is that because there are so few men around to choose from, you find yourself in the weird situation of sleeping with someone just because you feel, somehow, that it's easier than not doing it.'

The second woman had agreed, and described how she had felt a similar pressure once, while living in the Marshall Islands. 'In London, where I was living, there were so many people around that I never felt any pressure to have any relationships at all. But once I'd been in the Marshalls a couple of months it was like there was this incredible unspoken pressure to pair up. I had it off with two guys, both aid workers like me, but one married and the other a guy with whom I had almost nothing in common. It was sad, really … but just about everyone was doing the same thing – and no one, as far as I could tell, was particularly happy about it. It was really negative, almost incestuous.'

The first woman laughed. 'You begin to wonder if you're just some kind of sex maniac after a while …'

Marilyn hadn't known what to think. She probably hadn't thought consciously of anything but had got on with her day, washing some clothes and preparing for the night ahead. She certainly didn't see herself as a sex maniac, but for some reason being a sex maniac struck her as almost preferable to being unable to cope alone. It wasn't quite as pathetic as being lonely.

She'd kept her eyes on Tobin all the way to the skua bin, hoping that watching him might help her thoughts to clear, allowing her to understand what was going on between them. But it didn't. She only knew that she liked him, she liked him a lot, but that more than that – she felt grateful to him. He had, she thought, understood her.

The umbrella had caught her eye immediately. Brightly coloured and wedged against a corner of the skua bin, it had stood out from its dull surroundings like a clown at a hospital Christmas party. She had hesitated only an instant before pulling it out and opening it, twirling it above her head as she looked up, entranced by the roundabout of colour that flashed overhead. 'Do you want it?' she asked Tobin, while continuing to hold on to it so tightly that it was clear she had no intention of giving it up.

'No, you're right,' he said. Only then had she glanced at him and acknowledged his expression, a look of slight contempt that had softened out of an awareness of the genuineness of her pleasure. 'You keep it,' he said. 'I'm sure it will come in handy.' She'd nodded happily, continuing to twist the umbrella in her hand. 'If it rains I'll borrow it off you.' He was laughing as he spoke, and it had taken a while for her to understand.

'It hasn't rained in all the time I've been here,' she replied, laughing too.

'It hasn't rained for thousands of years.'

It took a few seconds for his words to sink in, and as they did, she found herself spinning the umbrella more and more slowly, lowering it to her feet, where it toppled to its side.

'Who left it here?'

There was, she knew, no answer to that question and it hadn't mattered when Tobin had shrugged. 'No idea. A tightrope walker? Or a golfer? Don't know.'

She had packed the umbrella the day before, including it with the rest of her luggage, which was weighed in, along with herself, before she left Scott Base. She and her bags had weighed over a hundred and ten kilos, which had surprised her. It was as if in the space of only several weeks she had grown obese and unrecognisable. The night before she had telephoned Chris, telling him she was coming home early. He hadn't understood at first, and she had had to repeat herself, shouting so that anyone passing in the corridor or sitting in their rooms might hear. 'I'm coming home tomorrow. Tomorrow!'

He'd asked again and again, 'Why, what's wrong?' and it was all she could do not to scream, 'I can't stand it here a moment longer!' That would have been the truth, but instead she'd replied, 'I can't talk about it now, I'll tell you tomorrow.'

Even then, a part of her had doubted that she would make it home. The gulf between where she was and where she wanted to be was too great. Her travelling back to New Zealand seemed as unlikely – as impossible – as travelling through time. Even as she had sat that morning, fabricating a story about her cats in order to appear sociable to her neighbour at breakfast, she hadn't felt confident she would see them again. And yet here she was on the Starlifter, an announcement from the flight deck informing her that the plane would touch down in approximately fifteen minutes. In a quarter of an hour, the captain had just assured them, they would be in Christchurch.

She had said goodbye to both Tobin and Andrea but neither of them had come to see her off. Tobin, she knew, was somewhere in the Dry Valleys, and Andrea had made no attempt to climb down from where she had been sitting on the edge of her bunk, swinging her legs as she watched Marilyn collect and bundle her bedding and towels before depositing them, for the last time, in the laundry basket. Unlike some of the other people on the base, Andrea hadn't tried to hug her, but had sat with her arms wrapped around her own body, rocking slightly as if at any moment she might lose her balance and fall to the floor. It was only as Marilyn hesitated in the doorway that Andrea had opened her mouth, mumbling, 'He did the same thing to his girlfriend – that's why she left him. She told him she was pregnant and he didn't know what to do …' She sighed wearily. 'He told me a few days ago. He feels really bad about what has happened …'

She looked away. 'He's a good guy, really. He means well …' A laugh escaped from Andrea's lips but was swallowed almost immediately.

Her words had caught Marilyn off guard; at any other time, even the day before, she might have questioned Andrea further, but the information had come too late. She just felt angry.

The fact was Tobin had left her alone. Not long after sleeping with her, around the time they had found the umbrella in the skua bin, he started to avoid her. She hadn't noticed at first, assuming only that he was caught up with work, that he wasn't ignoring her so much as attending to some other, more pressing business. But then it had become all too clear. Seeing her approach in the corridor, or sitting at a table at lunch, he would turn away as if drawing some cloak of invisibility around him to protect him from her gaze. She guessed that he found her loneliness pathetic and her behaviour dreary, and that he was irritated by her – but as there was nothing she could do to change the way she felt, she drew back, refraining from seeking him out. The humiliation of his rejection was already embedded deep within her body and she didn't want to hear any words of explanation or defence from him. It was better for her to simply disappear, to experience the hollowness of isolation more keenly than she had thought imaginable.

She recalled how, as days passed without her speaking to anyone except about work, she would find herself questioning callers from New Zealand about the weather. Most of the people assumed she was just making small talk while they waited to be connected, but occasionally, after some prompting, they would describe the day and, with a note of weariness in their voices, conclude that the summers were nowhere near as hot as they used to be; that it was raining all the time. That was what she had wanted to hear. At the mention of rain, she could smell warm drops on a dusty path – a smell so intoxicating that she would often lose track of where she was, jerking to with a start as a voice would break into her thoughts with a question: 'What line is the caller on?'

At night she would unfold the umbrella, twist it on the floor and watch as the colours blurred – a spinning top, one spoke of which would inevitably catch the corner of her bunk and cause it to crash.

She had observed the coloured window on her pregnancy test without surprise. If the information had penetrated her thoughts at all it had been only in the manner of a communication announcing the death of a distant relative. She knew she was supposed to feel something but she didn't know what, exactly. It was too much effort to respond, and besides, she had always known that such a thing might happen – she had taken no measures to prevent it, after all. If anything, she felt most surprised that life could be created in a place so lifeless and devoid of children. That was the biggest shock; the rest – the facts that now confronted her – were too difficult to respond to. Her breasts hurt and she needed to go to the toilet more than usual, but apart from that there was no marked change in either her body or her mind.

And then one night she had woken in a sweat. For the first time, though she had known about it for several weeks, she felt pregnant. In the minutes that followed she had felt so scared, so panicky that she had had to open the shutters to the room. She could no longer keep her thoughts hidden in the dark but needed the light of day in order to confront them. She had stood by the window for an hour, not knowing what to do, her heart thudding as she tried to focus on the scene before her, trying to make sense of what had happened and how she would deal with it.

Towards two in the morning Andrea had returned to the room, seen her standing at the window and, not knowing why, remarked only that she was tired and that she would be grateful if Marilyn would close the shutters so they could get some sleep. Her voice had sounded so flat and withdrawn that Marilyn hadn't been able to say anything. She simply did as she was told, before leaving the room and walking through the double doors at the end of the corridor, where she had sat on a bench by the door, surrounded on all sides by blue coats and boots. Still unable to think clearly, she had read through the names on the Velcro name tags, picking through the layers of clothing until she knew the name of every jacket that swung from its wooden peg.

Into the pocket of the jacket named Tobin she had placed a message, a short note scribbled on a piece of tissue paper that read, 'I need to see you.' Whether the note had been read or not she didn't find out, but discovered the following morning that Tobin had gone again, this time on another field-training trip – one that would keep him away from the base for several nights.

From then, a disjointed silence had taken over the base. A silence that was somehow, confusingly, accompanied by exaggerated sound. It was as if everyone or everything capable of making a noise had left the building, and yet the noise itself had remained. It was too difficult to make sense of but it was almost familiar all the same.

Once, years ago, she had visited Chris at work. It was when he was working in the maximum-security wing of the prison and somehow, despite all the rules and regulations, he had let her in one night – taking her only as far as his office, where they had spent ten minutes. What she had experienced then was almost identical to what she experienced now: a sensation she could only describe as being surrounded by people who were visible but somehow absent. It created an atmosphere that had scared her then and it frightened her now. Empty sounds like echoes of the departed had assailed her, adding to her discomfort: the swing of the doors at the end of the corridor, the ding of a telephone replaced on its receiver, the sudden, sharp scrape of a blunt knife and fork across a plate – all of these things set her nerves on edge, making it impossible for her to relax.

Perhaps if someone had talked to her, asked her how she was feeling, she might have confessed and things might have improved, become more real, but as it was, no one knew of her condition and no one guessed. Her desperation, which to her was as bloody and palpable as a heart visible through a surgeon's incision, went unacknowledged, and thus left her powerless.

She hadn't planned to address Tobin over the radio. The idea had never even entered her head, and, had it, she would have been appalled. Nothing in the world would have tempted her into making such a public announcement; she would rather the earth swallowed her up than broadcast her condition, the situation she had found herself in, to strangers. What was more, she felt no bitterness towards Tobin; it was not his fault, so there was no reason why she should show him up before so many people.

But then, sitting at her desk that night, she had suddenly become sick with fear. Breathing had become difficult. She had found herself gasping for air as a pain unlike any she had experienced before had taken hold of her body. She had thought she was going to die; she was convinced of it. Nothing she could do would prevent her death. It was not the anticipation of her last breath that terrified her at that moment, however, but the knowledge that she was alone. In a world of six billion people not one soul had any idea what was going through her head; there was no one out there who could do anything to help. And it was that sense of hopelessness, that inescapable emptiness of her isolation, that had engulfed her and caught in her throat as a cry – a final plea for help.

But even as the words formed on her lips, she had lost the strength to utter them. What had started as a cry had ended as a mumble, a faint confession: 'I don't know what to do.' And then everything had gone very quiet, very still, and for what seemed a very long time – minutes rather than seconds – the only thing to penetrate her thoughts was the pounding of her heart, a rapid drumbeat that enveloped her, cutting her off from her environment, forcing her into a place more lonely and frightening than any she had ever known.

Then, as she was about to give up all hope of hearing a response, the sound of a voice penetrated the room. Faint and hesitant, as if travelling across a vast distance, it was not Tobin's voice that reached out to her but the voice of a man she barely knew. He made no attempt to save her but spoke quietly, haltingly, as if, like her, he had not planned his words, and was unsure why he was talking. He spoke slowly, pausing often to draw breath, reminding her as he did so of someone who was not used to speaking, a man who had perhaps spent much of his life in solitude and who found the simple act of communicating unfamiliar – so alien, in fact, that he appeared disconcerted by the sound of his own voice.

His words, however, soothed her. He described for her the crash of the sea against the rocky shore at his feet, the cry of thousands of penguins rising and falling in waves behind him and the sight of a seal lazing in the swell, rolling with each surge, raising its head now and then like a fat man trying to judge his distance from the end of a swimming pool during a length of backstroke. He reminded her of a question she'd once asked; one he hadn't found an opportunity to answer before she had flown out from Cape Royds all that time ago. It was an interesting question, he'd said, but one for which it was difficult to provide an unequivocal answer. He'd gone on to tell her that in his experience the birds at Cape Royds tended to be quieter from midnight to four in the morning. But, rather than saying that birds slept at night, he'd told her, it was more accurate to say, simply, that a greater proportion of birds slept at night than during the day. Although, in describing his findings, he had sounded more confident than before – as if finding himself back on familiar ground – his voice had trailed off, to be replaced by the sound of the sea, which reached her faintly, a lullaby shush.

She waited for him to speak once more, but when his voice returned it struck her as more uncertain than before, as if whatever force had prompted him to speak a few moments before had suddenly abandoned him, leaving him self-conscious and slightly bemused. He spoke more cautiously, conscious perhaps that he was not only talking to someone he barely knew but that others might also be listening, tuned in to their conversation like a radio audience to a talkback show. His conversation had drifted to a standstill, filled only by the acknowledgement that he didn't know why he was taking up her time and a suddenly gruff observation that her boyfriend was probably waiting for him to finish so that he might get a word in. And then William had fallen silent and she had sat with the receiver pressed to her ear, listening, as if to a shell.

She looked at William now, his body separated from hers only by the space taken by Sally. Despite the fact that they had spent much of the day together, travelling within arm's reach of each other, he had done and said nothing all day to acknowledge that brief radio conversation. It was as if she had merely imagined his voice at the end of the line. Yet at the time, she had hung on to his words. Despite the fact that they were not the liferaft she had hoped for and were, in reality, no more than flotsam – splinters of wood barely strong enough to carry her weight – they had been enough. His observations, in being so matter of fact and unambiguous, had brought her peace, a respite from her fear. He hadn't told her what to do, had not even offered advice, but his words had connected with her and filled a gap, bringing an end to her isolation, and for that she would always be grateful.

A slight tremor rippled through the plane. She wasn't sure but she thought they must have landed. She glanced up and saw several other passengers looking around as if seeking confirmation or reassurance – she wasn't sure which – of something sensed but not confirmed. Minutes passed and nothing happened. They must still be in the air, she concluded. As she looked around, she became aware of Sally nudging her, pointing over her shoulder towards a man with a camera who was twisting in his seat, taking photographs through the window behind his head.

'We must be landing,' she heard Sally shout, but several more minutes passed and still she felt nothing. 'You don't get much idea of what's going on in here, do you?' she heard Sally yell, and she smiled in return, her body tense, anticipating the bump that would indicate they had touched down.

'That's it, we're down.' She looked at Sally and wondered how she could be so certain but then, seconds later, she heard it too, a rumbling roar followed by the sensation of being restrained, a tug as her safety belt pulled against her stomach.

Instinctively her hand went to her belly, but she could feel nothing other than the thick folds of her down jacket. A remark came back to her then, a final instruction yelled across the tarmac to her as she had boarded the aeroplane in Christchurch all those months ago. Chris's voice, she recalled, had been so loud and strong that everyone in the queue had turned, searching for the figure that stood behind the security fence, waving enthusiastically in the dawn light.

'Don't forget,' he had called after her, 'to bring back something interesting! Not one of those souvenir toys, but something real – something I can show my mates to prove you really went to the ice!'

She remembered her embarrassment at being singled out by his attention, and the manner in which someone ahead of her had laughed, 'He's a bit keen, isn't he?' And she imagined the colour draining from his face, his smile evaporating, as, word by word, she shredded his image of the Antarctic as if it was no more than a tattered black flag flailed in the wind. Now, when he looked at a map of the continent he would be unable to see his hero, Hillary, driving out across the pure, untracked territory before him. Instead, he would visualise his girlfriend on a bunk, her naked body shuddering like a seal humping its way across the frozen sea, as some man, a nobody, fucked her. She had destroyed his dream. Her fingers resting on her stomach, she absorbed the irreversibility of her actions and felt sick.

'Welcome back, folks!' Several instructions followed the announcement but she paid no attention. She leaned back against the webbing of her seat, willing the confused thoughts that twisted and tumbled through her head to settle, to give her one minute's peace in which to think. Her eyes scanned the wall opposite, flicking over the smiling faces of the passengers relieved to be home before coming to rest on the emergency exit. It was high above her head, located in the roof of the plane, a door which, if opened, would reveal not the ground but the sky. She kept her eyes on it as she imagined gazing through its gaping hole to the sky outside: the glare of the day softened by the onset of evening, a faint glow – shimmering green-pink like trout caught in a net – outlining the alps to the west as the sun slipped slowly, darkly from view.

ACKNOWLEDGEMENTS

First and foremost I would like to thank my husband, Alexander, and my mother, Wendy, for supporting me throughout the writing of this book. Without them I would not have been able to travel to the Antarctic, nor would I have been able to schedule any time in which to write. Likewise, I would like to thank Pam and Alister McLellan for all their help, and the staff at the University of Otago Preschool for looking after my son for several afternoons a week.

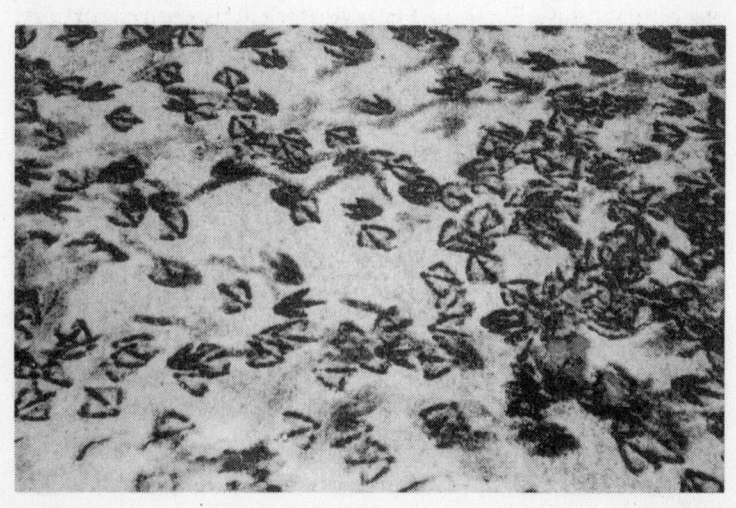

My gratitude also goes out to my son, Harry, for being so patient and such a good sport throughout the past year.

There are many people at Antarctica New Zealand I would like to thank: Lou Sanson, Natalie Cadenhead, Keith Springer and Paul Woodgate for facilitating my trip to the Antarctic. Also all the staff at Scott Base for being so hospitable during my visit. And I would like to thank all the scientists and educators I met while on the ice for their generosity and enthusiasm about my writing project.

I wish to acknowledge the assistance of Creative New Zealand in supporting both the Artists to the Antarctic Programme and my writing of this novel.

I would like to thank the following people at Penguin Books: Geoff Walker, Rebecca Lal and Louise Armstrong for their ongoing support, kindness and commitment to this project. I am deeply grateful to Rachel Scott for her careful reading and editing of this manuscript. Thanks also to Athena Sommerfeld for her cover design.

My interest in the Antarctic dates back to my childhood and I am indebted to my father for simply understanding; often driving the long way home, past Christchurch airport, so that I might catch sight of a Hercules or a Starlifter parked on the tarmac. I'm only sorry that he died before I travelled in one. Professor Bill Manhire has been, in many ways, my Antarctic mentor. I am extremely grateful to him for all the time he has spent encouraging and directing my interest in Antarctic literature and the Antarctic.

I would like to thank Dr Elena Glasberg for her helpful suggestions as the first draft of the novel took shape. I am also grateful to my friend, mountaineer Lydia Bradey, for permitting me to read her unpublished accounts of mountaineering and for the numerous discussions we have enjoyed over the past year.

Several people have been particularly helpful over the

past few years. Documentary filmmaker and author Alison Ballance not only guided and assisted me with research but also offered encouragement throughout the process of writing. I would like to acknowledge the wonderful contribution of Professor Euan Young, who not only provided me with information about skuas and penguins but also sent me a copy of his journal detailing his fieldwork while based at Cape Royds during the summer of 1959–60. I would like to stress that any errors with regard to skua behaviour in my novel are mine alone.

Composer Patrick Shepherd travelled with me to the Antarctic and we spent several happy days together at Scott Base and Cape Royds. In the year following our trip he has provided me with background material with regard to sound and music – but again, I need to stress that any errors in the text are mine alone. I would also like to acknowledge the generosity of composer Chris Cree Brown, who in the mid-1990s supported me and allowed me to observe him at work, both making sound recordings and composing electro-acoustic music.

There are three people I would like to thank in particular: climbing guide Aaron Halstead, and glaciologists Dr Becky Goodsell and Dr Neil Glasser. Despite having little or no knowledge of my writing project, they allowed me to join their party on the McMurdo Ice Shelf, permitting me to observe their fieldwork and tag along for several days. Their enthusiasm, generosity and willingness to introduce me to the subject of debris transport and deposition struck me as remarkable and made me appreciate just how indebted the visiting artist programme is to scientists and scientific events. I would like to thank them for allowing me to share their campsite and for making that brief visit one of the most interesting and happiest times of my life. Of course, I need to stress, once more, that any factual errors relating to

Bratina Island are mine.

It is to Aaron, Becky and Neil that I dedicate this book, with love.

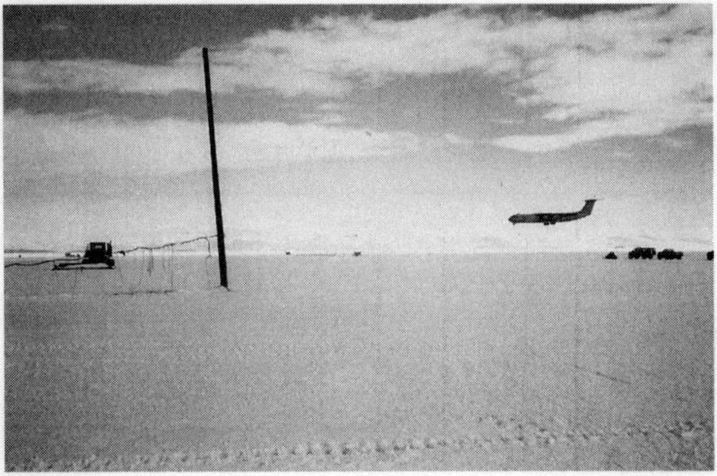

Butler's Ringlet

Laurence Fearnley

Warwick and Dean are living lives of quiet despair in rural Southland. Dean, a farmer, is single and lonely – if only he'd admit it to himself. Warwick is caught between his love for a place and his love for Sabine and Ecki, his estranged wife and child now living in Germany. Dean observes Warwick's struggle but has problems of his own: a domineering father he neither loves nor respects and on-going feelings of guilt and grief for a dead brother.

Suddenly Sabine and Ecki return to New Zealand, bringing the past with them to threaten the fragile worlds Warwick and Dean have created for themselves. In this story of male friendship, Fearnley reproduces the cadences and rhythms of rural life and offers insight into a provincial male world seldom explored in recent New Zealand fiction.

Delphine's Run
Laurence Fearnley

Since she left school at thirteen to look after her disturbed mother, Delphine's life has never been straightforward. Now, not yet twenty and employed on the Brest-Paris train, her life has become increasingly complicated. First, there is her daily relationship with flatmate Yasmina and infant son Sinbad, and the mysterious goings on of her friends Dany and Javier to contend with. Then there are her somewhat disconcerting conversations with a judge who travels first-class, and her growing infatuation with Charlotte, a marine biologist and supporter of official rights for the Breton language.

As the plot of *Delphine's Run* accelerates, we are forced to re-evaluate Delphine and her life. Is she an innocent player in a series of shocking events — or is there more to Delphine than she is allowing us to see?